THE DEATH OF THE BLACK MUSEUM

MARTIN DAVEY

Published by: The Black Museum

For my good friend Sam, an angel that lifted me up
after I had fallen.

CONTENTS

1. A COMPACT

The mist has been hiding the beach. But now the wind is awake and blows it into the sea, turfing it off the land like an unwelcome tenant. The beach is a poor, sickly stretch of land, anaemic and desolate. Scruffy tufts of grass are sprinkled across the dunes nearby. They look like discarded hair pieces, the wigs of giants who prefer to walk the land bald instead. The beach is empty save for two shapes. They look out of place, mere smudges at the water's edge. But when the low clouds that scud at a pedestrian pace overhead part for a second, the shapes sharpen and come into focus. One of them is a man, slight and furtive. The other is a great beast, hulking and savage. They have come to this empty place on the east coast to make a compact. The fens and the flatlands flow away in all directions, ever shifting, undulating and sinister. The sea, cold and steady, provides a backdrop that is huge in scale. No sail nicks that grey horizon, and no bird flies overhead. Only the wind dares whisper from the safety of the dunes nearby. The Beast is the first to speak.

"You leave no footprints, how so?"

The man looks over his shoulder and then back.

"Never really given it any thought."

The Beast tilts its head to one side as if hearing a sound in the distance. Then it snorts. Something has amused the Beast, but it does not say what it is.

"No matter. I have considered your proposal and I will take care of my side of the bargain. You know my price and what awaits you if you fail to make good on it. Crossing me would be folly. You know this."

The man pulls the collars of his greatcoat up tightly around his ears.

"Have no fear about payment. I will honour my promise. What will you do with your prize once you have it?"

The Beast growls and rakes the sand with one great paw.

Old Kind, the spirits of stream and hill were still active and potent. There was still a balance, and the Iceni would help to keep it that way for as long as they could.

Boudica was energised and happy. She knew her own future, what lay around the next bend and where her path was leading. It hadn't always been that way. The sacrifices that she had made in the beginning would have broken any other ruler and the promises that she at first regretted making, had proved to be right. And the great pact she had made? If she hadn't gambled and made it, her head would have ended up on the tip of a Roman spear long ago.

She looked at the Moon and mouthed a silent prayer to the White Eyed Mother.

"Make me fast and make me brave, my lady."

As Boudica waited for the Goddess of the Moon to bestow her blessing, a plane flew across the sky between them. It would be landing at City Airport nearby. If her Druid advisor had been there, he would have proclaimed it as some sort of magical fusion of the old ways and the new, and a clear sign that she would *fly* to victory. Or some other complete rubbish. She smiled and imagined the old fool's face. He was ancient but kind and he would be missed when he was finally summoned to the Heart of the Forest to sleep under the hill.

From nearby, the sound of a hunting horn pierced the stillness – it was nearly midnight and time for the race to begin. This was her favourite night of the year; it was a chance for her to feel like a warrior queen once more. She breathed it all in, the sway of the trees and the soft hum of the rushes by the waterside. Bats whipped past overhead, and there was the occasional yap from a nosy fox, hungry and searching for food. The Wetlands was an almost perfect arena, and she had won many victories here. Boudica liked how the lights from the windows of the apartment blocks at nearby Manor House made the surface of the water look as though it were strewn with small neon flowers that rippled endlessly. London in 2021 was a fine place to live. It was just a shame that she would have to leave it sooner than she wanted.

She gave the rein in her left hand a quick flick, and her well-trained team pulled away. All the racers gathered here tonight were from prominent *Under Folk* families. Rochester was here of course, drunk as usual, but not to be underestimated. Then there was Norfolk, a bastard of the first degree and his close friends, the Romans. There were a few new faces among the crowd tonight too. Boudica smiled. There must always be fresh blood. *Always*. Albion demands it. As she drew nearer to the starting line, she saw her entourage and family drinking in the blue and white tent with the golden livery. The Iceni were the Underworld's largest and most powerful family. Their empire stretched far and wide and their fortune was vast. They had a hand in most criminal enterprises and provided certain services for London's magical communities. More recently, they had branched out into the Mundane world – something that she was still not comfortable with.

As she manoeuvred her chariot towards the start, a mobile phone went off nearby, and the annoying ring tone caused Enbarr to shy away. Boudica made a clucking sound, and the horse snorted in reply. It was good to see some of her children enjoying life. She had always regretted not telling them more often to worship *life* rather than *money and power*. One of them would see the light, *hopefully*.

The crowds began to cheer and roar and as Epona and Enbarr sensed the occasion, they tossed their heads back and stepped high. They wanted to show the world why their queen had chosen them above all others. Then the hordes of the Iceni saw Boudica, and they cheered as she passed by. Flowers were thrown and great horns filled with mead were thrust into the air. Froth flew everywhere and showers of golden liquid rained down on the revellers. Some of the guests regretted wearing Givenchy and Prada.

The other families had pitched their tents nearby and she received loud catcalls and the odd insult or two. The banter and the songs helped make the evening what it was, and Boudica, if she was completely honest, enjoyed it immensely.

When she drew up next to one of the new racers, a tall and broad-shouldered girl that reminded her of herself in many ways, she suddenly felt her years and subconsciously stood as tall as possible and affected a slightly comical pose. The feeling lasted only a few seconds and she burst out laughing at her silly behaviour.

Acting like a first-time racer at your age? Ridiculous woman, get a hold of yourself, she muttered.

The girl in the next chariot held her team well. She may look like a novice but there was every chance that she would show no hesitation in smashing Boudica into the water or edging the Queen of the Iceni's chariot towards the trunk of a tree. Boudica would have to watch her closely. The colours she wore identified her as being one of the ghost children from the White City. They were good people, and she nodded to their champion. Once all eight charioteers had formed on the start line, one of the druids lifted a horn to his lips and sounded the first blast. On the second, they would be off.

The first circuit was slow; all the racers watched each other, looking for their opponents' weaknesses. The second lap was quicker, and already a few had fallen. Inexperience and a false sense of invulnerability were more dangerous than an empty chariot being pulled by a team of wild horses. Only five charioteers now remained. As they began the third lap, Norfolk was the first to move. His team of jet-black horses ran on fear. They were badly treated at home and had become mean and nasty, just like their owner. Boudica disapproved of the way he treated his horses, but she had a grudging respect for his abilities as a racer. When he decided to act, he did so without fear.

Boudica watched him swerve across the track and then, at the last moment, he pulled hard on his right-hand rein and used his riding platform as a battering ram. The last remaining Roman tried to pull back and avoid contact but he had reacted too slowly, and he followed his horses into the water. As the remaining chariots skidded around the bend on the approach to the tents, Boudica calmly threaded her horses through a small gap between two chariots ahead of her. As expected, the sudden sight of the Iceni Queen appearing on their shoulder caused both to panic, and they tried to close the gap, but it was already too late. Their wheels met, spokes splintered, and both platforms flew upwards, throwing both charioteers into the air like dolls. The broad-shouldered girl would have a few bruises to show for her first real race.

Boudica allowed the reins to play out a bit, and the horses felt it and started to speed up. They had been given their freedom, and the sudden burst of acceleration nearly threw her off the back of her chariot. *Gods, it was good to be alive*! The track ahead was empty – her horses were like two bright comets tearing the dark night to pieces, and the torches on the trackside were not lying. She was so far ahead that she could afford to look back. It would have earned a swift rebuke from the old Hibernian, but what the hell. Boudica shot across the finishing line and used all her strength to pull the horses back and reduce speed. The team had been travelling so swiftly that the chariot sped down the track and away from the tents. Boudica pulled hard at the reins again and shouted at her girls to slow down and stop playing around. They had destroyed the competition and were just showing off now.

Once she had them under control, she turned them neatly around and pointed them back in the direction of the crowds and the tents. Rochester, Norfolk and the other surviving charioteers eventually crossed the finishing line and thundered past. A few raised their arms in salute, and she acknowledged them.

A good ruler must never miss an opportunity to remind the enemy of its weaknesses.

That piece of advice had come from her late unlamented husband. He was a terrible ruler, but his advice was sound. It was just a pity that he hadn't learnt to listen to it.

She looked over her shoulder and saw that the other racers had decided to give their horses another lap of the track, and it was while her head was turned to watch them that it happened.

A monstrous black shape flew out of the bulrushes at the water's edge and hit her chariot so hard that she was thrown into the air and landed in the bushes near the trees. She was winded, her lungs felt as though they had been flattened by a blacksmith's hammer and her right arm felt dead. Boudica, who had survived much worse, reacted as she had done on countless battlefields and summoned the strength, from somewhere, to stand up. There was blood in her right eye, and she was dizzy.

No matter! said the small voice inside, *fight on, fight on and never kneel!*

Boudica set her back against the trunk of a tree and closed her bloody eye. She still had one that was fully functioning and one good arm. Whoever had attacked her had better be more of a man than she was, or he was going home in an envelope.

She could just make out the lake through the bushes and one sputtering torch. There was no sign of her horses or her chariot. No one would know precisely where she had fallen if the horses had bolted. Boudica tried to calm her breathing and at the same time she searched the ground nearby for something to defend herself with. For once, her legendary luck deserted her, and she was still empty-handed when the bushes in front of her parted and a fell beast edged towards her on silent paws.

"Black Shuk, you rancid animal, you know who I am and what you have done! Your disgusting black hide will be decorating the ground in one of my privies before the next moon."

There was no reply from the hound, and it attacked so swiftly that she was lifted from the ground once again and thrown against the trunk of a tree.

"Speak then, Beast, on whose orders are you made assassin? You are too stupid to attack me out of spite."

The creature closed the distance between them in one bound and placed one great paw over Boudica's mouth.

"You will know soon enough *Queen of the Iceni*. There will be a new king soon and he will make good on what you have neglected to!"

Boudica suddenly realised who had sent the great Black Beast of the Fens to kill her. *But she hadn't broken her promise to him*? The pact was still strong, what would he have to gain from this attack? Why take her soul now? They had agreed on a time and a place for that. She had told him that she would give it to him gladly, so why now?

Black Shuk's great jaws opened, and the scent of the death pits flooded out. Then the darkness came, and her last thoughts were stolen away on the tips of sharp yellow teeth and eyes that dripped with blood and despair.

Prince Faelan, heir to the crown of the Iceni, was the first to see his mother's empty chariot career around the bend and raised the alarm. Bedlam and confusion followed. Some of the Iceni charged into the water, hoping not to find an upturned chariot, others disappeared into the trees. Teams were sent to search the undergrowth and the nearby woods, but all returned empty-handed and forlorn.

As silence descended on the assembled ranks of the searchers, the torches nearby crackled, and the wind turned the sounds into the breathing of many dragons.

Prince Faelan pushed through the crowd and vaulted onto Boudica's chariot.

"Iceni! The queen is missing, *not dead*. Her body has not been found. She is lost but not gone. We must search this place until we have found out who has taken the queen and where she has been taken. Now, go! Leave no stone unturned!"

Then he returned to the Iceni tent. Rochester, Norfolk and the other Lords were assembled and waiting for him there.

"Let it be known amongst your people and the *Under Folk* that there will be bloody war if our queen is harmed. And believe me when I say that if we do call our banners to arms that none of you shall survive it. Please believe me when I say that. We will use every weapon we possess if we have been wronged, our reach is great and many of your fortunes could be vulnerable if we withdraw our support. Good night my Lords, pray for our queen if you will."

Rochester and Norfolk made their retreat. Soon their tents were gone, and so were the Range Rovers and the SUV's that had transported their followers to the races. All that remained were the Iceni. They searched until the sun rose, and then they too disappeared. They had found some clues – *but not their queen.*

3. A PAW TO THE GROUND

The next visitors to the Woodbury Wetlands were a class from the local junior school on a day out to observe the newts and the dragonflies. Their teacher and her helpers split the children into small groups and then followed them as they explored the park. One of the children was looking to catch a butterfly with a net on the end of a bamboo stick but had been unsuccessful so far. She found running after the insects in her Wellington boots rather difficult and had already fallen over twice, the mud on her coat was evidence of that.

She was about to give up and throw her net into the reeds that surrounded the lake when she saw a large grey cat sitting on one of the jetties. It was looking out across the lake and to a young mind eager to find magic and mystery in the world, she imagined the furry feline to be lost in thought or pining for a princess. Being a cat lover, the girl dropped her net and sat down next to the cat and began to stroke it. Her reward for sharing the love was the sound of contented purring. The cat enjoyed the attention for a few minutes and then grew bored and stood up. It arched its back, and then once it had stretched, trotted off to the entrance to the park. The girl went back to chasing butterflies – unsuccessfully.

The cat stepped through the gate and ambled up to a Hackney Cab parked on the road. The driver was being accosted by a family of tourists and he was busy pointing upwards, through the roof of the cab at his yellow light. The family did not understand his sign language unfortunately, so the driver opened his window and told them that he was on his lunch, politely but firmly. The family stepped away from the cab rank and started to grumble about how this sort of behaviour would not have been tolerated in their country. Their ire was increased when they saw the door open seconds later and a cat jump in.

The cab started its engine and pulled away, leaving a very confused and perturbed family of four from New York. On the back seat of the departing taxi, the cat made itself comfortable, pressed the intercom button with a well-manicured paw and said,

"Take me over to the West End, will you, Charles? I need to see a man about a queen."

"Right you are Cat Tabby sir, I'll have you there in a jiffy."

"Oh, take your time, Charles, I want news of what has transpired here tonight to rage through the Underworld like hellfire. I saw something that will be very useful to a certain someone or very valuable to one or two others. I can't wait to tell our good friend, Mr Dick Wittington, that our luck may have changed – dramatically."

4. ICKNIELD WAY

The rest of the boys had gone to Tallin for the week. Or was it Ibiza? Rob had decided instead to get some fresh air and stretch his legs with a yomp or two and some camping. He'd had his fill of stag parties and lads' tours to Europe's finest flesh pots. There was only so much lager you could drink, automatic weapons you could fire and scantily clad young girls you could ogle in the pole dancing clubs. To be honest, he always felt a bit ashamed of himself and a little disgusted that he and his mates were the reason why these girls did what they did. Still, he was no saint, and he was not going to start preaching to anyone about anything.

He'd been staying at pubs for the last week. They had all been amazing – roaring fires, good food, singing every now and again and soft beds. He had been accepted onto the Royal Marines Potential

Officers Course at Lympstone in Devon. His mum and dad were so proud of him, and he'd been killing himself at the gym and running across the moors until his blisters had blisters, so drinking for a whole week and starving himself of sleep wasn't really an option. This was what he liked the most anyway, a heavy Bergen on his back and a clear sky. There was also the feeling that you'd achieved something at the end of each day. Miles walked and places seen. Also, his bank balance would still be healthy when he got home.

Rob climbed over a turnstile and started walking up the hill. There was a massive oak tree at the top and he was planning on stopping there for a sandwich and a bit of a rest. The guidebooks said that this was the route that the Iceni tribe and Boudica would have taken to journey across the country. It was one of England's oldest roads. Apparently, after the Romans had defeated her army, Boudica had tried to escape back to her stronghold, East Anglia, along this very track. He liked the idea of walking in her footsteps. She was a warrior and he wanted to be one too. When he got to the rise of the hill, he saw a man standing below one of the great oak's branches, looking away over the fields. Rob got the impression that he was waiting.

When he approached, the man raised a hand in greeting. Rob returned the gesture. The man was not dressed for hiking, and he looked out of place. He was very tall, dark-haired and he looked sad, as if he had been left there for a long time.

"That pack you carry looks heavy young man, why not rest a while and give your shoulders a breather."

Rob was streetwise, he'd grown up in a big town and he knew how to look after himself. Still, there was something about the way that the man talked and moved that put him at ease. He did not feel threatened by him and decided to stop.

"It doesn't feel as heavy as when I started out, it was a shock putting it on and walking the first mile," said Rob.

"All journeys are like that aren't they? Some people never set foot on a new path for fear of failing, and others feel empty if their road never changes. Have you far to go?"

Rob removed his pack and set it down.

"Only a few more miles of this leg of the journey, then I head towards the coast where I hope to get a bit of sailing in."

"Across the flat lands to the water? The weather looks as though it will stay bright for you, it will be a wonderful journey, I envy you."

The sun had heated the ground all day and the grass was warm and soft. Rob sat down next to his pack and took out his lunch. It consisted of a ham sandwich, an apple and a bar of something that was supposed to give you energy. The only thing it had given Rob so far was stomach cramps, so he put it back in his pack. He offered the man half of his sandwich and was quietly grateful when his offer was respectfully declined.

"So, what brings you out here? We're a few miles from anywhere that you could park a car and there are no pubs nearby."

Rob found it easy to talk to the man. Normally he was a bit shy, and it had been remarked on during both of his interviews for the Royal Marines. He was attempting to cure himself of that.

"I always come here, to this exact place and on this day each year. I have an agreement with a *friend.* She meets me here and we talk about old times and try to resolve a few issues, nothing romantic, although sometimes I wish it were. We met here a long time ago and it's become a bit of a pilgrimage for both of us. Today is the first time that she has not appeared."

Rob chewed on his ham sandwich and swallowed. The man sounded sad and disappointed, and he looked back towards the vast trunk of the tree. It was as if he were trying to will this special friend into being. The seconds passed by and the man suddenly turned back and remembered that Rob was there.

"Oh, excuse me, Robert, my manners are atrocious. May I sit?"

Rob waved at the spot next to him and the man sat down.

"It's getting late in the day now; do you think she will show up?"

"Oh, it is far too late for her now, Robert. I'm afraid that we will not meet under this great tree *ever again*. Part of our agreement is that if one of us does not attend at the given time then they must pay a price."

Rob tidied his sandwich paper away and started to munch on the apple. The sun was dipping, and the shadows were growing fat.

"What sort of price? Will she have to buy you dinner or something like that?"

The man managed a rueful smile.

"I'm afraid it will be a little bit more costly than that. It has been nice to meet you, Robert – you will pass your course and wear your green beret with pride. I must be away now, goodbye."

"Thank you, I'm sorry, did I mention that my name was Robert or that I was joining the Royal Marines? My friends tell me that I've turned into a bit of a bore on the subject, it's just that I don't remember telling you."

"Good luck, Robert. Walk straight down the Icknield Way until you reach the small stone wall and turn left – the Golden Torque public house is just over the rise. Wish the children of the Iceni well as you cross the bridge, and you'll receive a warm welcome from the Landlord. I think he may even feed you and put you up for free."

And with that, he strolled off in the opposite direction and by the time Rob had lifted his heavy pack onto his back, he was gone.

I don't remember telling him about the Marines thought Rob as he continued to walk in Boudica's footsteps.

5. THE CANOPY

The sky above the Time Fields was a lie. A deceit. No, it was worse than that, it was an affront. Little more than a dead space that crackled with silent thunder and dark lightning. Underneath this foul canopy stretched a landscape of ghost worlds. And in them, were creatures and spirits that were not even good enough for the Pit.

He wanted to tear it all down and destroy it. Let it all be levelled and burned. Chasen had grown sick. He had succumbed to a terminal disease called anger. It had spread through his entire body like a primitive cancer. And from his heart, that mighty organ, spite and violence was pumped.

Chasen was one of the Black Museum's new custodians. Formerly an angel of the Host. Now, in his mind, a jailer and a warder at the most unusual prison ever built. Once he was a mighty warrior. Trusted with great and important errands. A shining light in the ranks of heaven's finest army. *Now this*. Madness had come to call, and this unwelcome guest had been made very welcome – indeed. Chasen, had begun to hate everything and everyone. But there was one person that he elevated above all others.

Ever since that little bastard Judas arranged for us to become turnkeys and lackeys at this Black Museum of Scotland Yard, we've seen no natural light nor even an open sky! We should be flying through the stars and standing shoulder to shoulder with our brothers and sisters. We were champions of the Heavenly Host! We should not be confined in here and made to keep watch over ghosts and evil spirits! How did Judas convince the Archangels to sanction this imprisonment? Because that's what this is, it's incarceration, punishment and torment. I shall bring Judas down, and if I can't hurt him, I know someone that will delight in finding a way to make him suffer.

Chasen continued to speak to himself as he flew over the Time Fields. When at last he grew tired of venting and shouting into the dark sky, he angled his wings forward and began to lose height. He had found a place to set his anger free. He had discovered it quite by chance and now he was on his way there – again. Chasen had found solace in the torment of others. For an angel of the Host, he had fallen very far.

Chasen had a partner called Hutriel. He was also an angel of the Host and had been ordered to serve Judas in the Black Museum alongside Chasen. Unlike his old friend, Hutriel had preserved his anger for the enemies of God. He was not a true warrior. His skill lay in diplomacy. He and Chasen had been tasked with watching Lucifer the Morningstar, whilst on Earth. They were a good team, able to solve a problem with a sword or a soothing word when and if required. But now, the despair and rage that had consumed Chasen had driven them apart. Hutriel felt a great sorrow for his friend, but he was still of the Host and he knew that if Chasen's behaviour was known then he would suffer greatly for it.

Hutriel was watching Chasen carefully, following him and observing from afar, and he despised himself for it. Hutriel had embraced his new role, he had been stung by the decision that tied them both to this strange place, but he had taken his medicine as the mortal children say. He knew that they were being punished and what's more, he knew that they deserved it. Chasen was too arrogant to see the situation that way and he was suffering for it now. Something inside Chasen had perished and the loss of it was turning him mad.

Hutriel had noticed that the mood of the Time Fields had changed in the last few months since their arrival, and not for the good. It was a prison, and it should be a place of contemplation and punishment, more akin to Hell than Heaven of course, but there was no need to torment the prisoners as Chasen was doing. That was not their role. They had stepped across the line when dealing with DCI Judas Iscariot, and Chasen had not realised that Judas was part of a much bigger plan, to their cost. But God's will is God's will and if they were supposed to be here then Hutriel would make sure that *he* did not falter again. If that meant speaking to Chasen or even betraying him, he would do it for a chance to re-join the Host.

He saw Chasen far below him, gliding through the void and when he saw him veer away to the right and drop down, Hutriel's heart fell with him. This was the same place that Hutriel had followed him to not three days since. He saw Chasen land outside a small cottage and began to circle in the air, not so close that he would be seen and not so far away that he couldn't hear. A whisp of smoke that looked like black string was trying its hardest to escape from the chimney stack and failing miserably. The windows of the cottage were empty, and the door closed. Outside the cottage were row upon row of perambulators, and inside each one was a crying baby. Chasen landed right in the centre of their ranks. The noise was dreadful, and the stench was fierce. Chasen raised one hand and sang a short song and when he had finished all the babies had fallen asleep.

The door to the cottage swung open suddenly and its handle clattered against the stone wall. The doorway was a black rectangle and from it a woman rushed out. Her name was Amelia Dyer and long ago, she had murdered 300 children in her care. She was disturbed, insane, and the crazed look in her eyes indicated that she was still in her body, but not connected to it. Her madness had sliced the bond between perception and reality some time ago. Her punishment, after she had been hanged by the neck until dead, was the care of the thousands of infants that surrounded her cottage. But, as with the other inmates, she could not interact with what she saw. Amelia could hear their cries and do nothing about them. She could smell their soiled nappies and never be able to change them, and she could not do what she wanted most of all. Which was to reach inside each pram and squeeze their little necks until the silence came. Every day was the same for her. And she deserved it. What she wanted, was quiet, peace, tranquillity, but the babies cried on and on.

Chasen watched her as she wandered around the massed ranks of the children with her hands over her ears. As the silence reached her, Amelia started to smile a strange, lopsided smile, and then her hands came away from her ears and she began to float on the sea of tranquillity. She closed her eyes and lifted her head up and her body began to shake, tremors of relief coursed through her, and she let out a silent howl. Chasen waited until she had stopped crying. He gave her a few moments of peace and then, like a spoiled brat that has allowed another child to ride its bicycle, he pushed her off by clapping his hands together loudly. The children began to wail once again. Thousands cried out, begging to have their empty stomachs filled or their red raw bottoms changed.

The change in Amelia was instant. Her hands shot up to cover her ears and she started to cry and shake uncontrollably. Chasen stood by and began to laugh. He watched her scramble back inside the cottage and slam the door, but he had not finished. Again, and again, he sang. Quiet followed cacophony and Amelia descended even further down into the darkness of her own insanity.

Chasen, continued to laugh at his *special joke* and from high above him, Hutriel shed a tear, not for the babies or the murderess – but for his friend. They had spent a lot of time in each other's company and had become close friends. But this angel was not the same angel that he had come to love and trust. Chasen was not in the ranks of those that were cast down from the City of the Heavens, in the First Fall of the angels; but maybe he should have been. It was clear to Hutriel now that Chasen had lost his way. His heart was black.

Hutriel hung there in the grey sky. His white wings made a hole in that dark firmament and he could sense a change in the Time Fields. Tension. Hostility. Anger. It was all around him.

What kind of custodian allows that to happen? thought Hutriel.

He watched Chasen fly away and followed the sound of his laughter back to the Black Museum. Dark times lay ahead. Judas must be told, before things really got out of hand.

6. THE GOLDEN TORQUE

The motorcycle courier turned left into the mews and dropped a gear. The throaty roar of his bike fell by a few decibels and he coasted to a halt in front of Number 26 Fen Court. The name 'Iceni International Ltd' was engraved on a polished brass plaque on the wall to the left of the main door. The courier flipped out the kickstand on his bike using his right foot and then, with an economy of movement that would have impressed a Black Belt 5th Dan, he dismounted and reached for the keys in the ignition. Said keys were attached to a bright yellow plastic slinky that was in turn connected to the rider's jacket pocket. Rummaging in a pocket for your keys after the 500th delivery of the day necessitated such an arrangement.

He reached out with a gloved hand and turned the key and the slinky shot back into his pocket like the tongue of some jungle tree frog. He dismounted, unclipped the fastening on his parcel box on the back of the bike and removed a package. It was the size of a small to medium pizza. He checked the address and then walked straight through the automatic glass doors of the bank and popped the package on the counter.

The young man behind the counter, dressed in the sort of uniform you'd expect to see in a manga film or an exclusive restaurant signed the courier's chit and waved him goodbye. The young man read the name of the package's recipient and quickly pushed a button on the underside of his desk. Seconds later, a hidden door opened behind him. Another man, dressed identically to the first emerged and the package was picked up and taken to the boardroom, six floors above.

Prince Faelan was exhausted, as his reflection in the highly polished wooden table in front of him showed. There was still no word or clue as to the whereabouts of his mother and tensions within the family were rising. As next in line to the throne and ruler in Queen Boudica's absence, retaliation for her abduction was expected. Physical or economic, it didn't matter which one of the two, only that it happened. Faelan did not want war but nor did he want to appear weak and slow to act. His mother's Druid counsel had offered their services and advice and if some news of her plight did not arrive soon then he would have to go to them and make a plan.

Faelan sat back in his chair and tilted his head back and tried to relax his aching neck and shoulders. He was giving serious thought to having a nap or getting on the first flight to somewhere hot and far away from the current situation when there was a faint tap on the door. Sunbathing or sleep would have to wait.

"Enter!" Faelan sat up and tried to look like a future king.

The door flew open and one of the guards ushered a servant in. The boy was carrying a small package. Faelan waited until the door had closed once again and he was alone before examining it. He found the tab on the side, slipped the tip of his index finger under it and prised it up. Once he was able to grip it properly, he ripped the flap off and opened the box. There was one item inside.

Faelan removed it and then shouted.

"Get back in here!"

The guard came running.

"Get onto the courier company that delivered this, I want the rider and their despatch operator here within the hour. Check the CCTV footage from the front door too, I want that bike's registration number straightaway."

"Y-y-yes sir!" stammered the guard.

"And on your way out, get my secretary to call my brothers and sisters immediately, I want them here as soon as possible. I don't care what they're doing, tell them that it is vital that they get here."

Faelan picked up his mother's Golden Torque. It was solid gold and fashioned into a collar with the head of a stallion at each end. It was the symbol of his people, sacred and some said, imbued with great power. Boudica had worn this for hundreds of years. To his knowledge, she had never taken it off and never allowed it to be touched by any hand other than her own.

If it is here now, she must be dead, he thought.

"And I am king," said Faelan to the empty room.

The words sounded small. There was no substance to them, it was almost as if he were trying them on for size. Faelan sat down again and felt even worse than he had done before the knock on the door. Below him, six floors down, all hell was breaking loose. Messengers would be scouring the city of the Under Folk for princes and princesses and armed guards would be appearing in the offices of courier firms all over Zones 1 and 2.

His youngest brother, Morcant, was the first to arrive, closely followed by his oldest sister, Fedelmid. Drustan and Oebfinn arrived together. Once everyone was seated, Faelan produced the torque and the room fell silent.

"It was delivered an hour ago by a motorcycle courier. The rider has been found and one of our people is talking to him. The despatch operator for the courier firm has supplied us with the names and addresses of anyone that has booked a delivery slot with him in the last seven days. One of mother's advisors has verified that it is hers; the druids have divined that the strands of hair attached to it belong to her. There was no blood, and the torque is undamaged as you can see. There was no note and there has been no contact since it arrived. Why it was delivered by a human from the Mundane world is still unexplained. The torque could have come to us by any number of ways. I fear the worst."

The room was silent and then as if following some invisible signal, all of the Iceni children started shouting questions and slamming the table. Faelan allowed them this outpouring because it was needed. When the cries began to fade, he held both hands up, palms facing outward, a silent appeal for peace.

"Brothers and sisters, we are all tired and our people demand that we strike out, but against who, and where? Shouting even louder gets us no nearer to the truth. I am being urged to speak to the Druid Council, pressure is building, someone or something is steering us towards all-out war and destruction. Or at least, that is how I feel."

Drustan spoke first.

"How do we know she is dead? This proves nothing so far."

Oebfinn, the youngest of them all, normally so reserved and quiet, found her voice.

"Mother would never allow for it to be taken from her, but there is no blood on the torque nor signs of a struggle or fight. Could she be unconscious somewhere, in a ditch, waiting for us to find her?"

"How then has the torque come to us? If she gave it up freely, which I don't believe she ever would, why has the messenger that delivered it not alerted us to her location, why take the torque and return only that? It must be a challenge. Someone thinks that they can take our mother from us, and our wealth and our great power. The Under Folk have long considered us to have grown too large. There is envy all around us and our expansion into the Mundane has not been received well by our friends and our enemies," said Morcant.

The conversation went on long into the night and few things were resolved. None of them truly wanted to accept that the queen, their mother, was dead, but the torque that lay on the table before them all was proof that the symbol of the Iceni power had been taken, and whoever had taken it was saying that anything that the Iceni held dear could be ripped away from them, at any time. They were not feared any more. This was an affront, a slap in the face with a spittle chaser. Their enemy was still in the shadows, but they could attack at any time and without fear. The only thing that they could all agree upon was that the Iceni were under attack, and if they did not show strength now, then their enemies would not wait to show the Iceni theirs.

Prince Faelan watched his kin depart and then sent word to the Druid Council that he would like them to attend him the following day. Then he sent for the

Warden of the Church Roads. The Iceni would need his blessing in order to move their forces across the country if things continued to turn against them.

7. SEWER'S END

DCI Judas Iscariot and Sergeant Lace of the Black Museum at Scotland Yard were covered in blood, and up to their knees in liquid refuse. The recent storms had given the sewer network beneath the capital a bit of a Spring clean, but the stench was still unbearable. Judas and Lace were truly thankful of the morticians Vaseline that Bloody Nora, the Black Museum's friendly pathologist had insisted that they smear beneath their nostrils before descending into London's biggest toilet. Bobbing gently in the water just ahead of them both was the dead body of a troll. It was roughly 6 to 7 feet tall and not in the best shape. Trolls are normally bulky animals, flat-faced and hairy with short, stocky limbs. This one looked like it hadn't had a square meal in weeks, and it had troll mange to boot. Great clumps of its hide had been pulled out or had fallen out of their own accord to reveal a sickly yellow skin underneath. As his torch passed over the hairless holes, Judas couldn't help but think of cheese and his stomach gave an involuntary heave; he couldn't tell if it was hunger or a little bit of nausea stirring in his gut.

Lace and Judas had tracked the Beast down to this level of the sewer network after a tip-off from one of the Under Folk snitches that Judas employed from time to time. He had hoped to find the troll alive, and to bring it in for questioning, but whoever had hired it to carry out the murder of a wealthy warlock from SW18 had got to it first. It appeared that they were in a sewer and at a dead end at the same time.

"There's not a lot more we can do here, Lace. Let's secure the body to the bottom of the ladder. We'll have to bribe Bloody Nora with some orange-flavoured Hob Nobs to send a few of her tame lab technicians down here to collect it. She'll find out what killed it for us. We'll take that belt and the pouch over there. You grab them. We don't want our only pieces of evidence floating down to the Lake."

"Lake?"

Sergeant Lace was new to the Black Museum. She'd been involved in an earlier case and had impressed Judas with her bravery and tenacity. She was good to work with and staunch when trouble came to call, which was becoming more and more frequent, unfortunately. She was fascinated with the Under Folk and the spirits that lived in the Black Museum and was always full of questions.

"There is a dark underground lake a few miles from here, Lace, and in the middle is a little village – or town, it could have grown in size since I was last down there. It's quite a feat of engineering because it's made up of old washing machines, jerry cans, shopping trolleys and quite a few rubble skips – stolen to order, of course."

"Who lives there, sir?"

"Hard to tell these days, Lace, you get a fair few Gentlemen of the Road down there and quite a lot of the *Enchanted*, some Fae and sewer folk, all trying to flog their wares or hide from someone they've shafted.

When this has all been cleared up, we'll take a trip down there and you can get to know whoever is keeping the peace."

Lace nodded enthusiastically – she was ridiculously happy and positive at the strangest of times. He felt like reminding her that they were still standing in a sewer tying the body of a scabby troll to a metal ladder. She just smiled and started to wade over to the far side of the sewer where the pouch that the troll had been wearing on its belt had snagged on a rusted iron pin protruding from the wall. She took a clear plastic bag from her pocket and put her hand inside it. Then, she grabbed the pouch and turned the bag inside out like someone picking up a massive dog turd in the park. After twisting a small clasp around the neck of the bag, she deposited the pouch into the rucksack she wore on her back.

Judas finished securing the dead troll fast to the bottom rung of the ladder and then they made sure to note down which section of the sewer they were in. Once that was done, they began the long walk back to the surface. The sun was rising by the time they emerged from the darkness, but the road sweepers and the die-hard party animals paid them no heed as they walked back to Scotland Yard. Lace took herself off to the female changing rooms, causing some disruption as she undressed. Her police issue overalls were really kicking up and there were some comments to the effect that an incinerator might be better than a washing machine for them.

Judas was showered, changed and having a cup of coffee when Lace entered the office. Not a lot surprised her these days; she'd been introduced to all manner of magical creature and seen some incredible sights already, so the cat sitting in the chair opposite her boss, casually chatting about the weather and passing the time of day just like an old chum down the pub didn't faze her at all.

"Lace, you know Cat Tabby of course," said Judas.

"Good to see you again, Cat, I trust the wounds are all healed?"

Cat Tabby stretched and turned to watch Lace as she crossed the room to sit behind Judas.

"Perfectly fine, Sergeant, nice of you to ask. I was about to ask you the same thing. The dear old Captain of the Night gave us all a bit of a run-around the last time we worked a case together."

Judas nearly fell off his chair.

"Worked a case together! Very good, Cat, you still have your sense of humour. Talking of funny stories, what do you want?"

"Still sharp as a tack, inspector, straight to the point as always. Never mind that I was nearly killed getting vital information that helped solve one of your cases not so long ago. And the pain and the nightmares … still a lot for a cat of my size to bear, inspector. A kind word and an open heart wouldn't be too much to expect would it now?"

"The only thing that worries or scares you and that master of yours is an empty bank account. Come on, we haven't got all day."

Cat Tabby sat up smartly. He was all business now – gone was the fawning feline, he was in negotiation mode and there weren't many better at it than he.

"You won't have heard about this yet, word has it that you've been underground, looking for the cove that stoved that poor warlock's head in. You won't have heard that the Iceni Queen has been murdered – or abducted. They still haven't found a body, but it could be either. Boudica ran a tight ship. The Iceni are power players in the worlds of the Under Folk. Prince Faelan, the next in line to the throne has made it known that if her whereabouts aren't revealed, or her body isn't offered up – then it's war."

It was Judas's time to sit up smartly.

"Cat got your tongue, inspector? You've heard of the Iceni I take it? Very dangerous people, lots of fingers in lots of bakeries. Most of the big tribes owe them money or favours. If Boudica does turn up dead, the Under Folk are going to be ripped apart. Tribe against tribe, Fae against the *Enchanted*, it's going to get very heated in some parts of town very soon if nothing is done."

Judas stood up and walked over to the window. Through it he could see the angels swooping over the rooftops, delivering parcels, picking up deliveries, cleaning the windows of London's high rises and generally putting a shift in and earning a living. This was his London and he'd been put here to save as many souls as possible and keep the bad guys in check. War amongst the Under Folk would be catastrophic right now. There was a lot of tension between rival factions, Warlocks were getting murdered and there were lots of blue pins in the map of London and its surrounding areas on the wall. Each one was an unsolved case, and the Black Museum was acting strangely too – there seemed to be a lot of unrest in there, more than usual, in fact. Something was stirring up a lot of ill-feeling in the Time Fields. Judas turned away from the world outside and looked straight into Cat Tabby's golden eyes.

"So then, Cat Tabby, purveyor of porkies and the odd bit of useful information, what do you have?"

Cat Tabby slumped back into the chair, his long, slinky tail, flicking this way and that.

“Well, inspector, it just so happens that I was over at the Manor House coliseum the other night. I like a bit of chariot racing, and it was while I was casually taking a little look at some of the runners and the riders that I saw a very unusual customer creep into the woods, where it made a lot of effort not to be seen. Then it waited for a certain, distinguished person to come around the bend and it attacked. I saw it all, from start to finish, inspector, and I even heard most of what passed between them when they spoke to each other. It might be useful for someone like you to hear what someone like me has to say. Of course, if you think that dependable comes to help when called by others, Cat Tabby is swinging the lead, then I shall be on my way.”

Cat Tabby’s perpetually swishing tail beat the time to its owner’s narrative like a composer’s baton. Judas just smiled. He’d known Cat Tabby for most of his nine lives so he could tell when he was lying. Unfortunately, this wasn’t one of those times.

"As the keeper of the peace and as far as I'm aware, the only sheriff in town, you should be telling me what went on the other night at the chariot races as a matter of course. Doing one's bit as they say. But, seeing as you're you and I'm me, what do you want, Cat Tabby?"

"Well seeing as we're all being so honest with each other, *we*, which is Dick Whittington and I, want to get back into the Real Estate business and were thinking that you might have a word with the Women of the Chapel and see if they could *'do their bit'* to stop a war from happening, and a lot of good, innocent magical folk from getting killed or butchered."

Lace, who had been watching Cat Tabby closely during his conversation with Judas felt a massive urge to usher the feline from the building with the toecap of her boot.

"The last time we met, you did something brave without the promise of reward, Cat Tabby. You ended up quite pally with Meg, she of the brightly coloured and very expensive silk scarves, and the capacity for violence if miffed. Why don't you go straight to her and see what you can work out together? She still leads the Women of the Chapel, doesn't she? If war is on the horizon and you can help us avert it, the money or the property shouldn't come into it."

"Sergeant Lace, your master chose well when he recruited you, fine words, spoken well. Let us just say for the time being that the Women of the Chapel and my good friend and colleague, Richard Whittington, have had what we might call a falling out, on a point of honour, if you like."

Judas leaned in.

"He touched her silk scarf, didn't he? Wanted to see if the rumours were true about what she concealed underneath it, didn't he? The bloody idiot! He's lucky to be alive."

"Well put, inspector – on the button, the head of the nail and in the red bit of the target. When he returned to London, he was in poor shape, and he now has problems in a *delicate region*."

Lace started to laugh, and Judas sat back in his chair and did something he hadn't done for a long time. He smiled.

"Look, Cat Tabby, after what you say happened, I don't know if anything I can say would have any bearing on Meg's decision to help you two or not. Especially after what you just told me. But I will try if you tell me everything about the Iceni and the events you witnessed. There are other property tycoons among the Under Folk."

Cat Tabby waited for Lace to stop laughing. Every time he was about to start talking, she erupted into a fit of giggles; it got to the point where she excused herself, rather than cause Cat Tabby any further embarrassment.

"Now that the comedy cabaret has finally finished, I shall tell you all, inspector. But before we start, I should say that I did think about going to the Iceni first but decided against it, on the grounds that they are a nasty bunch, and I wasn't sure that I'd get out alive – or paid. The attacker was Black Shuk. He doesn't leave East Anglia much these days and he is hard to miss if you are a distant relative, as it were. He's a right handful though and he is a killer, lots of folk have perished by those claws. He smashed Boudica's chariot to pieces and went after her. She was badly injured but still full of that warrior anger, stood up to Black Shuk, but he just put one of those big paws of his on her and that was that. She kept saying that 'she was ready to go with him' and that she 'hadn't broken their promise'."

Did you see this 'Black Shuk' kill her then?"

"No, inspector, I didn't, one second they were there, in the middle of the thicket, her bleeding all over the place and him pawing at that golden necklace of hers, and then *'poof'* – they were gone!"

"Is that the way that he works, does he take his victims anywhere special, does he eat them or hide them away, fatten them up, that sort of thing?" asked Judas.

"He had a thing for fire at one point, inspector, but as for a signature as it were, no, there's nothing he likes to do, apart from kill. He wasn't always that way though, turned bad some time ago, he's angry about something that was done to him, that's all I know."

"Okay, Cat Tabby, this is what I'm going to do, I'm going to look into this and if what you say is true, I will try and get something sorted out with the Women of the Chapel. If they won't help there is *someone else* – they may want to do me a favour, that's the best I can do right now. If you remember anything else in the meantime you know where to find me."

Cat Tabby left as quietly and as quickly as he had arrived. Judas went back to his desk, leaned back in his expensive German designer leather chair and started to rub his thumb over the surface of the silver coin he always carried with him. It was one of thirty that he had received in payment a long, long time ago.

8. THE DIENER

Victoria had been preparing the dead bodies for the arrival of a very special visitor. She had also spent a little more time on her own appearance, too. A new dress, a haircut that was long overdue and a new pair of glasses – the old ones made her look like a cross between a forger and a malnourished gamer. She was going to be wearing her lab coat all the time and have her hair scraped back. It was hospital policy of course, but she felt as though she should make the effort. Regardless, it made her feel good. One week ago, she had been woken from a deep sleep by the nuisance that was her mobile phone.

It was new and she hadn't had a chance to set it up the way she wanted. The ringtone was too loud and so achingly trendy that she felt embarrassed every time the thing rang. Initially, she thought it was Richard, her boyfriend … the rotten Richard, drunk again and having lost his keys or wallet deciding to treat her to his nocturnal fumbling and bad breath. She swore that the last time was the last time; but she had needs, just like everyone else. In the beginning it was great; he was funny and gentle. Then he started leaving his pants on the floor, expecting them to be picked up and placed into her washing basket, then to rise from the dead, freshly laundered, with a hint of ocean spray and subservient serving wench. She told him not to come over again, but he had appeared one night, sober and shaven, offering a bottle of so-so wine and an apology. Victoria accepted the wine but ignored the apology.

She was getting ready to shout something nasty, but then she heard the voice on the other end. It wasn't rotten Richard at all, it was the man she knew only as the Chamberlain. She was awake instantly – the Chamberlain spoke, and she listened – then, when he rang off, she found that she was unable to go back to sleep again. Tonight, her king, the Lord of the Dieners, the Silent King of the Resurrection Men was coming to see her. He was due within the hour, and he was looking for new soldiers, so she had been working around the clock to make as many bodies as presentable as possible. The hospital was busy, yet another strain of Covid had been detected and people were worried. That meant more admissions and more walk-ins to A&E. Corridors that were normally empty soon filled up with gurneys and wheelchairs. When that happened, everything got stretched and quiet places, like her morgue, suddenly became very interesting to registrars and hospital managers. They didn't see corpses; they saw space for more beds.

To hell with them she thought as she slammed and locked the big mortuary door. There was only one way into the morgue now, and that was through the delivery bay. Victoria had disabled the lights and all but one of the camera feeds as instructed by the Chamberlain.

The hands on the clock on the wall sliced their way through the silence and Victoria settled down to wait with a cup of tea from her thermos – she didn't trust the vending machines – and a steak slice that she'd found in her locker. It tasted okay, even if it was three weeks past its best. She was halfway through it when the man in the dark suit stepped out of the night behind the morgue and into the little black and white world of the screen in front of her. She recognised the Chamberlain straight away. Two more men joined him, heavy-set men with thick heads and sharp blades, no doubt. Then the king arrived, and Victoria flipped the switch that would release the lock to the door at the rear of the morgue.

"Victoria, it's good to see you again, you do our guild a great service," said the Chamberlain.

"It is my pleasure to serve, as always, my Lord."

Victoria was feeling more alive than she had in months. But now as her senses were heightened, she heard the sound of water once again, felt the pull of the tide and the roll of the waves. It was always like this when she was in his presence. She remembered the noose and the baying of the crowds. She remembered how the smell of the hemp rope they placed over her head had made her gag, and feeling her stomach turn as she dropped through that infernal hatch. Then there was the shame. Everyone who swings on the gibbet soils themselves. Her neck had been snapped and she was suffocating, but all she could think of back then was that she had shat herself and that everyone could see it. Victoria was beginning to feel uneasy and scared, but then she heard a strong voice calling her back to the present day, and it made her feel safe again.

"Victoria Hepplethwaite! You were hung by a mob for the heinous crime of stealing bread for your baby. You died once, my dear, you do not need to live through it again. When your body was presented to me by the children of the Mudlarks, I mended it and brought you back to life. All those that laughed and jeered at you as you danced the hangman's jig are now nothing more than ash and bone. You have lived more lives than all of them combined. Do not remember that day and do not torment yourself. All is well."

Victoria saw him then; the Chamberlain and the bodyguards had moved to one side and the Silent King stood at the centre of the room. He reached out to her –

he wanted to take her by the hand, but she fell to her knees instead.

"Now, now, Victoria. There will be no bowing today, nor will there be any need for you to feel threatened or cowed. You are one of my subjects and a much-loved one at that. Stand up and take my hand, I should like to know what has been keeping you busy, and away from my court and *your friends*."

They talked and Victoria was genuinely pleased that the Silent King wanted her to talk of her life, he wanted to listen to her words. He didn't grow bored or impatient and she felt so comfortable in his presence that she wanted to hang up her lab coat and return to his court that night. He was a beloved king, and a good ruler and Victoria knew that the best way to serve him was to do her job and find him as many suitable followers as she could.

"My king, here are ten good bodies, young men mostly. Car crashes whilst under the influence, a couple of suicides – social media pressure mostly, it's killing more and more of them it seems – two fatal stabbings and the rest are heart attacks or drug related."

The Silent King moved around the room, lifting a shroud here and reading a toe-tag there. He seemed content.

"You have done well yet again, Victoria; they will all make good subjects. Mr. Stick and Mr. Twist will take them away now, and then I will bring them back from the dark world of the dead at the next high tide. We must be away now; the Chamberlain keeps looking at his watch. Pretending to adjust his cufflinks is an old trick of his, but it is true, the night is nearly over, and we have much to do. Be well, Victoria, we shall see each other again soon."

Victoria bowed even though she had been told not to and the Silent King acknowledged it with a smile. A lorry reversed into the bay and the bodies were loaded onto it. The Chamberlain and the Silent King stood to one side, their heads together. Victoria wanted to know what they were saying but knew that it did not concern her; she was happy just to serve. Mr. Twist took his seat behind the wheel of the lorry and Mr. Stick joined him in the passenger seat. For two highly trained bodyguards it was a total dereliction of duty and a massive mistake not to have seen to their king's safety first. In their defence, who in their right mind would want to try to kill the Silent King of the Resurrection Men?

It was lucky for them that Victoria had remained alert. She saw the hooded figures emerge from the darkness and shouted a warning. Her orders had been to turn off the lights at the rear of the morgue so that her Lord might leave unseen. She had obeyed the order without question, but now she felt as though she had cleared the ground for the murderers. They loped across the tarmac of the loading bay towards their quarry like upright foxes. Their knives were curved and when they caught the light, silver smiles appeared in the gloom.

"Stop!"

It was the first thing that came into her mind, not 'beware' or 'look out', just 'Stop!'

The Chamberlain and Mr Stick were the first to die – both had moved swiftly to engage the attackers and had died bravely. Meanwhile, Twist and Victoria manhandled their king back inside where she immediately cut the power to the whole building. They heard the assassins in pursuit, smashing through the swinging glass doors that signposted their target's escape. There were muffled thumps as they fell over each other, and the sound of metal drip trays crashing to the floor as they floundered around in the darkness and the unfamiliar terrain of the morgue. Victoria knew the corridors and the rows of curtained cubicles like the back of her hand even with the lights off, and she guided her king and his remaining bodyguard to the safest place she knew – the cold chamber at Rose Cottage.

The 'Cottage' was the term that doctors used when describing the morgue in front of patients, lest it worry them or scare them even closer to death. It had been a little 'inside joke' of the morgue staff to change the directional signs on the walls from 'Cold Chamber' to 'Rose Cottage'. At the time she thought it insensitive and childish but now, she blessed every one of them. When the emergency system at the hospital detected that the power was off in the morgue, it would turn it back on straightaway. In the darkness, their pursuers were flailing around like birds trapped in a giant vacuum cleaner, but very soon, they would be able to hunt in the light and in their larger numbers would make short work of finding the king.

She hoped that they would search everywhere but a place called 'Rose Cottage'. If she had the time to cross her fingers, she would, but the sounds of pursuit were growing louder and creeping ever closer. They were not far away now, possibly even in the next room. Victoria took a deep breath and pushed the king through the door to the cold chamber and when the bodyguard had closed it behind them and locked it quietly, she escorted them both to a large silver door on the opposite side of the room.

Victoria used her hospital swipe card to unlock the great slab of steel on hinges before them. It took a very long 10 seconds for it to open. And in that time, she imagined again and again that their pursuers had found them, and brought their shiny, smiling knives down on her and the king. But the door to the chamber entrance remained closed, the lights had gone back on everywhere, but no dark shadow appeared in the glass of the door and no gloved hand clutched at a door handle and shook it. Victoria, the Silent King and Mr. Twist stepped inside the most secure room at Rose Cottage and pulled the door behind them.

When the door closed with a deep and very reassuring clang, they all let out a huge sigh of relief. The light inside the chamber was fierce. Victoria could see that Mr. Twist was covered in blood. Some of it appeared to be his own, but when she asked if he needed help, he declined politely. The adrenalin was still surging through his veins, burning him from the inside like liquid anger. She could see that the murder of his friend and partner was still raw. There would be little point in asking him to stand down, so she didn't and turned her attention to her king.

"Who would dare to attack me?!" His voice, normally so level and clear was flirting dangerously with outright anger and disbelief.

"To kill my Chamberlain, and my men? They must know that war is but a stone's throw from an attack like this. What power in all the *Under Folk* rivals mine own? There is not one tribe, not one great house in all the magical realms that can summon an army big enough to take to the field against me, save one."

The Silent King began to pace up and down; his hand stroked at his chin and occasionally he flicked at a strand of hair that fell forwards onto his face. Mr. Twist was watching the door. He had no counsel to offer, and Victoria, well she was a lowly Diener, a morgue attendant, what could she offer? So, she kept quiet and tried not to think of the Chamberlain and Mr. Stick and the pools of warm blood forming like red lily-pads underneath their pierced bodies.

"It can't be her!"

Victoria was surprised by the intensity of the king's voice.

"Her? Who is *she*, my Lord?" said Victoria.

"The Queen of the Iceni. Only she is powerful enough and brave enough to attempt this heinous act. But why now? We were so close to the end. It makes no sense?"

Victoria knew that the king was talking to himself and stayed quiet.

She sat down and rested her back against the cold wall of the chamber. On the other side of the room, decisions were being made and stratagems formulated. Then the king stopped pacing and talking to himself. He turned to Victoria.

"Open the door, Victoria, we are going to war."

She stood up quickly and Mr. Twist reached for the door handle.

"They c-could s-still be out there," she stammered.

"My men will be here by now and once this great steel portcullis of yours dropped down on those scoundrels, they knew the game was up. If there are any of them standing outside this door, I will make a special effort to resurrect them, because they are truly brave, if a little stupid."

Mr. Twist dipped his head towards the lock and Victoria quickly swiped her key card against it. There was a hiss from the hydraulics; the door shuddered forward an inch and then it began to swing on its overworked hinges. Victoria was scared – she looked to Mr. Twist for reassurance and found only anger and malice in its stead. He was as white as a snowdrift. Most of his blood was on the floor, but he looked strong regardless. His eyes were alert, darting this way and that, searching for his foe. Every muscle was strained; he was ready to engage the enemy. Victoria turned to the king and saw a look on his face that she had only seen once before in all her long life. She was scared. Not for herself or her king – she was afraid for whomever had caused that look to be there.

Rose Cottage was empty. Victoria heard a familiar alarm sounding far away in the main building. She escorted the king and Mr. Twist back to the loading bay at the rear of the morgue. As her Lord had said, there was no sign of the attackers. They had fled. The Chamberlain and Mr. Stick were where they had fallen. Their deaths had been noble but the corpses that lay glued to the tarmac with their own blood were husks of the human beings they had once been. The Silent King walked over and knelt beside the Chamberlain.

"My good friend and advisor, we have walked many a mile together, your counsel has always been good, and I am honoured to have called you *friend*. I cannot raise you from the dead again. I wish that I could, but it is against the old lore of Albion and even I dare not break that lore. So, it grieves me to say it; you must pass on. Be well, old friend, and know that you will be remembered. Not many of us can expect that."

The king began to bless Mr. Stick in the same way, but he was cut short in his praise of his bodyguard when his army arrived with thunder and the great humming of war machines. There were no tanks, only giant black SUV's and swift, impatient motorcycle outriders. They swarmed around the building like dark angry hornets. The riders kept slapping the sides of their helmets, activating the intercom that was wired into their headwear, talking to each other, communicating with each other, like some sort of mechanised hive-mind.

The king turned to Victoria, and she dropped to one knee.

"You will never bow to me again, Victoria Hepplethwaite. Without you, I would be dead, and my body would be anchored to the bed of the Thames by a supermarket trolley. I will have need of you soon, Victoria. Until then, do not worry about what went on here tonight. I will speak to the Hospital Board myself. We'll call it a power cut for now."

A big, burly man took the king's arm and gently ushered him towards the nearest SUV, assisted him inside, and slammed the door. The vehicles had arrived like a thunderstorm, but they left like the lifting of a mist. Victoria watched them go and was about to head back inside when she saw the flat, dark shapes on the ground. Blood always tells.

9. THE BROKEN FENCE

The Gilded Goat was sitting in one of the special rooms that are set aside for the Under Folk that drank at the Lamb and Flag. He was nursing a glass of white wine that had long since turned warm and undrinkable. Nearby, two dwarves were arguing in hushed tones over a large gemstone that pulsed with a green light on the table in front of them. Each time either of their voices rose above a whisper the stone burned orange and yellow and they both calmed down instantly. From where he was sitting the Gilded Goat could see that the dwarves didn't own the priceless gem, *it owned and controlled them*. There were many cursed trinkets doing the rounds. The Gilded Goat had recently been offered a dark ruby. It was the size of a cricket ball, and it could create doors in walls of stone and steel, making burglary and robbery altogether easier. He didn't like to fence cursed objects; they were far too much trouble and there was always an unhappy ending for fence or thief.

He was trying not to be noticed by anyone, which was hard when you were as well-dressed as the Gilded Goat, and you walked upright on two legs. He glanced down at the Rolex on his wrist for the fifteenth time, urging the second hand to spin faster by force of will and to bring his guest and hopefully his saviour to the pub as quickly as possible. He always met Judas here. They had watched many a bare-knuckle boxing fight here together. The front of the bar had been the boxing ring and fighters had been known to fall over it, sending tankards of gin flying. The Gilded Goat tried a sip of his wine and nearly retched. He realised quickly that it wasn't just the alcohol that was making him feel sick.

He had been robbed. He had been well and truly cleaned out and fleeced down to his bare floorboards. He was the best *fence* in London, and he was in trouble. If you wanted stolen gems, magical artefacts, stolen grimoires, cursed blades and magical books converted into cold hard cash – he was your goat. He was trusted and well connected. If it got out that the one and only Gilded Goat had been relieved of stolen goods in his care, he would be ruined and almost certainly murdered. That was why he was meeting with Sergeant Lace of the Black Museum, here at the Flag; she was DCI Judas Iscariot's right-hand woman and already gaining a reputation for being fair and fierce in equal measure. If Judas had sent her in his stead, the Gilded Goat was reassured and feeling slightly less suicidal.

The two dwarves finished drinking and stood up. The gemstone on the table flashed impatiently and they both reached for it at the same time. Another exchange took place between them. It was funny to watch – the hisses and the hand gestures were graphic. An argument was taking place, but only dogs would have been able to hear what was being said.

The door to the special room opened and Sergeant Lace walked in. She nodded at the dwarves but got nothing back in return. The Gilded Goat stood up (ever the gentlegoat) and extended a hoof. Lace shook it and sat down. She was of average height with short dark hair and bright green eyes that were trained to look for the signs of deceit and danger. Lace had only been with the Black Museum for a short time, but she hadn't wasted any of it. When she wasn't backing Judas up, she was in the Time Fields of the Black Museum, talking with the ghosts and spirits of murderers and the most famous villains of all time, learning how they plied their deadly trade so that it couldn't be repeated in the here and now.

The Gilded Goat turned and reached for a bell-cord by the window. He gave it a firm tug and seconds later, one of the servant girls appeared at their table.

"May I tempt you to a cool libation, Sergeant? Wine, beer, gin or something stronger? The mead here is very good, imported from Valhalla they say."

Lace unzipped her jacket and slipped it over the back of her chair. She was wearing a white t-shirt with the name of a Californian surfboard maker over her left breast. She looked incredibly underdressed sitting across from the Goat in his Kilgour two-piece summer suit and crisp Italian shirt.

"A beer sounds great. We haven't had the pleasure of working together as yet and I don't want to put your snout out of joint, so how do you want me to address you? Gilded Goat, Goat or do you have another name I should use?"

The Gilded Goat gave out a little bleat of joy which made the serving girl giggle.

"You may call me Goat if you like, Sergeant Lace."

He turned to the girl and ordered two beers and she slipped away to get them. When he was sure that they were the only two creatures in the room he leaned across the table and started to tell Lace why he had asked her to come and meet with him.

"Before we start, may I ask after the inspector? I hope all is well with him and the Museum?"

"All is well, or at least we think it's well. The Black Museum is acting up, but then, it's always a little fractious in there. I'll be sure to tell the inspector that you asked after him. Now, what can we do to help?"

The serving girl returned carrying two tankards on a wooden tray. The beer was frothy and very cold, and it put them at ease straightaway.

"That is good, isn't it?" said the Goat.

Lace nodded and wiped the moustache from her top lip with the back of her hand.

"Well, Sergeant, the thing is, and this is very hard for me to say, I have been robbed. Everything that I was holding for a couple of colleagues of mine has been pinched. I returned to my lodgings two nights ago to find that my whole stash has been taken. The thief came up through the fireplace, left its sooty footprints all over my Chinese rug and then went back the same way."

"What was in the stash, Goat?"

The Gilded Goat took another pull at the beer in his tankard. Froth stuck to his hairy chin, and he let out another little bleat.

"I had a few very rare items, Sergeant. A collection of the original Heart and Soul playing cards, if you can believe it. Play a hand or two with these lovely picture cards and you could win your heart's desire or even a clean, unsullied soul. Rare as rare can be, Sergeant. And I had a fully charged Moonglow staff too. Tap someone or something with it and no one can see it or them, unless there is a moon in the sky. Very useful indeed. I had a few other trinkets, but the real treasure was a fairy crown. How on earth it had come into the current owner's possession, I am not at liberty to say, but it was worth a kingdom to the Fae, and I knew a buyer that was wealthy enough to pay for it. All gone, every last groat and tarnished gem. The sellers are expecting their money and the buyers are getting hot under the collar to see their new purchases."

"Any idea as to whom it might be, Goat? Have you crossed anyone that you shouldn't have recently, reneged on a deal or put someone's nose out of joint?"

The Gilded Goat, noticing that Lace's tankard was empty reached around and yanked at the cord once again. The girl arrived, cleaned the table and returned barely a minute later with two more. The Gilded Goat was nervous and polished off half his beer in one go.

"There isn't a soul that I have done business with that hasn't been very happy with my services, Sergeant, not a one. I try to keep both parties in any transaction as far apart as possible. That way, they have to keep civil like, and all negotiations go through me, keeps everything above board and keeps the hot headed cool, like this here tankard."

Lace smiled at the Goat's attempt at levity, she could see that he was scared out of his wits but was trying hard to keep a brave face.

"Let me have the address of the property and your key and I will go over and have a look. Is there anywhere you can stay while we look into this for you? I can speak to the chief if you like; the Black Museum isn't a bundle of laughs, but you will be safe there."

The Gilded Goat nodded and then raised a hoof to one of his little sharp horns and scratched at it. It made a sound that reminded Lace of a skiffle band.

"I have a few places to stay, Sergeant. Thank you for the kind offer though, and please pass on my best wishes to Judas. Now, I must be away before darkness falls. I'm not afraid of what it may contain but these damn hooves of mine can be heard from miles off!"

He stood up and handed Lace a set of keys and a scrap of paper with his address on it. Lace watched him go and then started to make a few notes on what they had talked about. Once she'd taken a look at the crime scene, she would go back to the Black Museum and have a word with one of the inmates. A ghost called Raffles, who also went by the title of 'The Gentleman Thief'. He would know a fellow thief's modus operandi straight away. She got up and put her jacket back on. Time was not on their side right now.

10. THE BASE OF THE NEEDLE

The Embankment was busier than normal. Not quite rush-hour, which should be renamed crawl-hour, but a little more frantic than expected for this time of the day. The cars and buses were vying for supremacy of the tarmac. Tricky potholes, hidden away in the gutters, were snagging drivers and riders alike. Millions of pounds would be spent in tyre-changing emporiums and on innertubes from cycling websites. London loves cyclists but treats them mean. The light was escaping over the rooftops and the streetlights had come on. Clever electronic sensors had been fitted to the lights, so that they turned themselves on now.

Morcant loved the city of the Mundane. He was a prince of the Iceni and a prominent figure in the world of the Under Folk. The last few days had been savage, and his kin were feeling the loss of their mother and queen. His driver was weaving through the traffic, and they were making good time. This was the second full family meeting in as many days. Practically unheard of in all the time that they had been here. Things were changing and Morcant was worried that they weren't adapting to that change fast enough. As the youngest male, that was not his problem right now; that onerous honour belonged to his older brother Faelan.

"Good luck with that," he said to no one.

The car came to a halt at the base of Cleopatra's Needle. Morcant waited for his bodyguards to secure the area for him, and as he watched, he shook his head at the shuffling commuters passing from left to right and vice versa in front of him through the car window. Not one of them looked up and saw the wonder of the Needle – life must be pretty interesting for the rank and file to pass it by without a glance or a thought. But it didn't look that way; these people cared more for reality TV stars and small rectangles of phone screens that were anything other than smart.

The car door was wrenched open and Morcant was ushered up the gangplank of a ship that had been converted into a night club and a suite of rooms for people to disappear into.

Faelan has chosen badly again thought Morcant.

If the Silent King were behind the attacks and the kidnap of his mother, then being near, or on, the water wasn't such a bright idea. The king had rescued most of his people from the deep water of the Thames. Was it a show of strength or stupidity? Morcant and the rest of the family were about to find out.

Once aboard, Morcant was directed to a huge, private room at the stern of the ship, on the starboard side, which was yet another tactical blunder. The door opened automatically and Morcant stepped inside. The atmosphere was chilly – either someone had set the AC unit incorrectly or there had been developments.

Princess Fedelmid and Oebfinn sat on one side of the table facing his older brothers, Faelan and Drustan. The heir apparent had not taken his seat at the top of the table. Morcant decided not to pick a side just yet and lowered himself into a leather armchair that would not look out of place in a gentlemen's club in Pall Mall. The choice of seat did not go unnoticed and Morcant thought he saw a slight tic at the corner of his eldest brother's eye.

"Now that we are all here, Morcant, we need to start making some decisions and then acting on them. Our mother, and queen, has not been found, dead or alive – we have scoured this city, from their top to our bottom. There is no word of her from any quarter. In the East, nothing! West, nothing! North, nothing!"

"I think we get the point, dear brother." Fedelmid was looking down at the table, but her voice filled the room, so Prince Faelan stopped broadcasting, settled back and waved his hands above the table, as if to say the floor is yours.

"Brothers and sisters, our people and all of our connections know nothing and have found nothing. I believe that now is the time to bring in some help, someone independent, respected and impartial. I say that we should speak with the Master of the Black Museum. He can go to places that we cannot and speak with creatures and angels. What do you think?"

"Open our doors to an outsider? Mother would never allow it, and neither should we." Prince Drustan had not been very vocal yet, but he spoke what many around the table were thinking. Princess Fedelmid pressed on.

"We are powerful and wealthy, that's true, feared in some places, that is also true, but we have stretched ourselves, and I believe that we have made enemies amongst the people who live above the Under Folk. This city is dangerous, it is a place where whole streets and neighbourhoods disappear overnight to make way for houses that no one lives in and marinas for ships that never sail."

"Fedelmid, we must expand, if we do not then others will. Soon, we will become the minnows and the sharks will feed upon us."

"That is precisely why we must bring in someone else, Faelan. We need another perspective on this."

"Why do we need an outsider, sister?"

"Because, Oebfinn, we are marching into war right now. We have threatened some of the other tribes already. Words spoken in haste at the coliseum when mother was taken, words that cannot be taken back. What do you think that Rochester, and the people of the White City are doing right now? They are not waiting for whoever is responsible to show their hand, it is too late for that. They are making plans, just as we would, and if they are anything like us, blood will be spilt."

Morcant shifted in his seat. The movement caught Prince Faelan's eye.

"And you, little brother? What do you think we should do?"

"I do not think that war is the answer. But I don't believe we should show weakness either. If the Silent King takes one of ours, we should take one of theirs."

Princess Fedelmid sighed and threw her head back and looked at the ceiling. A hatch overhead had been turned into a glass skylight and she wished that she could float through it and join the stars. Her mother had taught her well and she took a breath and then looked around the table at her brothers and sisters once more. Faelan and Drustan wanted conflict; Morcant as usual was neither here nor there, physically or emotionally. Oebfinn was far too young to really appreciate the gravity of the situation they were in. So, she made a decision and then acted upon it.

She got up, marched to the door and opened it. A servant had been stationed there in case they had need of anything. She whispered something in his ear, and he trotted away down the narrow ship's corridor. Moments later there was a quiet tap at the door and when it opened, DCI Judas Iscariot of the Black Museum at Scotland Yard stepped inside. It was going to be a long night. At first there was suspicion and anger that someone from the outside had been invited inside the family, then there was disbelief that anyone other than an Iceni could solve the problem and discover what happened to their mother. Then there was an ending that Fedelmid had dreaded and a small victory for Faelan and Drustan.

"Princes Faelan, Drustan and Morcant, Princesses Fedelmid and Oebfinn, I appreciate that you have taken time to listen to my counsel. As the Master of the Black Museum and keeper of the peace amongst the Under Folk, I must warn you that if you go to war with the Silent King or anyone else, I must get involved. The forces you have at your command are impressive, but I advise you not to go down that road. God himself has put me here, and he has given me an Archangel with a huge, bloody frightening sword, to do my bidding – sort of. You just don't have any evidence that it is the Silent King. Until that materialises, I must remain impartial. I'm sorry, but those are the rules."

Princess Fedelmid nodded to Judas, who got up and left.

Morcant was the first to speak.

"What's with that silver coin that he rubs at? It was in his hand all the time, spinning around and around. He doesn't look all that fearsome to me."

"He's immortal, and like he says, he's got powerful friends, so let's not underestimate him," said Faelan.

"We won't underestimate him, brother, we'll just keep him in the dark. I agree with Morcant, if they come at us, we kill right back."

"So, Faelan, Drustan, you advocate violence and reprisal. I will stand by you, but I will not lift a finger until I am sure of who it is that we fight against. What say you, Oebfinn, little sister?"

Fedelmid turned towards her baby sister and waited for her to answer. Oebfinn looked around the table and chewed at her lip. Fedelmid knew what she was going to say before she said it. This was her mother's great mistake; she had taught them all to fight, but few of them to reason.

"I will not go against the will of the family, if it must be blood, then let it be theirs and not ours."

Faelan turned to Morcant, his was the last vote.

"As I said before, I don't think we should go to war – yet! But if we are attacked, we should defend ourselves, robustly."

"Always in the middle of the stream aren't you, Morcant? Why not dive in one side or the other? Make a change – make a decision for once."

"I just did, dear Drustan, shall I repeat it?"

"Don't tax yourself, little brother, at least the Golden Torque is safe and secure in our vaults. We can all rely on that even when we cannot rely on each other."

Judas walked down the Embankment. His brain was whirring and spinning like a top. He'd hoped that the conversation with Cat Tabby had been more of the feline fixer's twaddle, more of his massaging of the truth to get himself and his partner in crime, Dick Whittington, back in the game. Unfortunately for all concerned, Cat Tabby was on the money, this time. Judas had kept the identity of Boudica's attacker to himself. If he'd made it known that Black Shuk was responsible, the Beast would have been hunted down and the real brains behind this coup would never be discovered.

11 RAFFLES AND THE GOAT

The hotel is alive with the padding of footsteps. Leather slippers swish here and there, punctuated occasionally by the odd sharp stab of stiletto on a well-polished tile floor. There is also the familiar and heavy tread of a Brogue or a Derby shoe. Bells ring from atop the walnut counter of the main desk and chimes from large brass clocks tinkle through the air. Smoke from cigars and pipes floats around the room like the lost children of adult clouds, and green palms are wafted gently by fans high above on the ceiling. In a highbacked leather chair with brass studs that have been polished until they gleam like nuggets in a clear stream, sits Raffles, known to many as The Gentleman Thief.

He is as much a part of the Black Museum as Jack the Ripper, albeit, Raffles has earned the respect of his jailers and helps them to solve crimes rather than commit them. He is a tall, elegant man, well-dressed at any time of the day. His manicured fingers are adept at picking locks and palming playing cards, for the man likes to gamble in life and in sport. He is handsome, healthy and bored out of his mind. Sergeant Lace is counting on that fact to help her get to the bottom of her current case – the Gilded Goat.

Raffles sees Lace approach and a smile better suited to the lovechild of a fox and wolf spreads across his face. Lace notices it and prepares herself for the charm onslaught of Raffles the dandy.

"Sergeant Lace, my dear, you should trade in those great big boots of yours! Let me take you to a dear friend of mine, he'll have a pair of wonderful shoes made up for you within the hour and then you can get those beautiful ankles on show."

"The inspector told me that you'd be like this. You know, Raffles, I opted to join the Black Museum so that I could get on with solving crime and helping the needy, not to get my ankles out, and I'm certainly not going to go weak at the knees at a bit of old-fashioned and well out-of-date charm."

Raffles pretended to be offended, clutching at the lapel of his smoking jacket and looking dismayed at having his ankle fetish kicked into the high grass.

"Sergeant Lace, please. If I have offended you, how do they say it in the real world now, *get over yourself!"*

Lace smiled at the old man's attempt at bringing 'street' parlance into this Mayfair hotel inside the Time Fields of the Black Museum. She had spoken to Judas about the Gilded Goat case straight after she had returned from investigating the scene of the crime, the Goat's luxury Holland Park flat. He had suggested that she go and speak with Raffles. If anyone knew anything about breaking and entering without anyone knowing that you'd broken and entered, he would.

"The inspector sends his greetings and apologises for not coming to call. We're a bit manic up there I'm afraid."

Raffles inclined his head, a small bow but significant. Judas had helped Raffles once or twice in the past and his current situation, which was rather splendid, had been arranged by the Master of the Black Museum.

"The inspector and your good self, have but to ask. I shall make sure that there are no further remarks about your beautiful ankles, rest assured."

Lace just shook her head and smiled. He was an old rogue for sure but as Judas had told her, he was genuine and what the other felons called, an 'honest thief', and he could be trusted to do the right thing.

"Shall we?" said Raffles, pointing toward a table near one of the big windows on the opposite side of the hotel reception. When they had both sat down, Lace drew out her notebook and flipped over a few pages. When she found the right one, she turned it around and set it on the table so that Raffles could see her notes and the little sketch she had made of the Goat's fireplace, the supposed place of egress. She nearly burst out laughing when he removed a monocle from his pocket, gave it an expert wipe with a monogrammed silk handkerchief and placed it over one eye.

"Hmmmm, very nice, very nice indeed. No soot on the carpet, grime or dust on the mantle or the table nearby. Good, very good. The curtains were as you found them?"

Lace concurred with a nod of the head.

"This lamp, here in the corner, was it turned to face the window?"

"Now you mention it, it was. I thought perhaps it was to signal someone from the street."

"You're guessing now, Lace, that isn't what it's for at all. Moving on. Was there a piece of string attached to a small silver spoon laying on the floor towards the back of the room?"

Lace looked at Raffles now and saw not the smarmy, upper-class twit that he wanted her to see. Here was a professional. A big beast in the world of crooked.

"Yes, there was. Behind the table and chairs at the rear of the room. It was on the floor, the string was intact, but the spoon looked like it had been burned. Couldn't quite work it out. I thought that maybe someone had tried to fuse the lights?"

Raffles sat back in his chair and winked so that his monocle fell out. He caught it quickly and smoothly and then pocketed it in one fluid movement.

"Not quite, Lace, but good. I can see why the inspector recruited you. The 'string and the spoon hex' doesn't get used that much these days. But it is effective and powerful."

"The 'string and spoon hex'? No, you've lost me there," said Lace.

Raffles smiled and continued. If there was one thing he enjoyed more than breaking into an impregnable bank, it was holding court and allowing others to bask in the glow of his brilliance.

"Your friend, this *Gilded Goat*, tell me more about him. What is he like? What does he do?"

Lace realised that she was in for the long haul now and after a polite cough and a remark on how stuffy the hotel was, Raffles ordered some drinks and she settled back and told him everything she knew about the Goat.

It was shortly after the fifth G&T that Raffles thumped the table and caused at least four gentlemen nearby to splutter into their port.

"This Gilded Goat of yours wants to be a human! The way he dresses, the jewellery, the way he talks, the place he lives! I guarantee you that he has been talking to one of the *Cunning Men*. Only one of their sort would be able to help him. The hex that was used, only the Cunning Men use it. Whoever it was, and I have a good idea about that, came down the chimney and into the house using the fireplace. If I had been able to turn myself into smoke, I would never have been caught. Once they were at the bottom – 'the string and the spoon hex'. Anything that was in the room, say a guard dog or a vengeful spirit, any protective measures, would have gone straight for the spoon and then once they'd touched it, poof! Into the bag you go."

Lace was scribbling everything down into her notebook. She saw Raffles differently now. He'd worked out the *who* and the *why* in a few hours, working from a drawing in a small pad, without anything else.

"You said you knew who."

"Sergeant Lace, if I asked you to come and have a drink with me once your investigation is over, would you accept?"

"It's that or the ankles, isn't it?"

"I think I would prefer the company now, what do you say?"

Lace looked at the old rogue and decided that he'd earned a drink or two.

"Give me the name first."

"In my line of work, I don't normally produce the goods until payment, or until caught."

"You're in luck, Raffles. I am the police, after all."

"You drive a hard, and unfair bargain, Sergeant Lace, but I find myself cornered, as they say. The man you are looking for is James Murrell. He was the most famous of the Cunning Men. Half witch, half something else. Dabbled in alchemy, fancied himself as a bit of an astronomer at one point. Very dangerous though, Lace. He made a pact or two with some nasty characters, demons or others of that ilk. He performed several *exchanges* at the height of his powers."

"Exchanges?" Lace was scribbling again and didn't look up.

"Transferring the soul of one form and putting it into another, Lace."

"What happens to the soul in the body that doesn't want to be moved?"

"You'd best ask your master about that. Shall we say, next Friday at 9?"

"Let's just see if we can clear this case up before then, Raffles. But you have my word, if we have, then it's drinks at the bar, and I promise not to wear the boots."

12. BREADCRUMBS

Judas had decided to call it a day. The map on the wall in his office was pierced here and there with blue pins. Each one represented a crime scene of an occult nature. Staring at the blue pins had made his eyes tired and red. The troll that he and Lace had found in the sewers was causing Bloody Nora and her team of investigators a few headaches. The water and the sewage had masked or contaminated any clues that may have been useful. Still, if there was something to be found, Bloody Nora would find it. Judas reached for his silver coin once again and began to rub at it in small clockwise circles.

He'd come to this city long ago; he'd seen it grow and prosper. Then he'd seen the Second Fall of the Angels. They'd chosen London as their second home over New York, Paris, Berlin and a host of other cities that could have offered them something different, something more. Judas couldn't put his finger on it, so didn't try to. He put his coin away and put on his jacket and coat. He left Lace a note, asking how the meeting with Raffles had gone and to call him if there was any news. Lace had taken a great deal of the weight of the day-to-day running of the Museum off his shoulders. But there was still something not quite right in there, he could feel it, just out there on the boundary of his senses. A dark presence perhaps, maybe the Museum was growing or just needed pruning? Judas was too tired to think too hard about it right now. A cold beer, a chat with an angel and then home, to dream of a witch with the whitest skin and a crescent moon birth mark that moved across her shoulder in a perfect arc.

Judas walked through the main reception of the Yard. The usual cornucopia of drunks, streetwalkers, city boys who had consumed too much bugle and angry from Walthamstow, who'd had their car pinched and wanted something done about it, were all shouting at the desk sergeant. His name was Smalling but there was nothing small about him. He played rugby for the Force and was regularly taking advantage of the dental cover the Met provided. He had a wonderful smile that unfortunately, most people never got to see. Smalling was perfect for the front desk, a gentle giant with the patience of a saint, unless you happened to be in a ruck or a mall with him.

They exchanged greetings and then Judas was out. The rotating cheese wedge that carried the silver letters that spelled out Scotland Yard continued to turn like the wheels of justice, slow and steady. There were no film crews today, so no one in Parliament had been caught being naughty – yet. Judas crossed the river, heading south. Overhead, the angels swooped. The night sky was full of tiny red lights and flashes of silver and gold. The red was from their digital delivery pads and the rest, that was their wings catching either moonlight or tungsten from the streetlamps.

He'd just started heading towards Soho when he saw her. It was clumsy, but it was supposed to be. She made sure that he had seen her. He tailed her for about five minutes, following the breadcrumbs and then he stopped. The detective in him should have carried on, but he was tired of doing her bidding and of doing God's, who he was starting to believe had forgotten about him entirely.

"Sod it!"

Judas turned smartly on his heel and carried on heading in his own direction – for a change.

The Lamb and Flag was his favourite drinking den in the whole wide world. Forget the smoky Kasbah, or the Speak Easy, this was proper drinking in a real, authentic boozer. He loved it, because he had drunk warm beer and imbibed other, illegal concoctions, with Dickens and Wilde here. There was a seat that he always tried to get near the main window that opened onto the very bottom of Floral Street. He could watch the world go by from there and forget all about *the job* and *his* crime, the greatest of all crimes. Dark in the winter, bright and airy in the summer, the 'Bucket of Blood', as it was known when there were bare-knuckle boxing matches staged there, was the last place in all of Albion to watch a proper fight. Since then, the décor had not changed much, the beer was more expensive, and all the fights were free, provided you had them outside.

He sank the first pint a bit more quickly than he realised, and it was just as the foam was sliding down the empty glass and he was reaching for his wallet that Princess Fedelmid appeared. She was carrying a tray and on it were the next two rounds of pints, for them both.

"Why didn't you follow me? I was going to take you somewhere much nicer than this."

"I like *this* my lady. It's been around nearly as long as me, and it's still going, which is reassuring. It's a sign, perhaps."

The princess sat down next to him and removed the full pints from the tray in an expert fashion, then she passed the tray over to a barmaid that just happened to be walking past.

"It's almost like you planned that," said Judas.

Princess Fedelmid was above average height, athletic and powerful like her mother. She was formidable, Judas could see that, and he was immediately on his guard. She did not disappoint.

"The last time we spoke, you said that you would not interfere or intervene unless you had evidence, unless you knew for sure that the Silent King was responsible for my mother's disappearance – or her murder."

Saying the words was hard for her. She paused and sank one of her pints in one go.

"A bit warm and a little too fizzy for me, but overall, it is passable. I shall order us another couple of these."

"Fine by me," said an impressed Judas, before trying to drain his pint in the same fashion.

"I don't believe that the Silent King is behind this. It's too reckless for him, he doesn't need to do it – why bother with us? We have no conflicting business, no dreams of taking what is his, it just doesn't make any sense."

"What of the Golden Torque, Princess? How was it taken from your mother?"

The princess downed another pint in one go, causing a few raised eyebrows and some admiring looks from the seasoned drinkers seated around them in the pub.

"Faelan wants the crown, Drustan wants what Faelan wants. Oebfinn is young and wants to appear bold and ready, as our mother has always taught us to be, but she knows nothing and will take the easy path. Morcant is watching the wind. He will wait for it to blow true and then follow it. Of all of us, he is the one least like the rest of us."

Judas liked her voice; he could imagine her whispering something sweet and then roaring her orders across a battlefield like an angry ox.

"My lady, I hear what you say, all families have their fights and their secrets, but what are you asking me to do?"

Princess Fedelmid placed another empty pint glass down on the table. Judas was already starting to feel tomorrow's headache, but he persevered, nonetheless. He picked up his own pint, gulped it down, then immediately regretted it.

"You said that you would not get involved unless there was something more to go on, inspector. That is true is it not?"

Judas nodded.

"Before my mother disappeared, she was acting strangely – not overly, just different. She spent time with each of us, talking of the future, the way ahead, that sort of thing. It was quite unlike her. She was, *she is*, a wonderful mother, inspector. She disappointed the Romans on many an occasion, and she found a way to keep us safe. The last few years have been her reckless years. She rode more, gambled more, lived more and travelled more. There will be no surprise if the odd bastard or two comes calling in the future. What I am trying to say, inspector, is that I got the feeling that she was saying goodbye somehow. And then there were these secret meetings. No bodyguards and no records kept of who she was meeting and what she was meeting about. Once a year. Same day and same time."

The detective in Judas couldn't help but hear the last words of her sentence more loudly than the others.

"There is very little that I can do right now about these secret meetings, without a GPS printout or a statement from some magical being who might have been holidaying in a hedge nearby, but I am interested in how your brothers and sisters responded to the conversations they had with Boudica."

Princess Fedelmid bridled at the informal use of her mother's name but quickly realised that she was not in her world and that here, different rules applied. She motioned for the barmaid, and just as if she were on the end of a string, the girl appeared at the princess's elbow. Her eyes were wide and full of wonder and the girl was smiling as if she had just attained straight A's. Judas was not impressed.

"They are good people you know, Princess, not without fault I admit, and often a little bit wayward and violent, but leave your *Glamour* behind. You do not need it here. This place has its own rhythm. Let it be, we have more important things to discuss."

Princess Fedelmid shifted uneasily on her bar stool. She was royalty, and she had made a mistake. To do so was frowned upon. At court, or in the presence of other tribal leaders, she wouldn't have presumed to enchant or control. She had overreached, and the truth was, Princess Fedelmid had showed her weakness, she had farted in the lift. She had thought to project strength and display her power, but she had been clumsy. She felt his admonishment deeply. It was not meant as a rebuke, she knew that, but it stung – her mother would not have done the same.

"Forgive me, inspector, the last few days feel as though they have passed in the shaking of an hourglass. So much is going wrong, so quickly, and as you just saw, we are grasping for truth. It is my greatest fear that we shall settle for fear – and war will come to us all. I beg you and the forces of the Black Museum to help me avert this conflict. If it does come, then it will affect all the *Under Folk*. Believe me, Judas Iscariot, Master of the Black Museum, when I say that you have a shared interest in this. Faelan or Drustan see themselves wearing the torque. One of them might even be assisting the other, it is unclear, and I tell you, inspector, I am afraid. The Silent King is not stupid, he will see the truth of this before many others, and then he will decide, inspector. Should he wipe out the Iceni because they have dared to incite war with him, or should he take what is ours, because we have allowed ourselves to be manipulated?"

Judas let her words settle and watched as one of the barmaids collected empty glasses from the tables arranged in front of the pub. It had been a busy night so far and her hands were full. People were moving around and between the tables and it wasn't her fault, but she dropped a few of the glasses. They shattered on the cobblestones and all heads turned towards the noise. Save three. Two men and one woman separated from the crowd and formed a ring around Princess Fedelmid before the ironic cheer went up.

Judas smiled. He'd seen her bodyguards pretending to socialise when the princess arrived and guessed correctly that they were here for her.

“As you can see, inspector, we are taking this situation seriously.”

“So is the Black Museum, Princess. Trust me. It is.”

The princess finished her remaining two pints in one go and departed. Her bodyguards shadowed her as she walked down to the bottom of Covent Garden where a slate grey Aston Martin Vanquish waited for her. The bodyguards jumped inside a black SUV and then both were gone. Judas did not have a beautiful car waiting for him – it was the bus or shoe leather. The bus won.

13. THE ANCIENT MARINERS

Camden Lock is never still. Thousands of tourists visit it each day, looking for edgy London and cheap retro clothing from the stalls in the arches of the nearby market. Unfortunately, they arrive to find that the edge is terribly dull, and the big chains have moved in and choked the poor place to death. Expensive ice cream, artisan coffee, sneaker emporiums and well-fed pickpockets are in residence these days, and business is good. There are some interesting bars and pubs though, and after dark, the Lock comes alive to the sound of new bands, recently arrived in the capital in their barely street-legal transit vans, and touts selling marked-up tickets for clubs and comedy events at the Roundhouse.

Down on the surface of the canals, boats have been turned into taxis and landing stages have been reclaimed to make seating areas for chic new dining experiences. There is life and light down here, but paddle for a minute in either direction, and things change drastically. Here are the unwanted buildings, the empty warehouses and the canal barges that have been semi-scuttled so that one side or one end is underwater. Coffee cups and fast-food wrappers travel more miles downstream than these sad old boats. But there is one craft that is still intact and working tonight.

This one is called the Flying Fox. It putters towards an old, shabby warehouse and then unseen hands on the tiller bring it to a halt in front of the door to the building. It is an impressive piece of seamanship and the rubber buoys that hang down the side of the boat like overfed Christmas lights barely kiss the wall of the warehouse. The engine dies and its echo skims the surface of the black water and disappears around the bend. Then there is the sound of a chain being drawn, and a black rectangle in the wall of dark bricks appears.

Wulfric Walker, the current Warden of the Church Roads, watches the barge through the glass of a broken window in a building opposite. He's been waiting for the Flying Fox for four days. He thought he'd got the date wrong, and he was about to call it a day and leave, but here it was, bobbing in the water, only a few feet away. Wulfric stared at the Fox, willing its crew to make their move, but there was no movement from inside, and there was no law against mooring a barge either.

"*Patience, Wulfric,*" he muttered to himself.

It was rewarded moments later when the first three members of the crew of the Flying Fox began to carry their cargo inside the warehouse. Each one carried a huge crate. No normal man would have been able to lift one, but these were not normal men. These were the ghosts of men, sailors that had lived long ago. These creatures were the Ancient Mariners and they transported anything for anyone, anywhere. Wulfric started to lose count of how many crates were being unloaded, but there were a lot more than he had imagined.

One of the Ancient Mariners decided to take a break and sat down on the roof of the barge. He wore an old British Navy jacket and dirty grey trousers that had once been white. His face was yellow and whatever teeth he had been born with, were now gone. Around the creature's neck was a string of ears that had turned brown and there were also two ivory pins in his lapel that showed that he had once been crew on a whaling boat. After a few minutes rest and scratching at the imaginary lice he carried, the mariner stood up quickly and returned to his labour.

Wulfric had been watching him closely, which was obviously their plan, because now, a blade was at his neck and the stench of a dead man filled his nostrils. The Ancient Mariners had known he would be there, and they had set a trap for him. How easily they'd snared him – he'd walked straight into it, and there was only one place they were going to take him now, down to the odd place where the light dares not venture. The pressure on his neck from the blade started to increase and Wulfric was forced to take a step backwards and then to turn around. There were two of them in the room with him. Both reeked of decay; salt stains crisscrossed their clothes and deep lines were etched into their faces from too many miles at sea, under an unforgiving sun. To his disgust, Wulfric saw that the one opposite had several shrunken heads attached to his belt; one looked like it had belonged to a child.

He pointed towards the door, suggesting that they take him from the room but that wasn't the way they worked. The one behind would slash his neck open and then they would bundle him out of the window and into the canal. They'd leave him there for a day or two and then come back to use whatever parts of him they wanted to. It wasn't a nice way to go, and Wulfric wasn't prepared to take that trip with them, so he fell backwards and with an expert roll of the shoulders he launched his man straight at the other and bolted through the door.

They pursued him down the stairs and into the alleyway behind the old building. He was fast, but they were canny, and had positioned another of the crew on the tow path. It was the only exit, and they knew it. Wulfric skidded to a halt. His breath was producing tiny clouds of desperation in the night air before him, and he was starting to get the fear. The two from the room stepped out of the darkness and onto the tow path directly behind him and he was trapped. They all started to walk towards him; closer and closer they came. The one in front produced a nasty looking boat hook and jabbed at him with it. There was a clump of mud on the end, although Wulfric quickly realised that it was not earth but flesh, clotted and fly-blown. He had only seconds left but there is always a way out if you are a Warden of the Church Roads. Wulfric flicked open his dark blue Crombie coat and embroidered in its lining was the whereabouts of every single opening on the Church Roads, and there just happened to be one directly behind Captain Boathook. So, Wulfric ran forward, took the Ancient Mariner by surprise and together they fell through the invisible opening and crashed to the ground inside the Church Road. And now the tables were turned.

The mariner was confused – they were standing in the dark next to a canal only moments before. Now they were inside some sort of tunnel, and it was full of bright lights, so much light that he could not see properly.

"I guess you're wondering where you are right now," said Wulfric.

The mariner whipped around and brought his boat hook up but all he could see were blurred shapes.

"You're as blind as a bat in here, aren't you? Too bad. I'm going to leave you here to rot or until I can persuade someone to come back here and put you out of your misery."

Wulfric watched the ghost flailing around and turned his back on it, which was a stupid thing to do, because the mariner might not have been able to see very well, but it could hear him, and with a well-practised action, it pulled its arm back and launched the boat hook straight through Wulfric's shoulder. It felt like he had been kicked by a shire horse, but he knew that he had to put some distance between himself and his attacker. The blood was already soaking through his shirt and the wooden shaft sticking out of his back was throwing him off balance. He needed an opening quickly, or he was going to die of blood loss or be poisoned by bad breath. Neither option appealed. Wulfric knew the Church Roads by heart, and he shuffled as fast as he could towards the nearest one. He was starting to feel dizzy and cold. Wulfric knew what that meant. He heard the Ancient Mariner groping down the tunnel behind him and knew that it was now or Davy Jones' Locker, so he leaned to the right and just kept leaning until gravity gave him a helping hand. He fell out of the Church Road and onto the pavement in front of Scotland Yard.

Moments later, a phone rang in an office on the 7th floor and was answered by a DCI.

"Sir, I think we've got one of yours down here. Says his name is Wulfric, and he has what looks like a boat hook sticking out of his shoulder. Will you be coming down for him, sir? No. You want me to take him to Bloody Nora in the basement? Yes, sir, I will see to it myself. Right away, sir. Thank you. Goodbye."

The Met might be a huge oil tanker of an organisation, in that it takes a long time and a lot of room to change direction, but the men and women in the Met can deal with anything that life throws at them. Even a dapper gent appearing out of nowhere, with two feet of cold steel protruding from his shoulder blade.

Judas ran down the corridor, jumped in the lift and swiped his Black Museum card to send it down to the basement. When he arrived, Bloody Nora, a seasoned and well-experienced officer who knew what sort of thing happened up on the 7th, was carefully removing the boat hook from Wulfric's shoulder. The man himself was nearly unconscious. The lower half of his body looked like it had been dipped into a pot of dark brown dye. That was the blood, and his face was the colour of ash.

"Wulfric! Can you hear me?"

"I can if you stop shouting."

"What happened?"

"Came to warn you about the Church Roads … lots of weird things happening. Weapons are being moved, whole parties of Under Folk are leaving London … scared by something … caravans being attacked, markets shutting down, panic and fear everywhere."

"Inspector, I need to see to his wound and set up a transfusion, the questions can wait."

"Yes of course, Nora, let me know when he can talk, and you, Warden Wulfric, get some rest. I'm going to need a statement from you."

"Yes of course, inspector, can't think of anything nicer."

14. THE KING'S WOMAN

Nora had called later that afternoon to say that Wulfric would need the night to recover enough to speak to him properly. Lace was still out and about, trying to get to the bottom of the Gilded Goat robbery, so Judas made the decision to call it a day and go home. There would be no point sitting in his creaky chair, staring up into the stars through the dirty skylight all night tonight. Bloody Nora was in charge as far as Wulfric was concerned. He was in safe hands and whatever had used him for a dartboard would never dare make another attempt on his life whilst he was in the Yard. So, home it was and home he went.

The bus was trying as hard as it could to keep him awake, or break his neck, he couldn't decide which one. The constant starting and stopping was making him feel seasick as well and he decided to get off a few stops early and walk. The air was still and the threat of rain that the forecasters had predicted remained just that, a threat. There were a couple of fast-food places on his way home, but Judas opted for something healthy from one of the new supermarkets, instead. As he was browsing and trying to find any fresh fish that had been sourced from a country nearer than Honduras, Judas thought he saw something out of the ordinary, but when he looked again there was nothing.

The short walk back to his flat from the micro-market was uneventful and Judas decided that he was overthinking everything and seeing things where they weren't supposed to be. Paranoia is helpful, especially when you are a detective but sometimes it needs to be given the night off. Judas let himself in, double-locked the door and placed his warrant card and the black swipe card to the Museum on the small table in the hall. Then, he wandered into the kitchen, placed the bags of food on the counter and opened the fridge. The light inside went on and then something heavy hit him over the back of the head and his own lights went out.

When he came to, he was tied to his one and only armchair, the one that Lucifer the Morningstar chose to sit on whenever he came to call. Standing in the centre of the room was an old friend, who should have been dead long ago.

"Simon the Zealot, you were supposed to have left town after that business with the London Necropolis. I gave you a chance, looks like that legendary brain of yours has let you down."

Simon did not look good. He was normally a fan of suits that cost more than a loft conversion and spa days with Russian escorts. The tracksuit and bodywarmer combo were either a disguise, or he had fallen far.

"Judas Iscariot, Protector of the Weak and Lord of the Manor, this is going to hurt you and make me very happy indeed. Remember this? John's great knife – he jabbed you with it once, didn't he? Well, I'm here to finish the job and then I'm going to help the 'Baptist' to rise from his watery grave and we're going to get the gang back together again."

Judas looked at the blade and an involuntary shudder made Simon giggle. He knew that knife, knew it well, but he wasn't going to let it taste his flesh again. He was going to take it from Simon and then he was going to skin the little snake alive with it. Straight after he had worked out how to get out of this chair. Simon was watching him closely and had a good idea what was going through Judas's mind at that very moment.

"John the Baptist was a bully and he loved pain. I, on the other hand, prefer to watch rather than cleave. Tying bodies up became a bit of a thing for me, Judas. Not kinky, I just liked to do a good job, so there is very little chance of you getting free. I'd save your strength if I was you."

Judas was about to fling a witty retort in Simon's direction but the pain of the knife going into the top of his thigh stopped him in his tracks. Simon pulled it out and wiped the blood from the blade with one of the cushions from the sofa.

"I got those from Heal's, you little bastard!"

Simon giggled again and took a step closer to observe Judas's wound.

"That's very clever, isn't it? The wound seems to be closing already," said Simon.

Judas knew what was coming. He could not be killed but he could be put out of action for a while and with war between the Iceni and the Silent King looming like a giant storm cloud, and whatever was happening inside the Black Museum to deal with, being out of action was the last thing he needed. Simon, however, had nothing to look forward to, so he stabbed Judas in the shoulder and then went to the kitchen to get some salt for Judas's wounds.

When he returned, he was looking very pleased with himself. He'd found some more knives in the kitchen drawer. Judas watched as he laid them out on the rug in front of him. It was straight from page 1 of the Torturer's Handbook, thought Judas. Showing the weapons of torture to the victim beforehand loosens tongues and bowels and makes the work of the torturer much easier and quicker. Whoever had written it hadn't put a sub-section in for people like Simon, though. He didn't want this over quickly.

It was while Simon was arranging his instruments on the floor that Judas heard the unmistakable scratching of a lock-pick from the hall. Unfortunately, so did Simon, and he stood up quickly with John's blade in his hand. Blood dripped from the tip and onto the cream carpet. Judas was about to remind Simon of the extortionate cost of dry cleaning when the scratching stopped. Whoever was trying to get in had picked the lock and was about to make themselves known. Simon moved into the hall and raised the knife. But the door remained closed. Simon shifted his weight and moved to his right, changing his angle of attack. He may have been weak, but he was not stupid, and he would let the person on the other side make the first move. The door was his shield and his protector. Which was neither here nor there because as he stared at the door, a very attractive woman wearing a beautiful silk scarf around her neck smashed him around the head with a very unladylike looking cosh.

When Simon regained consciousness, he could see Judas drinking a G&T with lots of ice and a slice of lime opposite a well-dressed woman smoking a thin black cheroot. He tried to move but immediately realised that he wasn't the only person in the room that knew how to tie a knot. He groaned, not because he was in pain but because he had failed, again.

Judas heard Simon moan and turned to him and raised a glass to his old friend, and then, with all the irony he could muster, said, "Cheers!"

Simon started to sob which made Judas feel happy for the first time in ages.

"I thought I saw your scarf earlier on, as I was choosing my dinner for this evening, Meg."

"I'm getting sloppy in my old age, Judas, what can I say. Following you isn't as easy as it once was."

"When did you decide to come in and save me from a fate worse than death?"

"This one," she said, wafting her cigarette towards the blubbing Simon, "has been watching Scotland Yard for the past week. Sometimes he's there, and sometimes he's here. I slipped in while he was sharpening his butter knives, hid behind those very expensive coats you have hanging in the hall and then scratched at the lock a few times to bring him out. Works every time."

Judas was impressed, although he shouldn't have been. Meg was the leader of the Women of the Chapel, and she was as deadly as she was beautiful. They had helped each other in the past and had formed a mutual respect. Meg was also one of the Silent King's subjects. He had brought her back to life after she had been savagely murdered by Jack the Ripper in Whitechapel. She hid the only scar she carried under her silk scarves, and it was folly to touch her without asking first.

"I don't suppose that you were following me to ask me out for dinner or a city break to Florence?"

"You know why I'm here, inspector. You've been seeing a lot of the Iceni recently and my king would like to talk to you about the situation. We've been attacked, you realise, by the people you are consorting with. Some of our people have perished already."

Judas finished his drink and looked down at the ragged tear in his trousers. The wound beneath it had already healed but it was still tender to the touch. Judas didn't know whether it was the ruination of a pair of his favourite trousers or the indignity of being stabbed by Simon the Zealot that hurt the most. He would need to spend some time with Simon, but he didn't have any to spare right then, so he reached for his phone and requested a squad car and a cell at the Yard. Simon could wait. The Silent King could not.

Judas showered and changed his clothes. As he was dressing again, he caught sight of himself in the wardrobe mirror. The shoulder wound was turning yellow already and the thigh wound looked like a mere graze. The big scar, the one that ran from his waistline up to his clavicle, however, was still visible, white and knotted. The scar around his neck from the noose he had tied for himself in the olive grove was still there too, and seeing them again like this, with the fresh markings fading away before his own eyes, he realised something. God kept him alive to remind Judas of the pain he had caused all that time ago. Was it really anything to do with atonement anymore? Wasn't he just being kept alive so that he could be tortured repeatedly?

Judas finished dressing and had another drink while they waited for the police car that would transport Simon to the cells for the night. Meg stood by the window, looking down at the road. It seemed to Judas that she was trying to will the car to get here more quickly. He'd never seen her ruffled or impatient before, but then he'd never been summoned into the presence of her Lord and Master.

The car duly arrived and the two constables who'd come to collect Simon were briefed on their passenger's little quirks and how to avoid them. Then they were gone, and Meg waited by the front door as Judas collected his warrant card. Her car was nearby; it was an old E-Type Jaguar, white with red leather upholstery. Many motoring enthusiasts called the E-Type the most beautiful car ever built. It was cramped and noisy, but it had a charm of its own. Meg drove quickly but carefully through the traffic. The E-Type had a manual gearbox and Judas watched as she flicked up and down the gears, easing the car through gaps and maintaining the speed with little effort.

"Have you ever thought of becoming a bus driver, Meg? The one I took home wasn't driven like this."

"Not really my thing, Judas my friend, this suits me much better. How is the White Witch these days, still seeing her?"

Judas stopped thinking about cars or buses instantly. His mind was back on that train, the Ley Line Express, where he had met the White Witch, what felt like years ago. He was stung by the question and his hackles started to rise.

"Didn't know that it was common knowledge, Meg. How do you know about it and more importantly, why bring her up now?"

Meg dropped a couple of gears and put the pedal down to the mat so that they could clear a junction before the lights turned red. The short burst of acceleration forced him back into the leather; it gave ever so slightly and then released him back into position. Meg checked her rear-view mirror before speaking.

"Don't be so sensitive, inspector, why do you think I'm asking? Do you really think that the Silent King needs to threaten you or someone you hold dear? We're not interested in threats and murder, Judas, we're under attack and all the evidence we have, which is not much I grant you, points toward the Iceni. Your witch is safe."

Judas cleared his throat and wished he hadn't reacted so quickly. It was a mistake that he would not normally have made.

"Why do you ask then, Meg, if it's not something that you're going to use later?"

"Well, it was you who mentioned dinner or a city break, Judas. It got me thinking."

Judas felt himself turning as red as the car's upholstery and wound his window down a fraction. The cool night air came to his rescue and chased the blushes away. He wanted to say something clever, but he never got the chance because Meg turned right, drove down a ramp and into an underground car park, somewhere close to the river, in East London.

"Welcome, Master of the Black Museum and defender of the *Under Folk,* to the court of the Silent King."

Meg showed Judas to a lift at the rear of the car park. Her E-Type jag was the only vehicle there. Once inside, she pressed the button for the first floor.

"I thought kings lived in palaces," said Judas.

"Mine doesn't, that is one of the reasons why we all love him so much."

The door opened and Meg walked out. She crossed the hall and pointed out of the window. They were in the Limehouse Basin complex by the riverside. Tall, shining blocks of apartments surrounded the small harbour and sheltered the vast collection of narrow boats moored there. Judas pointed at the nearest tower of steel and smoked glass.

"That one?"

Meg just smiled, pushed through a door and took the steps down to the water and the boats. Judas followed. He couldn't see any guards or sentries and Meg was walking away from the million-pound pads with their private gyms and spas and their views of the Thames. She stopped by a rickety ladder and started to climb down it. A rowing boat was at the bottom and in it sat the crustiest looking old seadog in all of Christendom. He was casually back-watering with his oar, keeping the boat on station with little effort. Meg sat down in the bench facing the old sailor and Judas climbed in and sat next to her.

The old man whipped an oar up and pushed the boat away from the dockside, then with a few well-practised strokes he moved them out into the water and headed straight for the nearest narrow boat. Wood bumped softly against wood as the rowing boat was made fast against the hull of the bigger craft. Judas clambered up the side with ease which caused the old sailor to smile and acknowledge it with an approving nod. Judas returned the smile.

“People forget that I was a fisherman once upon a time. Thanks for the lift.”

Meg ducked inside the narrow boat and Judas followed. When she reached the far end, she stopped and looked back at him. When their eyes met, his scar began to tingle. It wasn’t the usual itch followed by the heat and then the burn that told him that he was in harm’s way; this was different. Judas decided not to take any chances and started to look for a way out, should things turn nasty. Meg adjusted the silk scarf at her neck and then opened the door and stepped through it and into the court of the Silent King of the Resurrection Men.

Judas wandered down the boat and looked through the open door. There was no ambush waiting for him or trap door hungry to swallow him. So, he stepped across the boundary between the Mundane world and into the presence of royalty.

The court was impressive. From the outside it was just a motley collection of crafts of differing sizes and shapes, bobbing up and down, providing resting places for seagulls and sleeping dogs. Inside was a different story altogether. Some magical force or otherworldly engineering had joined all the boats together and instead of a thousand different, separate floating cabins, there was now only one deck – a huge, open deck the size of Trafalgar Square. Beneath his feet was a polished floor that did not rock with the tide, and above there was a sky, created by at least a thousand lights. On the far walls were banners and totems. Underneath the glass canopy were creatures from every tribe and class in the *Under Folk*. Some he recognised as being wanted in connection with some petty crimes and of interest to the Black Museum. They recognised him too and started to edge away towards the exits. Judas made a mental note to come back here afterwards and feel a few collars. Meg threaded her way through the crowds and Judas saw guards for the first time since she'd picked him up that evening.

The crowds began to thin quickly, as if some silent warning had been transmitted around the room. The courtiers were departing in their droves; whatever business had brought them here today would have to wait. Tomorrow, perhaps, their pleas would be heard, and their arguments settled. Judas nearly tripped over Meg. She had stopped suddenly and was kneeling with head bowed. Judas looked up and into the eyes of the man he had heard so much about over the years. The Silent King sat on a tall, narrow throne. There were no arm rests so the king sat with his hands resting on his knees. He was sitting bolt upright, and Judas thought that he looked severe, and distant. He'd seen monks and Holy Men sit like that, as if they were trying to look through time, searching for something out of reach, like truth or enlightenment.

The Silent King stood up and stepped down from his throne. He stopped in front of Judas and looked him squarely in the eye. He was about the same height but much thinner. His cheekbones were well defined and there was something about the shape of his eyes that Judas could not place – yet. There was hardly any colour in the man. His hair was jet black and hung to his shoulders, and his skin was so clear and white that it could have been marble or milk. The king appeared to have read all that he needed to in Judas's face and turned away from him.

"Rise, Meg, you have done well. Please take your ease in the outer court. We shall speak after I have made my introduction to the Master of the Black Museum."

Meg stood up, winked at Judas and then disappeared through a door to one side of the throne. The latch on the door dropped and when Judas looked back to the king, he found that they were alone; everyone else was gone.

"What would you have me call you? Betrayer? Judas? Detective? Or the Law? You have many names here at court, I would not wish to insult you on our first official meeting."

Judas cleared his throat.

"Official meeting?"

"I have watched you from afar, Detective, and followed your exploits. You are nearly as old as I am you know, and we have certain things in common. Both of us have travelled far to be here and our sponsors want the same thing – give or take."

The Silent King motioned for Judas to follow him. A table had been set at the far side of the hall. A glass decanter was at the centre, red wine had been carefully poured into two goblets and a single candle flickered, making the wine shimmer.

"Please, take a seat, Detective, we have much to discuss, and the Iceni are on the march. We don't have much time for pleasantries I'm afraid. Hopefully we will be able to set that right at a later date?"

The king sat down and lifted a glass to his lips. Judas did not reach for his. The king saw this and smiled.

"We are not in the realms of the Fae, Detective, no harm will come to you for accepting a gift from me or taking a drink at my table. You are free to come and go as you please – for now."

Judas took a sip of the wine. It was very good, full-bodied and bold. The bouquet reminded him of a place he'd visited once, long ago. A place of heat and rolling sand dunes that stretched away so far that the curvature of the Earth could be seen. Judas recognised the spell straight away and replaced the glass on the table. The Silent King mirrored his actions. Judas took his silver coin from his inside pocket and turned it over and over in his hand. He noticed that the king was watching him closely now.

"This was part payment; the rest are hidden away. No doubt I'll live long enough to rub the smile from both sides of each one of them. I use it to focus the mind as it were, and to deter others who might think to sway me or try to put me off the scent."

"My apologies, detective. There are those that whisper in my ear from time to time, so-called advisors and strategists. They mean well but often overreach themselves, like today. It will be dealt with. I gave you my word that there would be no underhand or crooked dealings between us, so, the rules of our world must be obeyed, and I must answer three questions. What is it that you wish to know?

Judas put the silver coin back in his pocket and crossed one leg over the other.

"Did you kill, or order to be killed, Boudica, Queen of the Iceni?"

"No."

"Do you know who did the deed?"

"No."

"Do you know if she is still alive or where her body can be found?"

"No."

Judas watched the Silent King's face as he answered the questions, and he didn't need to be a detective to know that the king was telling the truth. There was something else written there in his eyes though, something that he couldn't hide. Judas needed more questions, but he was unsure that he would be allowed to ask any more. The Silent King reached for his glass once again and raised it to his lips. The candle had not flickered once since they had taken a seat and Judas wondered if time was actually passing. The king poured himself another glass of wine and offered some to Judas. The offer was met with a raised eyebrow and the king smiled. Judas held his glass aloft and the king poured some of the dark red liquid into it.

"All is well, Detective. Now, to business and to bloodshed. I asked Meg to invite you here, Detective, because we are, all of us, in a precarious position. An attack was made on my person recently. That action alone would have brought severe reprisals on whoever had committed it, but I have no real proof, so I cannot and will not act against them."

"Them?" asked Judas.

"We must go back to the beginning, Judas, back to the time of the Romans and the occupation, to fields of blood and broken spears, to the death of a once powerful tribe and the disappearance of a queen. I remember that night like it was yesterday, Detective. The sky was raspberry red over the battlefield and great fires were consuming the bodies of the fallen Iceni warriors. Some had called out to me; they did not want the sting and the pain of the fires or the long journey into the earth. So, I went to that field and what I saw made me sick to my stomach. It was a waste of a generation. No songs or tales would come from them ever again; Albion would be much the poorer for it.

"I decided not to resurrect any of them. Life was wasted on them, and it occurred to me that given another chance, they would just throw it away again. I walked away from the battlefield with a heavy heart, and it was just as I was about to turn onto one of the secret paths and disappear, that I saw her tent. It was pitched underneath the branches of a great oak tree. I can go unnoticed if I choose, so I chose to enter that tent. I can't tell you what compelled me to, Detective, it was just a foolish curiosity really. I wanted to see how the story ended for them.

"The Romans were coming, and they knew that their deaths would be long and painful. Boudica was in conversation with her remaining soldiers and advisors. I saw a few of them slinking away into the night like the cowards they were. In the time it took for me to wander around the tent, half had run away. In the end, there was only the queen and her children left and the sound of a tent flap snapping in the wind. She was angry and defiant to the end. She had procured some poison from a Hedge Witch and was adding it to cups and bowls for herself and the children. I saw it and decided to offer her another path."

Judas sat up in his seat. This history lesson was about to get to the good bit.

"Yes, Detective. I saved Boudica. I gave her safe passage into the realms of the Fae. I also gave her a Golden Torque that would protect her and give her a chance in a new world."

"W-why?" stammered Judas.

"Because she wanted to live, Detective. She wanted her country and her land to be free of the invaders and the slave masters from across the sea. There was fire inside her that I could not allow to die down. Nor would I allow the Romans to take her body back to Rome, to be dragged through the streets, pelted with faeces and fed to mangy dogs, whilst the only *civilised race* in the world laughed and fornicated their way into the abyss."

"So, the Silent King helps Boudica, and her children disappear from that tent on the Icknield Way. The Romans then tell a load of porkies about her whereabouts, and she resurfaces in the realm of the Fae some time later and is now one of the most powerful creatures in the *Under Folk*. But now she's gone, presumed dead, and no one can find her body."

"Precisely, Detective. I didn't kill her. We had an understanding. We met once a year at the great tree. This year she did not attend. It is the first time that it has happened. Shortly afterwards, I was attacked. For some time now, Detective, the Iceni have been extending their reach. They are becoming greedy, and they have chosen to expand into the world of the Mundane folk. I mentioned this at our last meeting, and she assured me that she would endeavour to re-educate her children. It appears that she failed, and I now presume that she orchestrated the whole affair and is in hiding."

Judas sat back in his chair and took out his little black police issue notebook and a well-chewed biro. He scribbled frantically for a few minutes and then replaced both in his jacket pocket.

"Are you hungry, Detective? I can have some food brought out if you would like to dine?"

"Thank you, but no. May I ask another question?"

"Of course!" replied the Silent King.

"Boudica and the Iceni disappeared. They had nothing – no wealth and no contacts and certainly no followers, but they have created a mighty dynasty and a powerful business empire. How?"

The Silent King stood up, reached across to the candle and extinguished the steady flame between forefinger and thumb.

"The Golden Torque, Detective. I gave it to her long ago. Its power is immense, a relic from a people that lived far away across the sea when the world was but an infant. Used correctly, it can help to persuade someone to do as you ask or convince them that you are a God or a Goddess. The wearer can travel in time and see far into the future. It is an unusual trinket but used in the wrong way it can destroy and bring great pain."

Judas stood up and brushed the creases from his coat.

"The Golden Torque was returned to the Iceni a few days ago."

The Silent King looked up sharply and Judas saw a change in the man.

"I presume that Boudica's neck was not inside it?"

"No," said Judas.

"The Golden Torque can only be removed by the wearer, or the next in line to the throne. Boudica is most likely dead, but at whose hand? Someone or something is helping the Iceni, Detective, and they are trying to start a war to disguise their identity. Regardless, I must defend myself and my people. I will bid you farewell, Master of the Black Museum."

Judas watched him stalk across the great room and disappear through a set of vast oak doors. He wanted to tell the Silent King what Cat Tabby had told him about the attack at the coliseum, and the appearance of Black Shuk, but Judas did not trust the Silent King completely and the last thing he wanted right now was for the Beast to be pursued and destroyed before the truth of who it was that was controlling it was revealed. And why exactly did the Silent King save Boudica, set her up with some magical charm and then demand only that she turn up for a chinwag every now and again? There was something more to this and he was running out of time to find out what it was.

Judas attempted to walk towards the door that he had come in through but all of them looked the same. He thought that he may have to ask for some help in getting out of the Silent King's court, but luckily, Meg reappeared. She had changed her silk scarf and the look on her face told him that she already knew what was happening.

"Shall I escort you back to the station then?"

"Please do," said Judas.

15. THE CATHEDRAL OF THE MARSHES

The A12 travels through the county of Suffolk and up and into the county of Norfolk, birthplace to one of England's most famous sons – Nelson. He was the master of the waves and an incredible seaman. But the sea is master here, and always has been, stretching back to the time of the Vikings and beyond. To know the waterways and the tributaries of both counties, is to know the magic of the land. It has secrets – some of them dark and some – terrifying.

Terry had finished the job at Woodbridge, a tricky decking project, multiple levels and lots of handrails and a rather natty, bespoke firepit. It had been a bit of a 'mare, but it had been finished on time and within budget, and he was pleased with his labours. He was taking the van back to Hellesdon now, to the yard.

It was a Friday, and he could already taste that first golden pint of lager slipping down his throat at the Pillars of Hercules in Norwich town centre. The lads were all excited about tonight's game at Carrow Road, home of the Canaries, Norwich City's football team. It was while he was thinking about the 'Reds', tonight's opponents from Merseyside, that he saw the thing fly across the road. He didn't slam the brakes on, didn't need to. It was just a big, black blur and two red flashes. One second it was there, in the headlights of the van, and then – gone. A reflection perhaps or a piece of loose wood chip in his eye? Terry drove on and as he turned towards the Cathedral on the marshes, the biggest church in these parts, he persuaded himself that it was the long hours and lack of sleep that had caused him to see the barrelling shape. A few miles later, his attention had already turned to more important things. *Could they get a win tonight? Or, at the very least, an exciting draw?*

Boudica woke with a start, and as soon as her eyes began to focus, she felt the panic rising from the pit of her stomach. She feared that Black Shuk had returned to feast upon her flesh, but she could not locate his presence. There were lots of deep shadows all around her, places where the creature could hide. She could not see or smell him. As the seconds passed, her heartbeat quickened. It got faster and faster and hammered so loudly in her chest she thought her heart might explode and save the hound the bother of finishing her off.

But there was no attack, not yet, so she sat back and closed her eyes; it was just a false alarm. She started to breathe deeply, sucking in the air through her nose, forcing the much-needed oxygen down into the depths of her lungs, and then expelling it in great blasts from her mouth. She had learnt the technique when she was a girl. Warriors she had known would often return from the battlefield or a hunting party with a wound or a broken limb. Boudica remembered watching the druids as they pounded the herbs they had collected into paste and smeared it on the bloody gashes and gaping holes where spear tips had lodged. The warriors would breathe in and out, readying themselves for the imminent snap of a joint being set back into place or the hiss and burn of a white-hot knife, closing a wound.

As she sat there, centring herself and replaying the events of the night before in her mind, she heard the sound again and tensed, ready to fight. But this time, she knew what it was and instead of screaming, she smiled and then laughed. A bird had made a home for itself in a hole in the wall, right beside her head. It had chirruped loudly, and the acoustics of the hole had turned the short, sharp tweet into something otherworldly and she had thought that the great black beast had returned. But no, it was just a sparrow or a curious crow. She pulled herself up into a half-sitting position and looked about her. What she saw confused her. This was no cell or dungeon – it was a church. A very old church by the look of it. Rows of wooden pews, stained dark over time, retreated in strict formation to the large oak doors at the back of the building. Stained glass windows stood resolute against the wind, and in a cruel twist, stopped the sunlight from coming inside. Years of grime had turned their bright colours to drab; grey shapes bordered with black lead. To her left was a pulpit, and beyond that a door. The floor was paved with thick grey slabs. They were not dusty or damp, so she knew that she was still in the realm of the living. A bible the size of a coffee table was perched on the edge of the pulpit and the wax of many candles clogged up the sconces on the walls. It was a well-kept church – small, but there was history here, lots of it.

The only odd thing about the church was the twin scorch marks on the floor that led down the aisle, and away from the pulpit. She inspected them, curious as to their meaning, then she noticed two deep scratches in the doors, and she knew immediately who had made them. Boudica had heard about this place; she was in *Black Shuk's* church. This is where he had attacked the congregation, spilling innocent blood on consecrated ground, and almost bringing the roof down upon them all. The priest had ordered the Beast to leave but Black Shuk had crushed his head beneath one great paw and then produced a hellish fire that blew the doors from their hinges.

Her body may still be in pain and reacting sluggishly, but her mind was alive, and it was working furiously. Did Black Shuk draw his power from this place? Was the church located in the present, or was it in some sort of twin world, or a different realm? If it were the latter, then escape might prove more difficult. Boudica tried to stand but her wounds were still fresh, and she felt the pain acutely. It was a strange sensation. The Golden Torque had always healed her swiftly, but now, with it gone, she felt the bruises and the knocks. With a grunt, and after shouting several oaths that would have had her ejected by the congregation, she managed to stand upright. Her head was pounding and her eye, mostly healed before the torque was removed, was functioning properly, once she wiped the dried blood away on the back of her sleeve.

Boudica decided to make for the doors. It was always better to try to escape straightaway – laying up and hoping that your strength would return in time to slay your captors never worked. It only served to weaken your position. She only managed two steps before vomiting. When she had finished, she somewhat sheepishly turned back to the pulpit and the cross behind it and raised her hands as if to say sorry. As she turned back to the doors and her escape, she decided instead to take a seat on one of the pews. Black Shuk had returned.

"Going somewhere, great Queen? I thought that you would have been out for another day or two at least, after the attack. I had to give you a nasty nip on the shoulder when we reached Ipswich – you were starting to get angry. That torque of yours has some power, doesn't it?"

The great beast, part wolf, part bear, part something not yet classified, padded down the aisle towards her. For a creature so large, it moved almost silently. When it drew level with her, Black Shuk sniffed at her shoulder.

"Almost healed! That bite would have taken the head off a goat in a trice. You are made of sterner stuff, my lady." Boudica sensed something about the Beast then and she tried to tease some more from it.

"My lady? Not a full moon ago you were butchering my horses and attacking me!"

"I did not harm either of your fine mounts. You know that my muzzle would have been red with their blood when I found you in the bushes if I had."

"Why spare them? Why attack me?"

"The Golden Torque, my lady."

"It will not work for you or accept you. The magic that gives it its great power is not to be taken, it must be given – by hand, from someone that loves you or someone of the same blood. Ripping it away from me will not help you. It may harm you though."

The Beast laughed at her. Its tail was longer than a spear and swished back and forth to a regular beat. She noticed that its hackles were dropping.

"I did not rip it from you, Boudica, great Queen of the Iceni. I know its magic and its lore. It would become a mere bauble to me, a piece of yellow metal that the mortals fight each other over. I did not take it from you, someone else did, and when I have completed my task, the Golden Torque will be handed over to me, all of the conditions of ownership will be observed and the spell that binds will be transferred in accordance with Faerie law."

Boudica watched the fire in the Beast's eye intensify and something started to chill her heart.

"What then is the payment for the attack and the theft of the torque?"

"You know that already, my lady. The Silent King will have told you."

"The Silent King! What do you know of him, or me?"

"You are not the only creature to have lived a long time amongst these people. As you burned the Romans' boats and slaughtered their soldiers, I roamed far and wide, listening to the land and learning what I could from the Old Ones before they sailed away into the mist. Do not take me for a dumb brute, my lady, it would not be worthy of you.

"You have been meeting with the Silent King once a year, at the same place and at the same time, come rain, snow, sleet or shine. What the full terms of your pact are? I couldn't care less, some I know, the rest I chose not to hear. What I do care about, however, is being free of these marshes. I have been trapped here, watching the world go on without me, for too long. The accursed man who stood in that pulpit, there, behind you, cursed me. And for what? Cows and sheep wandered into the bogs and the shifting sands hereabouts, but it was Black Shuk that devoured them. Travellers saw red lights in the mist and ran screaming for salvation. So much rot! And all of it, laid down at my paws. As if I would trouble myself with scraggy mutton and weak-minded fools.

"I will be forced to roam these dead beaches, underneath a sky that sits so low that it forms a wall that I cannot see over. Only something of great power, like the *Golden Torque*, can free me."

Boudica tried to stand again – if Black Shuk were here to kill her, then she would accept her fate on her feet. A warrior to the last.

"Well then, *Beast,* you know as much as you think you need to know, which is poor, even for a damned dog. But I can bring some light to this discussion, if you let me?"

Black Shuk launched himself at the queen. His speed was terrifying, but he did not bite or smash her across the room with his paw. Instead, he caught her before she fell to the ground and helped her back onto the pew she had just vacated.

"Be still, Iceni, if I wanted your head, it would be inside my stomach by now, and causing me great indigestion no doubt. Sit."

Boudica sat back against the cold wood of the pew and her head lolled forward. She hadn't felt this sick for a hundred years or felt such weakness in her knees. The Beast knew though; its senses were far more highly tuned than hers. She looked down and blood was seeping through her tunic.

Black Shuk turned around and walked out of the church. He returned shortly afterwards with a huge piece of moss in his maw.

"Try this, place it on the wound and be sure to rub some of my saliva in with it."

Boudica did as she was told and closed her eyes. When she opened them again, the Beast had moved over to the pulpit and was busy urinating over it.

"Petty. I know. It is one of the only things I can do to state my displeasure and show some sort of defiance. Watch closely, it will hiss for a bit and then it will disappear. The king of this church is strong."

Boudica sat up again. The moss and the dog spittle had worked incredibly quickly – she could still feel the wounds, but they were cold, and the pain was distant.

"I don't suppose that you would be open to a counter-offer? You have not named your employer – yet. Can he offer you the Golden Torque?"

Black Shuk snarled and stepped away from the dais and the pulpit.

“I cannot be bought and sold like some bauble from the village fayre. I have been retained and I have given my bond, for what it is worth, in these strange times. I must see this through, my lady. Now, rest as best you can, I must be away, there is a task that I must perform.”

Boudica realised that there was more to the Beast than she had first thought. She resolved to try and persuade it to see reason and common sense, and then she started to put a plan together to kill the Silent King for betraying her. Her wounds were not entirely healed yet – a few more hours, possibly even a day. However long she had left, she had to make it count.

16. MALICE IN THE MUSEUM

Judas had heard one of the young PC's talking about having a head full of wool a few days ago. It had amused him at the time, but now he sympathised. His mind was wandering. That wasn't unusual, it happened quite a lot, understandable really with a head as full of memories as his. Of course it wandered, but there was something else happening to him right now, something new and uncomfortable. He was distracted and shouldn't be – better men than he had lost their lives to well-placed smoke screens and cul-de-sacs of disinformation. He told himself to focus and concentrate. Judas was starting to work through a few possible scenarios when an angel flew over his head and the passing of its shadow on the pavement in front of him caused him to look up quickly.

This one was carrying a satellite dish under each arm and a huge bag slung underneath its torso with the name of the latest new media provider on it. Judas wondered if there had been a slump in the sales of ladders recently because the angels were doing everything – they could work at any height and in any conditions. He thought to himself that somewhere, a human businessman was spitting feathers that no new orders had come in for his company's latest and lightest, super-strong ladders. Could the human affection for angels be waning?

Judas put that thought to one side, entered the Yard and ran up the stairs, two at a time. It didn't matter how many times he did this; he always reached the 7th floor without breaking a sweat or increasing his heart rate by so much as a beat. He must be close to 2000 years old by now. Where was the grey in his hair and the complaining joints and the wheezing? He and God weren't friends right now, but there were times when Judas was relieved that *he who must be obeyed* had made him immortal. It wasn't that long ago that a WW2 German Zeppelin, powered by dark magic, had crashed into the Thames just between Embankment and

Charing Cross, and he had been on it. He had walked away from that, with a little help from a certain Archangel with a sword that could shave a few million tonnes from a meteorite – mid-flight.

It was only when he got to the door to his office that he realised what this silly itch was. He wanted to speak with the White Witch again. She was the onboard security on the Ley Line Express and they had become close. Judas resolved to call her. He could race into a den of child traffickers and lay waste to them all, but small talk and all that 'signalling', left him cold. Still, he carried the small leather pouch that she gave him and there was something about it that told him that the place or the time when it would be needed wasn't far off.

Sgt Lace was sitting at the back of the office with her feet up on the radiator that lived under the window. Every now and again it pretended to give off some heat, but it was more useful as a footrest really. Judas liked having Lace here, and he was about to say hello and announce his presence when he realised that he didn't need to. She had seen him enter using the reflection in the window. She raised a hand and he waved back. Judas was about to offer to make her a cup of tea when he suddenly thought of Sgt Williams. It was the first time he'd done so in ages. Williams was Lace's predecessor. A good man, staunch and true, but stuck in a loveless marriage and trying to eat his way out of it with fast-food and an increasing number of bets on horses that ran the wrong way.

Judas imagined Williams sitting across the room with his Racing Post in hand, trying to read some divine truth in the odds and instead betting on a horse because its name reminded him of an old aunt in Aberystwyth. He sat down and took his coin from his pocket, rubbing at one side of it. Lace had watched him come in and waited for him to settle before making a cup of tea for him. They took it in turns – there was no teabag hierarchy here. When the mug settled on the green leather blotter on the top of Judas's desk, right in front of him, he sat upright immediately.

"Apologies, Lace, my mind is full of spaghetti at the moment."

"It's wool, sir, not spaghetti."

"What is?"

"The saying is: *I have a mind full of wool.*"

"That's what I said, wasn't it?"

"Not really, Guv."

Judas put his coin away, lifted the mug to his lips, and drank. It was awful.

"Why do we do this to ourselves, Lace? The dust in this bag is disgusting, how anyone can call this tea is beyond me. Tomorrow, I am getting some proper coffee from an acquaintance. She gets her beans straight from the Levant."

"That sounds magic, sir."

"You don't like coffee do you, Lace?"

"Not much, sir, I can take it or leave it. Is that heresy?"

"It is where I'm from – *originally*."

Judas stood up and pretended to take another slurp from the mug, then tactically poured it away down the sink.

Lace was shuffling some paperwork around on her desk, occasionally looking up and scanning the room. Judas had noticed that she hesitated when she was unsure of something. It was almost like she had made an informed decision, one that Judas would back her unconditionally with, but she was still waiting for something else.

"What is it, Lace?"

Lace dropped the folders she was shuffling. She looked at Judas and then back to the folders.

"That easy is it, sir?"

"Lace, I watch people and creatures from fairy tale worlds for a living. Plus, I'm the most famous liar, cheat and nasty bastard known to man. There are books written about me! I can see things – plus, you're pretty easy to read."

Lace smiled and they spread their case files out on the table in front of them. The Gilded Goat was there, in his finery, emerging from one drinking den in the Underside and hastening to another, bag in hand and Rolex on wrist.

"He's been robbed, sir. Some pretty unusual items taken from his own home. He says he had lots of spells and wards for protection, but whoever it was waltzed straight through them all."

"What did Raffles say?"

"He told me to speak to a man called Charles Murrell, or Cunning Murrell as he was known."

"The one and only Charles Murrell, King of the Cunning Men … it's been a long time since I heard that name."

Lace looked up from her files.

"Anything to worry about, sir?"

"Lace, if he knows that the Black Museum are onto him, for anything, you'll break him inside a minute. He is a clever chap – don't be fooled when you meet him, the country bumpkin thing works on impressionable folk, but not you. He has some lore – magical power – but not as much as he wants. But this is the big thing where Charles 'Cunning' Murrell is concerned – he is able to transplant souls, take one from one body and move it to another. The host has to be pretty easy to fool, but the Cunning Man is rather good at it, so watch him. You work your own cases, Lace, that was our agreement, but may I suggest that you take Raffles with you? He is a thief after all, and he knows the cunning ways. He might come in useful."

Lace flipped her case file over and set it to one side. Normally, they would stick a blue pin or two in the map of Greater London, to indicate a crime of an occult nature or a dispute within the ranks of the Under Folk. This time, Lace stayed at her desk.

"Sir?"

"What is it, Lace?"

"I have been spending a fair bit of time inside the Black Museum of late and things are not quite right. Raffles wanted me to talk to you about it, says there is some bad feeling down there. Some of the inmates are hiding inside their own time fields, and some of our more colourful characters are starting to grow restless. Raffles thinks that there is a lot of poison being dripped into some susceptible ears."

"What do you think, Lace? Never mind Raffles, what does it feel like to you?"

"I don't have your experience or knowledge of the Museum, sir, but something has changed recently, and it coincides with the appointment of those two new angels – as warders and gatekeepers."

Judas wandered over to the filing cabinets. The one second from the end was vibrating and the air around it shimmered.

"Calm down!" shouted Judas.

The cabinet did not stop moving straightaway, and Judas knew that Lace was onto something.

"Go and see the Cunning Man – take Raffles if you want, your choice. I reckon our friend, the Gilded Goat, has asked for something from the Cunning Man, a spell or a transformation charm perhaps, and the Goat has reneged on the deal, hence the theft."

Lace smiled; all her pieces were falling exactly where she thought they would.

"The Gilded Goat wants to be human; he dresses like one, acts like one and desperately wants to be accepted as one! He's done a deal with the Cunning Man and for some reason the Goat has reneged on it, so the Cunning Man has nicked his jewels."

Judas nodded.

"I think you're right, Lace, and you didn't need to run it past me to know that. The Gilded Goat might turn out to be the least of our problems though. I think we can afford to let him sweat a bit for now. I need you to help me with my case, things are starting to take a turn for the abysmal."

"What do you need, sir?"

"I need you to head over to this address and to let me know when this man, the tall one on the left in this picture, stretches his legs, be it a metre or a mile. It's a night's work, Lace, you okay with that?"

"You don't need to ask me that, sir."

Lace dropped her blue file on the desk, collected her coat from the stand in the corner and disappeared through the door. Judas wandered over to the window and looked out over London. The neon beast was waking up as the sun set.

17. THE HILL OF THE HEDONISTS

People stopped and stared as the Aston Martin DB5 coasted past them. It was gunmetal grey in colour and its shapely chassis and fine, curving lines made it stand out against the boxes on wheels favoured by the locals. A German muscle car or an Italian thoroughbred sports coupe might have roared down the street and turned a few heads, but there was an elegance and a sophistication about the Aston, and everyone nodded, as if to say: *nice*.

Prince Faelan was reclining on the back seat of the DB5. His head was resting against one window and his feet, wrapped in the most perfectly supple leather of his hand-made Trickers shoes were resting on the passenger seat in front. Any car enthusiast would have killed him for that slight alone, but he was a prince and he cared little for the whims and the desires of the people from this world. The car coasted to a halt just outside the entrance to London Zoo. Primrose Hill was away to the right, home to the power brokers, the artists and the big beasts of the media. To the left, the canal – and the real beasts.

The driver got out, walked around the car and opened the passenger door, and then pulled the lever that made the passenger seat bow to the dashboard. She stood up and waited for the prince to lift himself from the back seat, something he had been finding more and more difficult of late. When at last he roused himself, she heard the tell-tale crackle of a wrap of cocaine being twisted open. Then there was the moment of silence as clumsy hands sought for a rolled up £50 note in the pockets of a Saville Row suit, followed by the huge intake of air that would suck the cocaine, baby food and talcum powder mix from the lottery ticket it had been wrapped in, up the strongest and less abused nostril and on and into the brain of the future king of the Iceni.

When Prince Faelan had licked his wrap clean, he disengaged himself from the red leather of the Aston

Martin's back seat and stepped into the cool night air. He could hear the DJ in his favourite club winding up the crowd already and he felt his pulse quicken. It might have been the coke, or it might have been the thought that soon, he would be a king.

Did he really care that his mother was gone? Did he give a monkey's about his family? No to both.

Faelan's driver took his arm and guided him to the door of his favourite club. There was no line here, no queue, no inebriated rich kids that have heard about the latest club from a friend of a friend in Zurich. Unless you were from the better houses of the Under Folk, this place would always be just a fairy tale.

An ogre was working the door tonight, one that Faelan didn't know, so he shoved his driver forward to speak to it. It was too early in the night to start slumming it with tunnel dwellers. His driver spoke to the hulk, and it just shook its great shaggy head. Then she crossed the ogre's palm with gold. The muscled mountain was about to throw it in her face when it saw the markings on the coins and opened the door as quickly as possible for a VIP – a *Very Important Prince.*

Penumbra was the name of the club. The entrance was at the bottom of Primrose Hill. Some form of charm had been weaved so that the door was hidden from view; only those in the know, knew about it. Faelan practically threw his coat at the fairy working in the cloakroom, and he didn't wait to receive the ticket for his garment either – he left that menial task to his driver. She followed behind in his wake, trying to make a mental note of who he had insulted, so that an apology could be sent the following day.

Faelan decided to sit in one of the booths on the far wall. A slight, semi-naked girl with fire for eyes appeared straightaway and took his drinks order. The prince devoured her with his cocaine-enlarged eyes as she skipped away to the bar. He would have her later, if he remembered, and if the 'gear' hadn't dampened his libido. He looked around the club. It was packed already and there was so much flesh on show that he started to become aroused. The music was levelling up, the DJ was working the room really well, and small pockets of people who looked as if they were starting to lose interest were hooked and pulled back to the dance floor. Faelan ordered more drinks and more drugs. He bought some company and then bored them to tears with stories about himself – half were lies, and the other half were made up.

At some point in the early hours the crowd started to thin, and the DJ retired for the night. He had played his pipes and the rats had danced to his tune. Tomorrow night would be different, the clientele would be different, but the DJ was supremely confident that he had the magic to sway them all. When the club was empty, Faelan's driver was asked by the club's management to wake him. She tried whispering into his ear to begin with, then she shoved him on the shoulder – no reaction. So, she took her life in her hands and slapped his cheek a few times. On the third attempt, Faelan woke up with a snarl.

He followed the driver through the maze of empty tables to the cloakroom to pick up his coat.

There was no need for a ticket because his was the only one there. The fairy pushed it across the counter and apologised for the cigarette burn in the sleeve. No one had seen who had done it, unfortunately. Such a shame, it was a lovely coat, maybe a tailor might be able to save it?

Faelan swore at her, repeatedly. It was only when the ogre and a few of his burly mates started to amble over to the cloakroom that Faelan decided that his evening did not need to get any worse. The driver picked up the coat from the floor and opened the door for him. The sudden rush of the night's fresh, cool air hit him hard, and he felt instantly sober, but that soon passed, and he staggered to the parked Aston like a man mid-heart attack. When he got to the passenger side door he stood there, waiting for the door handle to be released but there was no sign of his driver. Faelan spun around. He had got a taste for shouting at someone, and he was displeased that his driver was making him wait. He scanned the road in each direction. There was nothing moving and no sign of his driver either. He turned back to the car, and it was then that he saw the two great red eyes reflected in the glass of the car door.

Faelan felt a hammer blow between his shoulder blades, before he was thrown in the air and his face was being dragged across the tarmac. He could see blood everywhere; it was like looking through red sunglasses. His attacker was incredibly strong and fast and when it bit him in the side of the neck, Faelan could smell death. Then he saw a vast black hole behind a row of yellow fangs and screamed. The razor-sharp teeth bore down again, harder this time, and then they released him. Faelan opened his eyes – he knew he was not going to survive another attack.

"Why?"

Faelan wanted to see his attacker, he wanted to plead for his life, he had so much to live for and so much wealth and privilege to enjoy.

"I will be King of the Iceni soon; I can offer you much more than you realise."

Black Shuk placed one great paw on Faelan's chest and extended his talons so they dug into it.

“Please! Just tell me why and what you want!”

The Beast did not answer him but there was someone else there, just behind the great black dog, that did.

“You have nothing to give me, I can take what I want. Your mother is gone; soon you will be too. What’s to stop me setting the Beast on you once again and throwing the chunks it doesn’t eat into the canal?”

Faelan recognised the voice and it chilled him to the bone.

“Step into the light!”

There was movement and then Faelan saw who it was that had attacked his mother and now him.

“You think that you are king? You think that you can take everything that the Iceni has built for yourself? You will never be our king, you mongrel bastard!”

Faelan heard a whisper, and then the fangs came again. This time they did not stop or nip. They tore and savaged his body. The expensive material of his Saville Row suit and his Thomas Pink shirt were shredded –

and then it was the turn of his flesh. Faelan was dead and dismembered in seconds, and his killer was true to his word. What was left of Prince Faelan of the Iceni was dumped into the canal. The red flesh splashed into the water and the dark night stole it away.

18. THE DEAD SKY

The angel Chasen was sitting in the dark in the Key Room, and under a dark cloud of his own making. He had stopped asking Hutriel to sit with him. It was clear that their paths had forked, and Chasen, consumed with anger and spite, believed that Hutriel was walking away from *him*. He felt betrayed and he felt numb. The fire that once burned within him so brightly was naught but an ember now. Judas, the villain, had ripped his heart out and replaced it with some black, hungry thing that devoured love and kindness, leaving nothing for Chasen to believe in.

If only I could escape this place he thought.

He contemplated sleep but he knew it would not come easily, so he just closed his eyes and pressed his fingers into his temples until his head ached. He was seeking out more pain when he heard voices close by and stood up quickly. He could hear a faint mumbling and whispering, and he became alarmed, because he thought he saw movement in the gloom ahead. He unsheathed his sword and started to walk towards the sound. The Key Room defies any architectural logic – it is very long and running the entire length is a table, and on that table are the keys to every single cell inside the Black Museum.

They are not keys in the normal sense of the word; they are not made from iron or swing from a steel hoop on a gaoler's belt. These keys are objects, something that identifies the monster locked inside. A poisoner's key might be a small glass vial, the object they used to kill their victims with; a murderer's key might be a hammer or a hatpin. The key mirrors the crime. Chasen looked around but could see no one and was just about to leave when he looked down and saw a gentleman's opera glove, whiter than a swan's belly and pressed flatter than a shilling piece. There was something troubling him about the glove, so he bent down and picked it up.

"Help me, Chasen!"

As soon as he grasped it, he heard his partner's voice. Hutriel sounded weak and in pain. Chasen closed his eyes and concentrated on the glove in his hand, and seconds later, he was flying down through the darkness towards a bed of twinkling lights, cut in two by the curves of a silver river. Chasen felt rather than saw the ground rushing up to meet him and unfurled his mighty wings to their widest reach and they acted on the air like a sky anchor and stopped his descent instantly. His feet landed on the slick, wet cobblestones of a coaching yard. A street sign on the wall told him that he was in Whitechapel, London. He could see a large black hearse under the eaves of a well maintained stable further across the yard and a selection of bridles and decorative headpieces for the horses that pulled it.

"Hutriel? Where are you?"

There was no answer, and Chasen drew his sword.

"Hutriel, if you are unable to talk, make any sound, and I will come to your aid."

Again, there was no reply. Chasen leapt onto the tiled roof of the stables and held his sword aloft. He whispered the blade's name, and it came to life and pulsed with a white flame so bright that the skyline disappeared. After the initial explosion of light, the blade began to breathe – when it exhaled the fire increased and when it inhaled the streets went dark. He was looking out onto a warren of dark and lawless streets; they ran away from him in all directions like fractures on a sheet of black glass.

Chasen tried to get his bearings. A short distance away, *as the angel flies,* was the Cathedral of St Paul's. Ahead, he knew, was the river and to his right, the marshes and then the sea itself. There were some beautiful structures that he recognised straightaway, but there were twice as many buildings that punctured the skyline like rotten teeth in a broken jaw.

"HUTRIEL!" Chasen roared into the night.

A voice replied, but it was not the voice of his friend.

"He is not here, Chasen, once a true son of the mighty Host, and now a lowly and pathetic turnkey, wandering aimlessly through the sewers of the darkest prison in all of the worlds."

The voice was sharp – like the point of a needle, it scratched at the air and left it sore.

"Where is Hutriel?"

"He is far away from here I expect, cosying up to that rat Judas and the rest of the filth."

Chasen sheathed his sword. There was nothing to fear here, and as soon as the voice started to speak, he realised that Hutriel was not here and that he had been deceived.

"If my friend is not here, whoever you might be, then there is no need for me to be, either. I wish you a long and unpleasant confinement. So, goodbye."

"Now, now, let's not be too hasty mighty warrior, I can help you. I know things about the Black Museum, and I know ways to escape it. I've done it once before, it's easy if you know how."

Chasen jumped down from the roof of the stables and landed, once again, on the cobblestones of the courtyard. He stood there for the space of a heartbeat or two and waited. Sure enough, a lamp was lit and placed in the window of a building nearby. He walked towards it, slowly, watching the shadows for movement and readying himself for conflict with every step.

He reached the door to the house with the golden window and opened it. The feeble yellow glow of the oil lamp's flame shuffled across the floor to meet him. Sitting at the table on the far side of the room was Jack the Ripper, and he had come dressed for the opera.

"I could rip you to pieces for summoning me here like this."

"You could, but the next time anyone picked that infernal glove up in the Key Room, there I'd be. That's the way it works in here, Chasen."

The angel ducked so that it could enter the room. The average height of the average man in this era was on the short side and Chasen felt confined immediately. He pulled out a chair and sat down. Jack the Ripper's hand slipped into his dress cape, and it made Chasen smile.

"If you are resting your hand upon a weapon because it makes you feel safer, and more comfortable, believe me, it will be of little use to you. Now, what is it that you want?"

Jack removed his hand from the folds of his cape but there was no knife in it, no wicked blade or surgeon's scalpel. Instead, there was a nosegay. The flowers had long since wilted and turned brown, and all that remained was a folded cotton handkerchief with the initials EB stitched onto it. Jack the Ripper laid it on the small wooden table between them.

"Exotic," said Chasen, sarcastically.

"It is, isn't it. Doesn't look much, laying there, does it, angel? Nothing much to fear or to write to one's home about. That's its magic you see. This shabby looking article was the key to a certain Edmund Baynham's cell. He was the leader of a motley crew of young dandys and young thrusters who walked around the old city in days gone by swearing, drinking, and then slicing up the Watch. The queen had to intervene, or it would have been the rope for dear Edmund. He led his gang of fools and called them *the Cruel Gang.*"

Chasen watched the man across the table closely and he realised that they were not so different after all. *He* wanted to escape, and so did the little man in the black cape and top hat, sitting opposite.

"I am familiar with the object. What use is it to me?"

Jack the Ripper leaned in closer; he could tell when his audience was truly listening, and he was getting excited because he could see that the hook he had baited was so near to being taken.

"Edmund was taken and imprisoned, but moments later, he was gone. He went 'adventuring' in Europe. Who helped him escape from inside here, and more importantly, how did he get out? It's taken me a few hundred years, a few false attempts and rather more injuries than I would have liked, but I have discovered his secret, and I know how to get out."

Chasen shifted in his chair and the movement of his wings dislodged several plates and tin mugs from the dresser nearby. He didn't take his eyes of Jack the Ripper though.

"I take it that you need an angel to make your escape. Or, why lure me here? Your plan is only a half plan really, isn't it? Pathetic and ill-thought through, no wonder you are locked away inside here."

Jack smiled, a smile full of teeth – sharp, hungry teeth – and then reached across the table and turned the small wheel that fed the wick into the oil. The lamp sucked in the fuel and burned brighter, and Jack went for broke.

"Of course, you are right, *mighty Chasen*, I need *you* to get *me* away from this awful place. What is it that *you* need to escape from?"

Chasen watched the face across the table through the smallest of heat hazes and he felt sick to his stomach. The face was right, and the words that trickled out of its mouth like poisoned honey did their trick and worked their evil magic on him. He sat there, disgusted with himself, but his desire to escape plus his utter and unshakeable belief that he had been cheated tipped the balance in Jack's favour. So, they talked and talked of escape and vengeance until the wick burned all the way down. The sun came up like a milky sphere hidden in the cold mist of a new day in Whitechapel, but the darkness remained.

19. THE WEEPING GIANT

Judas woke up to the sound of his bedside clock getting its revenge for being swiped onto the floor on so many occasions. Louder and louder it screamed, and it would have carried on if Judas's hand hadn't emerged from underneath his dark blue John Lewis duvet cover and slapped it across the face. It managed just one more warbled cry, before it shut itself down.

Judas had pondered more than once: after waking someone up, do alarm clocks go to sleep? Do they watch the people they have tortured and just pulled from the safe, warm embrace of a 10-tog duck feather cloud of loveliness, as they hop on one foot around a cold room, disorientated and angry, and then chuckle?

Judas didn't have the luxury of existential observations at that moment because a new alarm had taken the other's place. Someone was hammering on his front door. *Really hammering.*

Judas crept through his flat, moving from room to room, quickly. He avoided the windows – there might be two of them or even more. The hammering on the door continued. Judas took one more look around the flat before slipping into the hallway. It wouldn't be the first time that he'd been attacked from behind, and it wouldn't be the last, but if he could reduce the risk by watching his own back for a change, then he'd be a fool not to.

He'd had a spyhole fitted into the door but did not trust it. There were far too many creatures and people in the worlds that he moved between that could tell you what colour socks you were wearing from the street outside. It was a cosmetic device more than anything, but Judas had a gut feeling that the hammering on the door was for his benefit, and not as a smoke screen prior to an attack. He'd been wrong before, but his scar was not burning, and he trusted that scar.

The hammering stopped. Judas stepped back, away from the door. Whoever was on the other side either had a sore hand after thumping the door for the last five minutes or had sensed his presence. Or there was another option – the person on the other side had drawn him to the door and now that he or she or it, were happy that he was where he was supposed to be, was about to blow the door to pieces with some unholy weapon or dirty bomb.

"Boss? Is that you?"

"Lace?"

"Bloody hell, sir! I've been banging on this door for the last ten minutes! They've found a body. Well, it isn't the whole body, it's the remains of Prince Faelan. The Iceni have claimed him already and say they're going to bury him straightaway, at some tree or something."

Judas risked a quick look through the spyhole. Lace was standing right in front of it. There were no furtive glances from her, indicating that she might be under duress and being told what to say. She appeared quite calm, and although they had only been working together for a short time, he could read her facial expressions. He opened the door.

Lace marched in and while Judas was showering and putting some clean clothes on, she wandered around his apartment and did what police officers generally do, which was to have a quick peak through the homeowner's things. There were lots of pictures on the wall, a few paintings, and here and there, black and white photographs in neat, boring frames. It was spotlessly clean, and all the appliances were state-of-the-art – and hardly used. The temptation to open a drawer or two was rising. Thankfully, Judas emerged from his boudoir just as she was about to.

"There's nothing of interest in there for you, Lace. Come on, let's get going."

Lace had one of the pool cars outside, a Ford Mondeo, silver of course, and dependable. Judas sent the new superintendent a text message as Lace pulled away from the kerb.

"How bad is it, Lace?"

"Uniform responded to a shout from one of the Regent's Canal team at 03.00 hours this morning. They were dredging the canal for *aggressive weeds*, shopping trolleys and used condoms, when they came across what they initially thought were lumps of chip fat and lard. Apparently, some of Camden's mobile fast-food purveyors dump their waste into the canal when no one is looking. The team leader that called the local station after they'd found what we now know is the remains of Prince Faelan, said they were all in shock. They said that they, the cleaners, thought they'd found some half-inflated red balloons, which turned out to be half-eaten lungs, a long white snake which was in fact a spinal column, and what they thought was an old, brown cricket ball that turned out to be Faelan's heart."

Judas thumped the dashboard and then quickly searched inside his jacket pocket for his silver coin. Lace pulled over to the side of the road.

"Sir? Where are we headed, sir?"

"Sorry, Lace, we're going out of town, to Norfolk, the Norfolk Broads to be precise – let me plug in the details on the sat-nav. It will take us most of the way there."

Lace watched as Judas quickly set the destination, and as soon as the lovely lady inside the box told her where to go, she drove away.

The drive was uneventful. As soon as they had left fortress Greater London, the countryside crept up on them. It was amazing to see how quickly the grey gave way to the green. Trees started to line the roads instead of lampposts and pheasants flew up instead of pigeons. It took them an hour and a half to get to the destination. It was going to take a little longer to get to the burial site.

Lace parked the Mondeo in a small but perfectly formed visitors' car park, near a river. Huge geese and swans were wandering around as if they owned the place, leaving little brown markers on the grass behind them, just to let everyone know where they had been. Lace instantly regretted wearing her white trainers today. Judas was hopping from one foot to the other like a novice hot coal walker. His choice of a pair of Church's loafers had been a mistake too.

Behind the car park was a small pathway that led down to the water's edge. Judas set off and Lace followed him. They walked along the riverbank for about a minute or two. It was beautiful there; the river ran on beside them and the trees bowed to it as it passed them by. The branches overhead started to creak, and their leaves rained down on them both as they walked on. The air became heavy, and Lace started to feel uneasy. Something unusual was happening. Judas sensed her anxiety rising.

"You've just walked back in time, Lace. Welcome to Druid country."

Lace was unfazed, as usual.

"Makes a change from *Homes under the Hammer*, sir."

"Indeed, it does, Lace. Watch your step now, once we climb over this turnstile, things might get a little weird."

Judas put one foot on the old wooden step and vaulted over. Lace did the same. When she landed and looked up, she was surrounded by a group of male and female warriors – white skinned, red-haired, and carrying some truly naughty-looking spears. Judas was already talking to their leader. Lace couldn't hear what he was saying, but after a few bobs of the head and placing a hand over his heart, the warriors stepped away and Judas walked on with Lace beside him.

On the far side of the field stood an enormous tree. It was two heads and two shoulders higher than anything else around it, and underneath was a white tent. Lace noticed the arrival of other people from gaps in the hedgerows. They weren't all taking human form though – little flying men and women swarmed overhead and great beasts and trolls, not unlike the one they had found in the sewer recently, lumbered through the trees and headed for the tent. When they were only a few feet away the flap of the tent opened and a tall man wearing a white, homespun robe stepped out. The hem of his garment was stained green from the wet grass, and he wore a small leather bag around his neck.

"Welcome all. Step inside – we are about to say goodbye to our prince."

That was it, no great speech or song of great valour, just an introduction to say goodbye. Lace followed Judas into the tent. There were hundreds of creatures already inside, but Judas walked through them. They parted as they saw him coming and here and there, a hand was raised in greeting, or a head was bowed in respect. The tent had been pitched under the Weeping Giant, a tree that was venerated by the Iceni and worshipped by the druids. The rear of the tent opened out onto the riverbank, and it was here that the remaining Iceni formed a guard of honour for the dead prince.

Judas saw Fedelmid and Morcant in the front rank of the Iceni. Their little sister was not present for some reason, and of course, the throne remained empty too. Boudica's body had still not been found. The Iceni were falling quickly. Faelan's shroud had already been placed on a raft made from the branches of the Weeping Giant. The river had stopped flowing as a sign of respect and the only sound was the murmuring of the druids nearby. A lament was being sung, but no one present could understand the words.

When it finished, the Druid Chief bowed to Princess Fedelmid, and she stepped forward and untied the rope that held the raft fast to the shore. The raft went neither left nor right. It defied physics and logic and instead, floated in a straight line away from the riverbank. There was to be no ceremonial archery contest today though. No burning shaft would arc through the air and set fire to the prince's body. The river began to cloud over and a low mist appeared, even though it was a fair and bright day. Everyone in the tent and on the riverbank bowed, and then, two great branches reached down from the tree and lifted the prince's body from the water. The Weeping Giant pulled what was left of Faelan to its breast and the shroud and the raft went back to their creator.

Lace was amazed, and it showed on her face.

"Try not to look too impressed, Lace," whispered Judas.

"Sorry, sir."

The afternoon unfolded, and the sun started to drop in the sky. The crowd thinned and then it was gone. Lace couldn't remember the ceremony ending, or Judas taking her by the arm, and leading her back to the turnstile. They stopped at a roadside café, the haunt of lorry drivers and salesmen with their spare suits hanging up in the back of their cars. Judas ordered a full English and Lace followed suit. The black pudding was awful, but everything else was just what the doctor ordered. They ate in silence. It was only after the young girl, who bore an uncanny resemblance to the chef, had cleaned their plates away that Judas spoke.

"Did you notice the way that the Druid Chief kept looking at Fedelmid? I couldn't work out if he was measuring her up for the crown or a raft of her own. What do you think?"

"You were telling me all about the family, sir. Isn't there a younger one, another princess?"

"Yes, Oebfinn. She's the youngest … well, when I say youngest, she's a few hundred years older than you. I wondered about that too. The Iceni are warriors, a bit of blood and a dead body, however hacked about it is, shouldn't really be cause for a member of royalty to miss the funeral."

Lace lifted her mug of tea to her lips and gulped it down.

"What do you think happened to the prince, sir? Cat Tabby was talking about a great black beast, wasn't he?"

It was Judas's turn to drink now. A huge articulated lorry rattled past on the road outside and the vibrations made the salt and pepper pots rattle too.

"Cat Tabby wants his fortune back, or at least some of it. The Women of the Chapel are the Silent King's subjects, and they have most of Cat Tabby's old property empire. Cat Tabby says that he saw a huge black dog. Its real name is Black Shuk, and it is very dangerous. Is Cat Tabby behind all of this? Is he trying to set the Iceni and the Silent King against one another?

If one, or both fall, Cat Tabby can step in and clean up."

Lace paid the girl at the till, and they continued their conversation in the car as they drove back to London.

"Is Cat Tabby big enough though, sir? Doesn't really strike me as the Napoleon of crime, to be honest."

Lace performed a deft bit of driving and undertook a slow driver who couldn't make his mind up about what lane of the motorway he should be in.

"You're right, Lace, if he has Black Shuk in his pocket, how is he controlling it? He's a cat and Shuk is a dog, doesn't quite add up."

"And Boudica, sir? We haven't found her body, no one knows if she is alive or dead, and the Iceni are dropping like flies. If they go to war with the Silent King, they're going to get mullered."

The Mondeo was making good time with Lace at the wheel and the steady thrum of the tyres blocked out any other noise and gave them both the time and space to work over the many different aspects of the case.

"The Silent King doesn't know everything yet, but he will, he has the network, and he has the power, and he'll want to know why I didn't tell him about Black Shuk at our last meeting. Then, there is this pact between him and Boudica. He thinks that she betrayed him – that would give him grounds to get a bit miffed, wouldn't it? Right now, from the outside, would it be a stretch to imagine that Boudica could be staging all of this to get out of her arrangement with the Silent King? She pretends to get abducted, pins it on him, cries foul and then returns triumphant. Everyone is on her side, she saves face and has the right to stiff him on whatever she owes him."

"That's pretty thin, sir. Cat Tabby wants his fortune back, Boudica wants to get out of her secret arrangement, the Silent King says he's been attacked, and all the while, the Iceni are getting wiped out? If this is all part of her plan she needs to think again – that's what I think, sir."

Lace indicated, pulled over to the left and parked outside Judas's mansion block.

"Someone or something wants a war, and we can't let that happen, Lace. While we were at the funeral, a lot of the tribal leaders in the Under Folk made it clear to me that if the Black Museum can't keep the peace, then they might have to find a way to police themselves. See you tomorrow."

20. DROWNING TO STAY ALIVE

Princess Fedelmid had been starved of sleep for two nights running by a rather unpleasant thought. She still believed that her mother was alive somehow, and that the Silent King was involved, but there was something else that she had begun to consider, and it made her feel sick to her stomach. Rather than call the Druid Council to a meeting, or gather the family, she had decided to call upon DCI Judas Iscariot of Scotland Yard once more. The last time they met, she had handled it badly, playing the princess rather than the concerned daughter. She would not make the same mistake twice and this time, she had something to share with him that she honestly believed would help to resolve this damaging and deadly situation.

She asked her driver to stop just outside Borough Market and disembarked. Her bodyguards assembled around her. Fedelmid had never felt comfortable surrounded by a wall of muscle, it made her feel as if she were walking inside a bubble, so her bodyguards had been trained to stay close but not to suffocate. In the event of an attack, all of that went out of the window, of course.

The Market, once upon a time, was the province of the fisherman and the farmer. Wide-eyed fish in great baskets, filled to the brim with ice, were sold to the buyers from the hotels, and meat from all four corners of the Isles were paraded around small enclosures, soon to become sausages or steaks or fillings for pies. Now, bars and restaurants had taken their place. There were still a handful of stands serving food, and on certain days there were street markets where you could sample designer cheese, and olives with ninety-nine different flavourings were scooped into recycled glass jars to sprinkle over salads in artisan bakeries.

For all its modern-day pretensions, Borough Market was still a vibrant and exciting place to visit. On thirsty Thursdays and weekends, the pubs were packed, and the drinkers spilled out onto the market floor. On this particular thirsty Thursday, Princess Fedelmid needed a drink before she spoke with Judas. There were plenty of places to choose from, but she decided to send one of her minions ahead and book a table at Roast, a restaurant built into the eaves of the market's roof. Fedelmid entered and was immediately guided to a table for one, with the best view in the house.

After a glass of a spectacular Chilean red, that was nearly as good as one of the wines from the fairy realm, and a plate of cured Spanish meats, Fedelmid set off for her meeting. She hoped that her hypothesis was incorrect, but that hope was a forlorn one. Darkness had arrived in the meantime, but there were still crowds of revellers in the Market and enough light from streetlamps and bars to navigate the narrow paths and the lanes that led away from the Market and down to the Thames.

It was while she was thinking of her mother that she realised she was alone. When she looked around, her bodyguards were nowhere to be seen and the streets were empty. Fedelmid felt the cold breath of fear on the back of her neck and her legs stopped obeying the commands sent to them from her brain. Something had turned the corner at the bottom of the lane and was moving towards her on silent paws. As it moved ever closer, she could see its red eyes and, in those eyes, she saw herself – frightened and weak and unable to move.

It was this image of herself, a little girl, wetting herself because a great dog was upon her, that saved her life, at least for now. Fedelmid became angry and she turned and ran. She had only made it to the corner of the lane when she smelled its breath and felt its claws rake across her back. Fedelmid stumbled but did not fall. The spirit of her mother was with her, and she refused to give in and succumb.

The Beast, a victim of its own phenomenal speed and its great mass could not get enough purchase on the wet cobblestones, and it careered into a parked car. The vehicle's windows shattered, and its alarm began to shriek. It would go unnoticed, of course. Londoners did not care much for car alarms, unless it was a Sunday, and the car was parked outside one of their homes.

Fedelmid took advantage of the Beast's misfortune to run as fast as she could towards the place she had agreed to meet the Master of the Black Museum. It was her only chance of salvation … only he could save her now.

Judas looked at his watch. He was five minutes early; being late had always been for the bad mannered and the inconsiderate, in his book. He was beginning to think that a pint at the Lamb and Flag would be a better use of his time when he heard the scream.

Fedelmid tried to punch the Beast's great head, to no avail. It was like trying to stab a rhino with a banana. So, she picked up a traffic cone and turned it upside down. Inside the rim was a plastic bag of sand that was used to weigh it down and stop the wind from blowing it to cone heaven.

"Come on then, dire wolf! You may have teeth, but now, so have I! And believe me, Black Shuk, I will not go as easily as my dear brother. You will remember me, by the wounds that you will carry for the rest of your life! So, come and have a go!"

Black Shuk opened its great mouth and thick strings of yellow saliva formed a spider's web between its fangs. Then it advanced, eager to finish its task.

Judas was running as fast as he could. The Thames's towpath, normally so full of tourists and workers heading home after another day of timesheets and watercooler moments, was empty. He feared the worst.

Princess Fedelmid had lost a lot of blood. She felt cold and the cosh she had fashioned from the plastic bag filled with sand had begun to feel heavy. Every time the Beast attacked, she had managed to keep it at bay, but her strength was failing her, and the Beast knew it. She looked around. There was nowhere left to run. Her only escape route was the river and she knew that she would not last more than ten minutes if she jumped.

Judas heard a scuffle, and then a howl that sounded long and low into the night. He was too late!

He had run too slowly! He knew who had been attacked before he rounded the corner, but he found no body, butchered and bleeding on the ground. What he did happen across was a dog the size of a transit van with eyes so red that they reminded him of hot coals in a furnace.

Judas stopped.

"So then, we meet at last, *Black Shuk*. And, as a policeman, I'd have to say that you are holding a smoking gun right now and looking a little bit guilty."

Black Shuk did not reply. He had no need to. The girl had gone into the river, and she would not be coming out again. Stopping to parley with the Master of the Black Museum was pointless, and as he had done so many times before, he disappeared into the night and was gone.

Judas knew better than to try to follow the Beast. It could have travelled to another realm by now and hidden itself in some vast forest that only sprites and the Fae folk could pass through. Instead, he went to the stone wall of the towpath and looked over into the water of the great River Thames. He had hoped that Princess Fedelmid had managed to grab a hold of one of the old wooden breakers in the water or found something to stop her from being dragged under. But there was no sign of her. She was gone and war seemed another step closer. Judas felt deflated. The adrenalin that had raced through his system was subsiding, and grief was now taking its place. *He'd lost another one.* The Under Folk would know about this straightaway, and the respect for the Black Museum would be lost forever. There could be a silver lining to this whopping great grey cloud of failure though. By the morning, he could be out of a job.

There was nothing he could do now, so he walked back to Scotland Yard along the waterfront. When he got there, he was told that he had a visitor. She was waiting for him in one of the holding cells. She had been brought in by a member of the public, wringing wet, cold, and covered in blood. The desk sergeant had given her some warm blankets and a cup of tea from the canteen.

"It kills or cures, inspector – you never know which one – but she looked like she'd been in the wars, so I thought it best."

Judas scrambled down the stairs to the cells in the basement. In number 7, he found Princess Fedelmid sitting in the corner of the cell with her knees raised to her chest, a horsehair blanket around her shoulders and worshipping a mug of police tea like the Holy Grail.

The Duty Sergeant had asked the best first aider he could find in the building to attend. He'd looked at her leg, and then prescribed wrapping her up like a Mummy and pumping her full of hot, sweet tea, until someone that knew what they were doing turned up. Her face was as white as the glow from the tungsten bulb in the ceiling above her, but Judas could also see defiance and strength.

The long line of the Iceni might yet carry on he thought.

When she was ready to walk, Judas took her to the lift and together they rode it to the 7th floor.

Judas didn't need to be a detective to see that Princess Fedelmid was out on her feet, only her pride and her Iceni blood were keeping her from dropping to the lino like a sack of King Edward's. He wanted to help her and lift her up, but she would not have thanked him for it, and so he was forced to watch her suffer. He pulled a chair out from under a table at the back of the office. Williams, one of his former sergeants, had snaffled this old leather chair from a crime scene long ago. It was cherry red and punctured at regular intervals with round brass tacks that looked like a robot's bellybutton.

Fedelmid lowered herself into it and sighed. She tried to pull the coarse blanket more tightly around her shoulder but succeeded only in dropping her mug, which thankfully was empty. Judas lifted the mug from the floor and took it to the sink at the back of the office. When he returned, she was fast asleep. It was just as well. Judas was the worst sort of patient in the world, always griping and groaning and fending off the well-intentioned care of others with his barge pole of pride.

He imagined Fedelmid to be the same and counted his blessings that she would not wake up as he tended to her wounds.

It took him about an hour to cleanse the wounds and then to dress them again. There was no chance of infection now, but she was dangerously dehydrated, so Judas improvised and called Angel Dave. The angel arrived within the hour. He was carrying everything that Judas would need to make a drip in a leather satchel that reminded him of the larger scale version that the Angels of the North had carried him to Newcastle and back in. Angel Dave was a friend, a dependable sort that Judas had rescued long ago from the gutter, and Dave did not go a week without being reminded of that.

Once they had set the drip up, and the first flushes of anything resembling a natural colour returned to Princess Fedelmid's face, Judas ushered his angel friend away. He had done more than expected – *again*, and it was up to Judas now to watch over her. He knew who had attacked her and he knew why, but he still had no idea who had sent the Beast. If it was the Silent King, he would have the forces of the Iceni, the massed ranks of the Under Folk and the might of the Black Museum against him. But the Silent King was not stupid, far from it. It was not him; he wouldn't make a mistake like that. That left only Boudica. But where was she?

21. CATS AND DOGS

Sergeant Lace was sitting in the passenger seat of a dilapidated Ford transit van. It was one of Scotland Yard's fleet of unmarked vehicles, and although it looked shabby on the outside, it was stuffed with mod-cons inside. It had heated seats, headrests and ergonomic car seats, those favoured by taxi drivers. The windows had a very faint tint at the bottom so that the lights from the in-car communications set-up couldn't be seen by a nosey passer-by. She wrapped herself up tight in her favourite blanket, watching the street in front of her, and making sure to use her rear-view mirrors regularly to keep an eye on the mews behind her. Judas had asked her to resume her watching brief on the Iceni as soon as they had returned from the countryside and Prince Faelan's death ceremony. The prince had neither been burned nor buried. *Ceremony* seemed the right thing to call it.

On her way to the *OP,* earlier that evening, Lace had made a detour to a small Waitrose supermarket and stocked up with snacks and bottles of water for the night ahead. There was nothing worse than being on a stakeout with a grumbling stomach and a parched throat.

The Iceni guards standing in front of the main doors of their natty mews address were being changed regularly. Whoever was organising the roster was well-trained and taking no chances. From her position she could see everything, and she doubted whether anyone could get near to that building without a silent alarm triggering and the troops swarming out.

No person could, but a cat? A cat could saunter down this mews and not raise the alarm. A cat could wander up to the door and solicit a cuddle or rub itself up against the legs of whoever was standing there.

Which is exactly what Cat Tabby did. Lace watched him trot up to the door, swishing his tail and purring like the 2-stroke motor of a remote-controlled car. The guards ignored him of course. They noticed him, but they did not allow themselves to be distracted, and Cat Tabby got to spend as much time as he wanted looking through the glass doors and spying on the Iceni. Lace had to admire the feline's nerve. Once he'd seen everything he needed to see, Cat Tabby walked back the way he came, and Lace watched him in the rear-view mirror until he turned the corner.

Lace folded her blanket up and laid it on the driver's seat. Then she made a note of the time, checked that the camera on the dashboard was still recording everything that was happening, and slipped out of the van to set off in pursuit of Cat Tabby. If dear old Cat Tabby was making a note of what was happening then there was a good chance that his partner in crime, or whoever he was doing business with was nearby, and Lace wanted to know who it was. During police training, instructors always set you the task of following a group of children down a busy street. Kids stop and start and turn quickly for no reason, they stop to look in windows at toys and tech and often split up, only to meet up again at the far end of the road. The reason for trailing them is obvious; there are a million and one ways for them to spot you, so you have to be three steps ahead.

Lace had finished top of her class, but Cat Tabby was proving harder to track from a safe distance than the whole cast of Grange Hill. He was so small and slight that he kept disappearing into the shadows and Lace had to keep stopping and staring hard into those little pockets of darkness. Luckily, Cat Tabby was on a mission, and he obviously didn't think that anyone was following him. Lace kept with him and all the while she was trying to work out what he was doing.

Cat Tabby had been up on the rooftops half the night already. The Iceni had more motion sensors on the top of their office than a Foreign Embassy building in Mayfair. He'd had to tread carefully up there but it had been worth it. The death of Prince Faelan had really put the wind up the Iceni. Boudica was still missing, presumed dead, and the mighty Druid Council were being very quiet, which was very strange. Cat Tabby was starting to get one of his 'itches'. The whole situation was crazy, so many moving parts, so much that he didn't know, and as the biggest source of gossip and information in town, it irked him no end.

He'd managed to get onto a window ledge, just outside what was obviously the main chamber for the family. There were a few chairs around the long wooden table, and one solitary pool of light at the far end. Someone had entered the room just as he was trying to get in and he'd nearly had kittens, but that person wasn't remotely concerned about intruders.

Prince Morcant wandered around the room, spinning chairs, and running a finger along the edge of the table. He stopped in front of a picture of his mother and stared at it. Cat Tabby couldn't hear much over the hum of the city in the background, so he tried to read the young man's body language instead, but the light was too poor to make sense of anything. Morcant turned away from the portrait of his warrior queen and started to move across the room to the window where Cat Tabby was hiding. Any sudden movement would have caught Morcant's eye, so he sat as still as possible and lowered his eyes.

Morcant loomed in the window above him and just when Cat Tabby thought that he would be discovered, Morcant's mobile phone went off. Cat Tabby perked up and turned both of his radar-like ears in the prince's direction. On a good day, Cat Tabby could hear a conversation in the middle of a thunderstorm as a fleet of on-call ambulances roared past. Some double glazing and a car alarm shouldn't be too much of an issue.

"*Is she dead?*" Morcant whispered.

The answer he received displeased him, but he hid it well.

"That's great to hear, and she's where? Which hospital?"

Cat Tabby strained to hear the voice on the other end of the phone but some fool on a Ducati Monster or some such muscle motorbike let rip on the street below and obliterated the conversation.

Prince Morcant ended the call and replaced the phone in his pocket. From where Cat Tabby was sitting, his face was not a happy one. In fact, he looked as mad as a goblin in a vacuum cleaner. Just before he turned away from the window, Cat Tabby thought he heard the prince mutter something along the lines of '*Black Museum'*. But who was the person he was talking about? Had Boudica been found? If she were at the Black Museum, there would be a lot of interested parties that would pay handsomely for that information. He just had to choose which one.

Lace saw Cat Tabby turn into a little side street ahead and she realised that if he were to slink under some railings or a wire fence, she would lose him. She checked her watch again and started to speed up. When she turned the corner, she stopped suddenly and tried to merge into the bricks on the wall nearby. Cat Tabby wasn't going anywhere because a huge black dog-shaped thing had him pinned to the ground with an enormous paw. Luckily, the Beast only had eyes and ears for Cat Tabby and the poor little feline was entirely focused on the red eyes of the horrible black mass on top of it.

Lace wanted to creep closer and to try and make out what they were saying to each other, but she couldn't speak dog or cat and decided that if Cat Tabby lived, she would pick him up later and let Judas have a word with him. The growling and the mewling continued for a short while and when the Beast raised its paw, Cat Tabby did not need to be offered an escape route twice. He shot off like a tiny grey blur down the side street and disappeared up a drainpipe at the far end. Lace realised that she was trembling and was sure that the Beast would hear the hammering of her heart before long, but her feet were not her friends right then and they refused to obey the signals she was sending them from the panic department in her brain.

The dog, or wolf or bear, or whatever it was, did not hear her or see her; its mind was elsewhere. The task it had been set was starting to get more and more complex, and now the Black Museum was involved too.

As Black Shuk padded away into the darkness, an unfamiliar thought came to call.

Was the prize really worth all this?

Lace watched its terrible form disappear into the night. At one point she thought it had gone down into the sewers through a drain and the next, she could have sworn that it had taken to the air and slipped away like a cloud of dark mist. Regardless, it was gone and so was Cat Tabby. She had no new intelligence other than the cat was more involved than it had been letting on. Was it in league with the Beast? She had no hard evidence of that either. Lace walked quickly back to the transit van and was glad of her blanket and a cup of hot oxtail soup from her thermos. When she looked up to check on her cameras, she realised that all the guards were gone and every single one of the lights in the Iceni building were dead. Something major had just happened and she had missed it. She could have kicked herself and was angry that she had left her post because she thought that something more important was happening somewhere else.

Lace reached into her pocket and called Judas. He picked up the call straightaway.

"Lace?"

"Sir, I've dropped a bit of a clanger."

"Go on."

"I was on the OP when Cat Tabby showed up and I decided to follow him instead of staying put as ordered. He met up with the Beast and they seemed to be having a conversation about something. I couldn't make out what, sorry, sir."

"And then what, Lace?"

"Well, sir, I got back to the van and the Iceni have gone, all of them. The building is like a tomb – no light, no sound, nothing."

Lace listened to the silence and tried not to read anything into it.

"Did the man in the photograph I showed you appear?"

"Not while I was here, sir. I need to go through the camera footage, but he certainly didn't show up while I had eyes on."

“Interesting, really interesting. Lace?”

“Sir?”

“Can you come back to the Yard now? I need you to do something very dangerous for me, you up for that?”

“I’ll be there in twenty, sir.”

Lace stowed her blanket and the thermos away and started the engine. Seconds later, she was weaving through the traffic and happily cutting everyone up.

22. THE JIGSAW AND WHAT WAS SEEN

Judas couldn't decide if he wanted to sit down in his favourite chair or stand by the window and count the angels as they flew past Scotland Yard. He opted for the latter and was amazed to see how many there were now. They were no longer carrying flaming swords or lances that rippled with lightning. Some of these winged marvels were holding down full-time jobs while others preferred the zero-hour contracts and the flexibility they brought. He wondered as he watched them flitting here and there, what the older residents of the city thought. Was it unnerving for them? Many were old enough to remember the Second World War and the threat of the V2 rockets and the Doodlebugs that blackened the sky and levelled the ground. Did the fast-moving shadows on the pavements cause them to stop sharply, as they walked down the street? Judas had been surrounded by angels all his life and even he was still surprised by them. When he next took some time off, he would go and see an angel he knew in the North and sit down with the old chap and ask him to tell Judas the story of the Second Fall. It was still a mystery to him. But right now, he had a mystery of his own to solve.

The pieces to his current puzzle were starting to fall into place. The only problem was that the places they were falling into were spread out and few and far between. Lace had seen Cat Tabby talking with Black Shuk – what did that little feline want from Shuk, or was it the other way around? Had Cat Tabby tried to muddy the waters right at the beginning by telling him that he had seen Black Shuk at the races? Faelan was dead, Fedelmid was recovering in a chair by the door, that left only Morcant and Oebfinn. Was this all part of a bigger deception? What was the Silent King up to? Was there another player, one that had not shown his or her hand yet? And, lest anyone forget, there was also the dead troll in the sewer and a Cunning Man to keep an eye on.

He heard the lift door open with a huff. It was a sound not unlike despair or resignation. Lace appeared seconds later carrying her overnight bag and some bigger overnight bags beneath her eyes. Regardless, she was still a ball of energy and as keen as mustard, and it made Judas feel more alive to see her that way. Once she had sorted herself out and made notes in her police notebook, Lace wandered over to Judas's desk and waited for him to invite her to sit.

Judas looked up and nodded at the seat opposite and Lace dropped into it.

"Well done, Lace, for following Cat Tabby tonight. Most people would have ignored him and carried on staring at a couple of bodyguards standing outside a shiny revolving door all night. Now, at least we know that there is contact between Black Shuk and Cat Tabby. Whether it was a chance meeting or one that they had planned, we know that they have made some sort of agreement, or Black Shuk would have bitten Cat Tabby's head off."

"He did let him go, sir. There was some sort of chatter going on and Cat Tabby disappeared as soon as he was able. If I was to make a guess, it looked to me like Cat Tabby was doing the other's bidding."

Judas sat back in his chair, and it squeaked.

"And you say that the man in this picture did not appear?"

"No, sir, not while I was there."

"Do you know what I think, Lace? I think that there is something that we might have overlooked. Everything is pointing towards the Silent King. He might have tried to double-bluff us and have himself attacked to make it look like an act of revenge on the part of the Iceni."

"That would tip the balance towards war, sir.

Who would stand to gain from that?"

"Well, Cat Tabby and his mate Dick, for one. With the Iceni out of the way, their grip on London's property market would loosen. Maybe he's feeding the Silent King with misinformation?"

"Sir? There is another angle. What if this was all the Black Shuk's work? What if there was some age-old grievance behind it all? Maybe Boudica owes him or has cheated him?"

"I hadn't considered that, Lace, but why rope the Silent King in?"

"Not sure, sir. Muddy the waters?"

"Muddy? These waters are as black as pitch right now, aren't they?"

Judas got up to stretch his legs and before long his silver coin was in his hand. He completed a circuit of the office, often staring into space and then into the faces of the people of interest that he and Lace must find the time to catch up with. He was about to peer at another when Lace caught his elbow.

"I think the princess is waking up, sir."

Fedelmid opened her eyes and tried to move her head but the headache she had dreamt of was most definitely not a figment of her imagination. Her body was sore – not just her elbows or her back, the whole bloody thing. It was good that her eyelids had escaped the beating, or she would have been blind for another day or two at least. She could make out several maps on the wall and some stocky metal filing cabinets under a window.

"How are you feeling, Princess?"

She turned, and wished she hadn't, towards the voice. DCI Judas Iscariot, the Master of the Black Museum and his right-hand woman were looking over at her.

"Better, thanks to you both. How long have I been asleep?"

"Lace will fill you in while I go and make some coffee. I would do it, but Lace thinks that coffee is the Devil's work."

Lace sat next to Fedelmid and proceeded to tell her what she and Judas had discovered so far. By the time the coffee arrived, and a mug of tea for Lace, Fedelmid knew most of what had happened, but not all of it. Lace had omitted the parts that Judas had declared off limits to anyone other than themselves. Fedelmid clutched the hot mug to her chest – she looked as though she were trying to pull it inside her, to steal its heat. Judas was watching her closely; he still hadn't decided if she was crying wolf or playing some sort of an intricate game. It wouldn't be the first time that he'd been mistaken about someone. His gut feeling was that she was telling the truth.

"Lace."

"Sir?"

"First thing tomorrow, I'd like you to head over to this address and speak with your old friend, Angel Dave. Then, on the assumption that he's amenable, and he's not busy with anything shady, I would like you both to follow the man in this picture. Stick with him – wherever he goes, you go. Angel Dave will be able to help you shadow him, from afar, and he can get you out of trouble, if anything happens. I think the person behind all this is going to show his or her hand now, or at the very least, shine some light on what on earth is going on."

Lace took the photograph from Judas's outstretched hand and studied it closely. Then she copied the address of the place where she would meet Angel Dave into her notebook. She was just about to close it when she realised something odd.

"The Devil's Tavern? That's a joke, right?"

"Just wait until you see the place, you should fit in nicely."

Lace looked up at him with a quizzical look on her face, but Judas was giving nothing away.

"Get some rest, Lace, tomorrow is going to be a long day."

Lace put her jacket back on again and squeaked back down the corridor to the lift. Judas turned to speak with Princess Fedelmid once again, but she was asleep. The warmth of the coffee had worked wonders and turned the noise of the world off for a few minutes at least. Judas returned to his desk and found that his brew had gone cold, so he set about making another and it was while he was meticulously grinding the coffee beans that he heard the office door creak open, and he realised that the princess had made her exit.

When he returned to his desk, he found that she had left him a short note expressing her gratitude and her apologies for slipping away. If the truth be known, Judas wasn't really one for goodbyes, and he needed all the time that he could steal to resolve this case. He sat down and leaned back in his expensive German chair, inspecting the cheap mass-produced tiles that formed the drab ceiling above his head. He wondered just how much asbestos was hidden away up there. It was against the law to insulate buildings with it anymore, but the Met had to make their savings where they could, just like everyone else, and removing asbestos and replacing it with something that Extinction Rebellion would approve of was costly.

He drank his fresh cup of coffee slowly and watched the steam from the rim of his mug make tiny serpents in the air. They were full of energy and intent as they left the heat, but their lives were short. The further away from the surface of the liquid, the more insipid and transparent they became. Soon, the coffee was cold in his hand and the serpents were no more. When he reached across his desk to place the mug down, he detected something that made him sit up with a start. There was a strange odour in the room, and it was not something that the sink in the small kitchen could have created. Judas stood up and walked around the office, sniffing at the air. He moved slowly along the cabinets, dallied for a few seconds by the window and stood motionless for the best part of ten minutes in the doorway. The smell was familiar to him, and his scar began to itch.

23. THE DEVIL'S TAVERN

The following morning, Lace woke to the beauty of a London dawn chorus. No starlings or blackbirds sang – this was the song of the bin men and the hulking great wagons that roared whilst the good folk they served tried to slumber. You could even smell one of these vehicles long before you could hear one, especially when they were reversing. As usual, the men in the orange suits were bellowing at the top of their voices, shouting to each other, and daring one another to feed the great grey beast faster and faster, so that they could get away to their other jobs, the ones where they did not have to inhale the stench of days' old rubbish and the hum of their neighbours' discarded Sunday roasts.

Lace was awake and alert in seconds. She had slept so well that her duvet was still in the same position as it had been when she slipped into bed the night before. A crash and a thud sounded outside her window. *Why did an empty plastic container make more noise than a full one?* she thought before jumping out of bed and heading for a shower.

The Antipodean shower gel that she had carefully chosen the week before made her feel slightly odd as she carried out her ablutions. She made a mental note to try something less fizzy the next time around. Once she was dressed and had eaten her regulation three pieces of marmite on toast she slipped on her parka and left her temporary accommodation. She'd been lodging with an old friend ever since the Captain of the Night had followed her home and tried to pull her head from her shoulders. She loved her flat, had saved and saved to get the deposit and done more than her fair share of overtime to show her mortgage lenders that she could afford it.

The flat was still there, albeit with a huge metal shutter over the front door and a sticker telling all that approached that the premises were police property and not to be entered. Her current digs didn't feel like home, but she wasn't comfortable with the thought of going back to her own place, just yet. Soon. But not just yet. She locked the communal front door behind her and made sure to drop her keys into her bag. Her good friend had let her have the flat for mates' rates and she didn't want to repay him by having it burgled while she was on duty.

The underground was particularly smelly this morning. At least two of her fellow commuters had not been too generous with the anti-perspirant or toothpaste. It made her want to gag. She was relieved when the tube pulled into Chancery Lane station, and she was able to escape the pong and the hum of humankind. Fleet Street was busy – it was still the home of the hack, even though most of the journalists had moved over to King's Cross or out to the desert of Canary Wharf. Lots of the old drinking holes and all-day bars were still doing a roaring trade. You could take the wordsmith out of the city but you couldn't take them out of a pub where stories were on tap, along with heavily subsidised drinks, as long as you were able to flash your press card.

The address that Judas had given her was just up the street. She wasn't at all surprised to find that it was not there. Judas had made a couple of remarks about the place, so it had to be a magical watering hole or only accessible if you were a wood nymph or something like that. The only indication this might be the place was a small plaque on the wall. The Devil's Tavern had been located here, but, so the plaque said, it had been demolished in 1787. Lace shook her head and wondered if this was some sort of test, which, of course, it was. She decided to take a seat at the bus stop nearby and wait and watch.

The first patron she saw enter was an angel. It dropped out of the sky above her and landed like a snowflake directly in front of the wall where the tavern should be. Then it leaned forward and stroked the wall with one wing. A shimmer formed where it had touched the granite and the angel stepped into it and disappeared. Over the course of the next ten minutes at least twenty angels repeated the action. She was never going to get in by herself, so she loitered outside and waited for the next angel to land.

When he did, Lace stepped forward and introduced herself – with her warrant card.

"Police. I would like to get inside; can you do the feather thing for me please?"

The angel looked confused and stared at the wall.

"Get inside where? That's a wall, officer."

Now it was Lace's turn to pull a face.

"I've been sitting here and watching a veritable troop of angels go in there, so don't give me that 'it's just a wall' nonsense. Get your wing on the wall right now or I will get a Maria over here and we can have a chat down at the station about obstructing a detective in the course of her duty. And if that doesn't convince you, I'll put my card behind the bar and you can have a few pints on me."

The angel smiled and brushed his wing down the wall, then as soon as the shimmer appeared he took her hand in his and they stepped inside the Devil's Tavern.

It was the smell that hit Lace first. Most pubs smell of beer and industrial strength carpet cleaner. The air in here was heavy with citrus and there was a freshness to it, like the inside of a new car. There was also a breeze – it was flowing around the room but there were no windows or open doors. It ruffled the wings of the angels, and she could feel her fringe lifting and falling. It was impossible, but this was a tavern that had been demolished in 1787 after all so she tried not to understand it. Instead, she scanned the crowd for her contact.

There were steps leading down from the door to the floor so Lace, standing on the top step and on her tiptoes, could just about see over the tops of the heads of the angels drinking in the pub. She could see Angel Dave – he was holding court at the back. Before she made her way over to him, she accompanied the angel who had helped her gain access to the bar and offered her bank card up to the barman.

"Are you *Black Museum*, miss?"

"I am. Here's my warrant card."

The barman, a larger than average angel with beautiful grey wings with a fleck of red running through them took the card in his huge hand and scrutinised it closely.

"The Black Museum don't pay for their drinks in here, miss, they are on the house, as a courtesy to your master."

Lace smiled and looked up at the angel she had entered with.

"I promised this one here a few beers on me, take what you need from my bank card, please."

"I think we can extend the hospitality of the house to young Lorient here … but not too much hospitality, you hear me now, Lorient?"

Lorient bowed low to Lace and then nodded to the barman.

"I would never dream of it; your gift is well received young miss, and I will not take advantage of your good nature."

Lace had not really had that much experience of angels, even though they had been living amongst the general population for what seemed like forever. What she was learning, very quickly, was that some of them were chancers and a lot of them were too charming by half.

Lace accepted a drink from the barman. He had to search under the counter to find a glass small enough for her, and then she tried to weave her way through a curtain of wings. The average angel is tall, a good two to three feet taller than the average male, and when there are lots of them in one place, and they let their wings hang loose, it's like walking through a warm snowstorm. Most of the angels saw her coming though. Word had spread quickly of her arrival and who she represented, and they flexed their wings to one side, or pulled them in even tighter, so that she could pass. Angel Dave was not surprised to see her. The small crowd of his friends had disappeared and the seat opposite him was empty.

"Welcome, Sergeant Lace."

"Hello, Angel Dave."

Angel Dave looked uncomfortable for a second before leaning across the table and whispering in her ear.

"It's *Davinor* when I am in the company of my own kind, Lace. Angel Dave is my street name, my nom de guerre, if you like. We're not supposed to take on human names really, it gets frowned upon by the upper order angels and they are a bit snooty, if you catch my drift."

"Davinor is a much nicer name than Dave, why don't we just stick with that?"

"If that is your wish, my lady."

Davinor performed a theatrical bow that would not have looked out of place in a 5th form amateur dramatics rehearsal.

"How gallant of you. You big show-off."

Davinor picked up his pint of Guinness and drained it in one.

"So, what does the Master of the Black Museum require today? Information leading to the arrest of the

Gollum of Golders Green perhaps? Or is it something easy, like liberating an ancient fairy-killing weapon from a troll's hoard?"

Lace sipped at her beer. It wasn't for dramatic effect or because she was ordering her thoughts. She was hot; the air inside the pub was close and heavy. Her temples were throbbing, and she needed to remove her parka because a small bead of sweat was running along her hairline at the nape of her neck and about to disappear under her collar. Davinor noticed her discomfort and placed a hand on her shoulder.

"It will pass, Sergeant Lace; we call it the *Host Heat*. Most, if not all our human friends feel it at some point. Drink. You will be fine."

Lace wasn't used to being touched by anyone, but she allowed Angel Dave, or Davinor, to continue. She drank and within seconds the hot flush passed, and she felt cool and calm once again.

Davinor sat back in his chair and raised a hand towards the bar. Lorient appeared straight away carrying a tray with two more pints and a smaller glass filled to the brim with wine. Davinor shook his head, and then smiled at the young angel.

"I asked for another round for myself and Sergeant Lace. I don't recall offering you a beverage."

Lorient pretended to look shocked.

"I thought you were asking me to come over with a round of drinks?"

"I was, but just a round of drinks for myself and Sergeant Lace."

"Oh well, I'll take it back, but the pub is very full and what if I were to trip and fall, and the ale were to spill? Old Red behind the bar would never serve me, or you, again. Is it worth the risk? Maybe I should just drink it instead?"

"That tongue of yours will get you in trouble one day, youngster. Away with you and don't antagonise Red. He has a fearsome temper when riled. Ask him about his last promotion when he flew with Michael. He has a story to tell, and unlike most that you will hear between these four walls, it's worth listening to."

Lorient winked at Lace and then slipped away into the crowd and made his way towards the bar.

"Is that true about the barman, did he really fight with the Archangel? The DCI doesn't say much about him, but it's normally along the lines of *he could slice a pyramid in half – with his hand if he so desired.*"

Lace was intrigued.

Davinor just smiled.

"Some of it is. Red is a very strong angel, a savage warrior, it is not wise to rile him, and it's true that he was in line to lead a cohort under Michael. It would have been his finest moment. He deserved the chance, but, on the day that Michael was to choose his next commander, Red was shot with an arrow, and he could not fly for many days afterwards. Michael chose someone else in his stead."

"Was it an arrow from an enemy?"

"Not quite. One of the younger members of the Host – and it's not Lorient, before you ask – was showing off and let fly with his bow by accident. The shaft bounced off a shield and hit Red in the backside.

It took four angels to hold him down, and another three to pull the arrow free."

Lace looked into Davinor's eyes. She was a police officer, and she could tell when someone was spinning her a line. She didn't have to wait to get confirmation of that because just then, all hell broke loose behind her. She turned towards the noise, but Davinor placed his hand back on her shoulder and whispered.

"Just watch."

Seconds later, Lorient came barging through the crowd and made for their table. His eyes were wide, and he had a look on his face that would have made coffee nervous.

"You said to ask him about his promotion!"

"I did, my young shaver; how did he take it?"

Lorient opened his mouth to explain but before he could get a word out a huge hand gripped him by the shoulder, and he was lifted into the air as though he were a tin of tomato soup on a supermarket shelf. All the other angels found something else to look at, as quickly as possible. They did not see or want to see Lorient being dragged to the door and then thrown out. All Lace heard from her seat at the back of the room was a howl of pain and then the sound of the doors swinging violently back and forth on their hinges. She'd watched films about cowboys on TV at home. Grizzled hard men and despotic cattle barons. Inevitably there would be a showdown and the hero would have to walk through the double doors of the saloon. The bad guys would come flying out of the saloon and the doors would take a pasting. The sound she was hearing right now was just like that. Somebody had gone out through them a lot faster than they had come in.

"That was a bit mean."

"Sergeant Lace! I don't have a mean bone in my body. Now, where were we before Lorient had to leave?"

Lace removed the photograph that Judas had given her from her inside pocket and slid it across the table. Davinor took it and examined it carefully.

“Is this who I think it is?”

“Yes, it is, and we’re going to follow him. That is, if you’re not busy getting little kids beaten up by warrior angels?”

Davinor looked hurt, only for a second, and then he smiled.

“On foot, on four wheels, or the other way, Sergeant Lace?”

“I think it’s going to have to be the other way. Now, before Lorient gets back and tells Old Red that you set him up, shall we?”

Sergeant Lace and Davinor, who would soon be plain old Angel Dave the moment they stepped out of the Devil’s Tavern on Fleet Street, made their way through the crowd, Lace collected her bank card, and they left the pub before all hell broke loose. It was the Devil’s Tavern, after all.

24. A CARD MARKED

Meg was standing and staring out of a window so vast that it had no right to call itself one. It should have been called a glass wall instead. On the other side was London. A city she knew better than any black cab driver or television historian. Meg was one of Jack the Ripper's victims, but she had been brought back to life to serve the Silent King. Around her neck was a beautiful Italian silk scarf. Today's was an explosion of yellow and pink with small horses printed across it. Underneath the scarf were the scars that the Ripper had created. Meg was the only one that still carried them. She could have had plastic surgery to hide them, but she kept them, and no one that knew her ever asked why.

The Women of the Chapel were five in number – there was Meg, Sally, Sue, Mary and Helen. They had all been prostitutes. *Fallen women* they were called by the hypocrites at church on a Sunday, and then it was *darling* and *sweetness* by the very same people in a bordello or alleyway on a Friday night. They'd been called unfortunates, drudges and trollops, but here they were, driving Aston Martins, holidaying in Florence and owners of half of Canary Wharf. The Silent King had given them back their lives and ushered them onto a path that had brought them to this moment. They thought that they had everything that they would ever need, but DCI Judas Iscariot of the Black Museum at Scotland Yard had shown them something they desired so badly they would kill for it. It was just a matter of when and how. And if Judas got in the way, well, they would cross that bridge if they were forced on to it.

A shrill beeping sound emitted from her mobile phone and Meg turned away from the wall of glass and sat down at her desk. She reached over and touched the screen.

"Girls, we have a mission … no, we have two missions now. The Silent King is getting his forces together. He is moving most of them along the Church

Roads and it's becoming more and more likely that we will be at war very soon. We will stand with our king, and it may be that we will have to complete a number of tasks that will upset some of our people and our business contacts. Are we all agreed that this is something we are all prepared to do?"

"I speak for myself on this – whatever the king needs, I'll do it."

"Thank you, Helen, what about the rest of you?"

"I'm in," said Sally.

"You don't need to ask, Meg, we are all in, aren't we, Mary?" Sue added.

"Of course, what's the plan?"

Meg smiled. Normally she avoided conference calls and video chats like the plague, but she needed to hear their voices at that very moment. Each one of them had suffered so much, and yet they truly lived, making the most of each day and fighting tooth and nail to be heard. If the truth be known, they all wanted to be remembered for what they were and not how they had died.

"The Silent King has asked that we speak to a few people on his behalf, we are to be his envoys. Some of the names on the list are well known to us and I think that they will agree with us that remaining neutral is in their best interests. But there are a few that will require either a heavy hand or a little persuasion. The one name that causes me the most discomfort is that of the Master of the Black Museum, DCI Judas Iscariot."

There was a silence on the line that proved Meg was not the only person who felt a little uncomfortable about asking Judas to turn a blind eye to whatever was going to happen. It was the youngest of them that spoke first – Lady Helen.

"The Black Museum? I'm not sweet on the guy or anything like that but he did make Cat Tabby sign over his property portfolio to us. Won't it be a little like stabbing him in the back?"

"Look, Helen, we're going to have to stab in the front at some point, why not now?"

Sally was always more lightning than thunder, but Meg intervened.

"Helen, Sally, Sue, Mary. I think we should go to Judas and ask him politely to take a step back and let the situation run. We do owe him, Helen is right, but so is Sally. We will have to push him further than he would like soon, and I think that if he were to stand against the king, it might make things easier for us."

Everyone tried to talk at the same time. There were raised voices and harsh words, and then after they had all let off some steam, there was silence, so Meg leaned forward and like a true leader, told them what they were going to do and how beneficial, in the long run, it would be for all concerned.

"Hold on! Look. I don't like this subterfuge any more than you do. I don't want to look into the eyes of someone who has gone out of their way to help us and then sell him down the river. Nor do I want to see a war. If I still have your trust and you will still follow me, this is what I propose. We advise Judas to stay out of it. He will refuse, he has to, because he is the law and he is on a mission to prove to his God that he has learnt his lesson, repented, and then he can get off his hamster wheel and go to the good place. He'll get involved, of course he will, and then he becomes our enemy, and that will make it easier for us to go to war with him."

"Meg, why do we want to go to war with the Black Museum? He's got an Archangel on his team!"

"Because, Mary, Judas also has the keys to the Time Fields, and we know that Jack the Ripper is there. I for one would like to spend some time in there – wouldn't you?"

The silence on the other end of the line was deafening and then, one by one, they all agreed to Meg's plan.

25. THE SWIFTS

Black Shuk's snout was hot and wet with yet more Iceni blood. He was killing them wherever he found them, and he was finding them far too easily. The look of surprise on their faces when he ambushed them was starting to get boring and he yearned for the thrill of the chase and the joy of the kill. He knew where they could be found because the traitor was cruel and impatient.

How many more would die before war was declared?

A score of their mutilated forms lay on the ground before him, and from where he stood, it looked as though some giant hand had reached down and then carefully dressed the battle scene, laying each man or woman out on the ground, making sure that there was a small space around each one, so that they could die in private. Most were dying quietly and embracing the darkness, moving slowly and steadily away from the here and now, to a place perhaps where they would meet their kin of old, or to walk across some great long bridge into the afterlife.

Black Shuk did not know who the Iceni prayed to or what stories they told each other to make death seem less frightening. He'd heard, long ago, that there was even a tribe of wood folk, tree dwellers, that believed that a giant crow would one day descend from the darkness and rip their homes to pieces to make a nest for its own black chicks, destroying their forest and them along with it. Black Shuk did not fear death. Death should fear him.

It was sheer stupidity, bordering on recklessness, to order any of your forces, even one as small as this, to travel by the Church Roads. Whoever was calling the tune now had no experience of battle whatsoever. No general or warlord would ever concentrate such numbers in so small a place. If Boudica had been in charge, this would not have happened. His employer had surprised him; he was wiser than he looked. Black Shuk surveyed the scene once more, and then loped away. The Warden of the Church Roads would hear of this by nightfall and then investigate.

The old church where the Queen of the Iceni was being held prisoner was alive with the song and exultations of a wholly different sort of congregation. Hundreds of tiny swifts were swirling around in the rafters, making a noise that sounded like a broken generator. She had been watching them fly in circles in the space above her for an hour at least. There was something in the way they moved that fascinated her. There was a unity, a sense of purpose and togetherness about them and she suddenly realised why she was so fascinated by their movements.

The swifts were leaving the building through a hole in the far corner of the church roof and then re-entering the church through another hole in the wall above the door. As soon as the infernal hound had left, Boudica had started searching for a way out. Pretending to be more wounded than you really were was an old soldier's trick and Black Shuk had fallen for it. There was no exit through any of the doors though it seemed. Whenever she had approached one, it burst into flames and the sudden and searing heat was enough to send her scurrying away from it. He might be a great hulking beast but there was old magic inside the hound, and he had shut her up inside the church securely.

Or so he believed. Boudica had not allowed her head to drop. Instead, she had looked up for inspiration, or it might have been to curse any God or spirit that were witness to her actions. Instead of despair, she found her escape. By her reckoning there were at least two ways out that Black Shuk had missed. So, she tied her belt even tighter around her waist, and then stepped up onto the dais, and then into the pulpit. From this lofty perch, she could see her way up. One of the old stone columns near to the pulpit had lost a large amount of plaster over time. These would be her hand and foot holds, then once she neared the top it would just be a matter of reaching up and taking hold of one of the beams and then she would be away.

The first beam she grabbed disintegrated in her hand, and she was lucky not to fall to the stone floor below. The second beam proved to be sound, and she was able to climb on and then stand. The swifts were rushing past her head, and she imagined she could hear them warning her that her jailer was close. Boudica used one hand to steady herself on the main beam above, and then she started to edge along the rafter. Each step she took sent showers of dust downwards. Black Shuk might be surprised by her escape, but he would be able to divine her method quickly just by looking on the floor.

When Boudica reached the hole in the roof she found that she had yet another problem to contend with. The swifts were completing their circuit of the church grounds more quickly than she imagined. As soon as the last bird had disappeared, it was barely a few seconds before the leader reappeared behind her. They were only small birds, but their velocity and the sharpness of their beaks was not to be underestimated.

Jump at the wrong moment and she could expect to be cut to ribbons.

This was not a moment to be scared though – she had come this far, her wound was not bleeding, and she could see the broads stretching away to the coast. The last bird flitted through the hole, and she jumped. The tiles on the roof scattered as she landed, and she half expected to go straight back through them and land on one of the pews beneath, but the roof held firm, and she slid down to the edge and then rolled off and dropped to the ground.

Boudica didn't celebrate, nor did she wait for a second to get her bearings. She knew exactly where she was, and she ran off in the direction of the broads as fast as she could. There would be no looking back or stopping to check to see if she was being pursued – those actions only slowed you down and gave your enemies the chance they needed to bury an axe between your shoulder blades. She could hear her heart beating so fast that she expected it to stop suddenly, and her legs were on fire, but she pressed on. She had changed a great deal over time, but the land had not.

Of course, there were these blasted roads, lots of them, grey snakes that poisoned the country. Old villages remained, and new towns erupted like cement pimples everywhere, but the land stayed true. Magic was locked deep down inside it – the land remembered the days of the Dark Druids and the arrival of the Sea Borne. She started to feel its power again. It had been so long since she had spent any time in the real world, away from the money and the greed. This was the real Boudica of the Iceni! She felt the years falling away, and the wind setting her free. The beating of her heart softened, and she felt more alive in that moment than she had done in years.

If she survived, things would change.

Boudica had been running flat out for at least twenty minutes by her reckoning and she was slowing down. Two hundred years ago, maybe even a hundred years ago, she would have eaten these miles up, drifted across the ground like the shadow of a cloud on the grass in a gale. But today was today and she came to terms with the fact that age always lost the most important race of all. She decided to stop and rest at the water's edge under the long strands of a weeping willow that stood on a bend in the river.

Further north was her true kingdom, the land of the Iceni and the seat of her power. If she could get there, even cross its southern borders, she would be able to contact the druids and they would be able to locate her, but it was a good ride away and she was on foot. No, best not to think like that. Survive the hour and the battle was not lost – survive the day, and the war was yours to win.

And what of the Silent King? What had made him turn against her so quickly? There had been a moment when she thought that he wanted more from her than just a meeting of minds and an opportunity to mark yet another year's passing. There had been a time when he had spoken to her of his loneliness. He had been honest with her, had allowed her to see and hear his plans for the future, but then, in an instant, as though some internal security switch had been pulled, he had closed himself off from her and disappeared.

He was sitting on his throne, no doubt, surrounded by his pale army of souls saved from the Thames and the sewers of London, already believing that she was but chunks of offal in Black Shuk's den. He would regret moving against her, she would make sure of that. The Silent King of the Resurrection Men might be able to bring someone back from the dead, but could he do the same for himself? She would find out soon enough – and so would he.

26. A WORD IN THE WIND

Sergeant Henshaw was manning the front desk when Judas entered Scotland Yard. The last two days had been a nightmare, and if he could have put in for a transfer, he would have done just that. The new Commissioner would have rubber stamped his request so fast that the stamp would have rebounded off the desk and more than likely done the man an injury. But the head of the Met was not his boss. His boss was God, and he wasn't listening to Judas, or maybe it just felt that way – it had been over a thousand years since their last chinwag, after all.

Judas wasn't having sleepless nights *per se*, but his night's sleep was getting more and more interrupted as the week went on. He had picked up the phone and started to dial the number for the witch he had met on the Ley Line Express, but something in the back of his mind told him that she would not appreciate being called in the dead of night just to help him cure his insomnia. She would want to hear his voice, he hoped, but the words would need to be different. He knew what he wanted to say but he also knew that he didn't have the right to say it. His time on Earth could be measured in minutes, or it could be centuries. It depended on the Almighty, as all things did, apparently. Henshaw nodded at Judas and pressed the secret button under the desk to open the security door for him. It hissed as Judas passed through and Judas almost turned around, expecting to see his old friend Lucifer the Morningstar perched on top wearing his snake costume.

On his way up to the 7th floor, he had time to focus. The steady day-to-day trickle of information and gossip had suddenly turned into a full-on Niagara Falls of panic and garbled grunting and posturing by tribal leaders and some of the leading lights in the worlds of the Under Folk. The situation was made even worse because Lace was away with Angel Dave following a suspect, and all the while, Boudica, Queen of the Iceni was still missing, presumed dead, and bodies were turning up all over the capital. As things stood, the tally was fairly even. The Silent King's forces and those of the Iceni were being hit hard. But alarmingly, there appeared to be a surge in the amount of collateral damage too. This was making the situation even worse and whoever was orchestrating this stupid campaign was winning.

Wulfric, the Warden of the Church Roads, was injured, and in Bloody Nora's care, so Judas was hearing only snippets of information from him. Unfortunately, those snippets were bad, and only getting worse. At one point, Judas was going to ask Nora to take charge of the messages because he was worried that Wulfric, through the tears of his own pain, might be embellishing the truth, but alas, his words were true and, if anything, they were being watered down to alleviate some of the pressure on the Master of the Black Museum.

Judas walked down the corridor towards his office. The door to the Black Museum's outer room was only a few paces further down. Usually, he would have stepped inside and listened to the voices of the murderers, taken the temperature of the Time Fields, but he was reluctant to do so, because the Iceni case was taking up so much time. The pressure of the current investigation was bearing down on him and usually, he would have just shrugged his Saville Row covered shoulders and gone straight to work. But something was bothering him, and he was starting to get angry. There were so many figures in the mist without faces, and their whispers were getting louder.

Judas entered his office and hung his jacket on the coat stand. As he was smoothing the sleeves, making sure that it hung straight, he suddenly felt the presence of his old sergeant. This was where Williams had hung his battered old coat, the one that had pockets big enough to stow newspapers, betting slips and packets of digestives without causing so much as a crease. He wondered where Williams was at that moment. He could be anywhere in the universe. He might be flying in some distant realm or lining up for battle alongside the Archangel Michael. Wherever he was, Judas wished him luck and hoped that he would see the old scallywag again sometime.

As he stood by the coat stand, he realised that the layout and most of the furniture was relatively unchanged. Williams's old desk was still there and the rickety old chair that squeaked when it was pushed backwards but silent when rolled forwards. The green desk blotter was still covered in doodles and scribbles, mostly written in biro, but here and there, another hand had written something and then someone else had covered those words in some of their own. The office was becoming like the Museum – dusty and full of old memories. Judas made a mental note to do something about it.

He started to look through the drawers in Williams's desk and was disgusted and intrigued in equal measures by what he found inside. He was just about to start on the other drawers when the phone rang. He picked it up and heard Henshaw's voice.

"There is a lady down here at the front desk, sir. She says that you know her, and I am to say that she is wearing a lovely scarf around her neck."

"I'll be right down, sergeant, thanks."

Meg had removed herself from the front desk and was waiting for him outside the station. She did not smile when he approached and he realised that this was a business call, and there was something about the way she stood that told him the time and place for levity had passed.

"Meg, it's a pleasure to see you again. How can I help?"

"Walk with me, inspector, this place makes me uncomfortable."

She turned away from him smartly, giving him no chance to read her face or suggest some other course of action. It took him a couple of strides to catch up with her. She was on a mission, and he had a feeling that she was about to give him some bad news.

"What is it, Meg? I have a case load big enough to choke a donkey and I'm understaffed and on sleeping rations."

"We're in uncharted territory, you and I. The situation we find ourselves in is getting out of hand, so much blood has been spilled and whether we want to believe it or not, the eve of war is surely upon us."

Meg's silk scarf was being set upon by the breeze coming off the river and he very nearly reached up to tuck it into the collar of her jacket.

"The bodies are piling up, Meg, and now we are starting to get some collateral damage as well. You know that I must find the perpetrators and bring them to justice. I am tasked with keeping the peace between our worlds, Meg. I told you once before that I can't take sides – if your king has been waging war on the Iceni, and you've been a part of all this then you know what will happen. And, if it is Boudica, then she will face the consequences too."

Meg stopped and turned to look over at the great River Thames. The water was grey and choppy. The tide was going out and the vessels plying their trade up and down it were working hard.

"It is not us, Judas, or, if it is us, then I have been played for a fool. I am normally privy to what is going on or about to happen. I can honestly say with hand on heart that the Women of the Chapel are not involved in this."

Judas leaned back onto the wall of the Embankment. Wherever he looked, London was

27. THE CALL OF THE COLLAR

He held it in both hands. It was heavier than he imagined, and the gold felt warm to the touch. When he gripped it tightly, he could feel a subtle vibration in his palms. The magic was buried deep inside the torque – hundreds of years of power, coiled and beaten into the metal, waiting to be set free and allowed to feast and devour. The druids told stories of its power. It was capable of opening doors between worlds and much, much more. His mother was eager to learn its ways in the beginning. She listened to it and drew great strength from it. Everything she did, the risks and gambles she took, they all worked, and those that dared to stand against them? They fell away.

Why did she stop? They could have taken it all!

It appeared to him, and to the rest of the tribe, that she had *chosen* to forget what was truly possible with the torque. They had escaped the Romans with their skin on their backs and the weapons in their hands. Who would ever want to be in that position again? The torque needed to be set free, and if it wasn't to be used in the pursuit of power, let it go and then rule by force. It was the Iceni way. Or at least it used to be.

He placed it inside his leather bag, zipped it up, and walked out of the boardroom. He was not challenged as he made his way out of the building. He took the stairs and then sauntered across the foyer. He felt in that moment as though he were invisible to them, that he was already on another plane of existence. He was above them. He was higher, their words were but murmurs, their lives … inconsequential.

His car was waiting outside. The car's engine was running, and the driver's side door was open. He placed the leather bag on the passenger seat and then pulled the door closed. The Bentley was a superior car. One did not need to drive a Bentley, one worked with it. He adjusted the seat then pulled away from the House of the Iceni with their heart in his bag.

Lace was sitting on the edge of a very tall building nearby, looking down at the mews. Their position had been chosen very carefully by Angel Dave. She thought she had operational command seeing as she was the only real police officer on the case, but Angel Dave had shown her that when it came to line of sight, and matters of an aerial nature, he was in charge. They could have been right on top of the Iceni building, across the road or just behind, but Angel Dave had vetoed her suggestions and picked the building they had made camp on the night before.

The surface of the roof was uncomfortable to say the least, and Angel Dave had suggested, with only the slightest trace of a smile, that Lace could snuggle up in one of his wings … a purely operational arrangement, of course. But she had decided that the flat roof, covered in grey gravel and sprinkled with pigeon droppings would do for tonight instead. With hindsight she would have made a different decision. She felt as though she had been given acupuncture with a hammer, and there was a musty smell to her jacket.

When she saw the man in the photograph that Judas had shared with her leave the Iceni building, she threw a handful of stones at the sleeping angel. He was a beautiful specimen – muscular arms and Hollywood cheekbones – but the angel could snore, and Lace took great delight in waking him up. He was by her side quickly, fast enough that he could see the car and its number plate.

"Okay, Lace, into the bag if you will, then we are up and away and on the wing!"

Lace looked at Angel Dave and then at the leather bag that the angel had brought with them. She thought that it was a sleeping bag or some sort of angel smock, to be used in rough weather or for making a shelter, or something. Angel Dave put the straps of the leather bag around his neck and then tied a thong around his waist. If the appearance of the angel was beautiful before, the image now was shattered. Angel Dave looked like a giant overweight pigeon wearing a butcher's apron.

"Get in, Lace! We'll lose him if he decides to get smart."

"Get in what?"

Angel Dave reached down and lifted a flap in the leather bag he was wearing around his neck.

"Get in here and do it quick!"

Lace looked at the bag and then up and into the eyes of Angel Dave.

"You want me to get in there?"

"The Master of the Black Museum flew to Newcastle to see the Angels of the North in a bag just like this one. It's safe, and you're flying with me, there's nothing to fear."

Lace took another look down at the mews and she knew that the suspect would be lost to her if she didn't act. Every second was precious now – the suspect was getting away. So, she took a deep breath and stepped into the leather harness. When Angel Dave leapt into the air she nearly vomited, but the thought of being in close confinement with the Indian takeaway she had eaten last night helped her to keep everything down. It took her a few minutes to get used to the speed and the rapid changes of direction. She felt small and disconnected from the world.

It was dark and claustrophobic inside the harness, but it was dry and warm. There was a small flap sewn into the leather and when it was caught by the wind, flashes of grey light shot through it, and they flickered all around her like the outpourings of an over-excited neon tube. Lace closed her eyes and tried to centre herself. The breathing exercises she'd learnt from one of the Met's many self-help pamphlets were working wonders. The initial panic she had felt was subsiding and now she was feeling much more attuned to her surroundings.

She tried to imagine what Angel Dave was experiencing out there in the clouds, but how could she? Lace leaned back and tried to enjoy the ride. She was closer to the air and the elements than she had ever been before, and she felt free.

The roads were practically empty at this time of day. It was no wonder the big film companies shot zombie movies and apocalypse blockbusters during the early hours. Give or take an early bird cyclist or a city-boy trader, hurrying in to make sure that someone was manning the Hong Kong desk before the markets went ballistic, the metropolis was a ghost town. He settled back into his seat and gave the Bentley a bit of a push. The engine accepted the challenge, and he was away. The Golden Torque was in the bag on the passenger seat beside him. His plan was working. They were all at each other's throats – his enemies were getting weaker and weaker with each passing day. It was time for the Iceni to die and the thought that he had tricked them all made him smile.

It was nearly time for this farce to end and there would only be one victor at the end of this battle.

28. ANGELICIDE

Hutriel watched the coach pull to a halt outside a tall imposing building. Whoever lived there, or had lived there, would have been wealthy, a minor noble, or some captain of industry perhaps? No matter, it was just the shadow of its real self, a black reflection, because they were all inside the Time Fields of the Black Museum now, and dark deeds were afoot. He watched from the rooftop opposite as the cloaked figure alighted from the coach. The horses, sensing the evil nearby whinnied and shuffled, their great iron clad feet scraped on the wet cobbles, and in the darkness, it sounded like naked blades being sharpened.

Hutriel had been dreading this. Chasen had been growing angrier by the day and now the madness of the angels was clearly upon him. Many of their kin had succumbed to this dark malaise before. Living among the mortal children was one thing – skulking around in the echoes of their heinous past was another. He had been slow to spot the signs and he felt guilty because of that lapse, but Chasen was one of the warrior classes and one of its proudest. Of course, confining him in here would always have gone this way. Hutriel just wished that this moment had fallen to another. He pulled in his wings and then looked up into the crackling firmament of the Time Fields and shuddered. This truly was a terrible place. Who could have dreamt it into existence? When the light appeared in the window of a room on the second floor, Hutriel took another step backwards and hid himself in the blackest of shadows behind a tall chimney stack. Chasen would be here shortly and then, if reason was defeated, there would be blood and conflict and one brother would have to murder the other.

Rain began to fall sometime later. Hutriel had lost all track of time inside this accursed place. It was forever night here – the sun did not rise, it merely dragged itself into the air and then expired swiftly, leaving the day dead on its feet. A pool of rainwater had formed just in front of him by the roof's edge. It acted like a mirror, reflecting the dark sky above, and he did not have to move from his hiding place to see his friend approach. Chasen always moved at speed, he couldn't do anything slowly. In the past it had been an endearing trait, but now, Hutriel could only see his old friend rushing into the arms of the one thing he had fought all his long, long life – the darkness.

The horses heard the beating of the angel's wings and kicked the stable doors open and bolted. The coach disappeared around the corner and the sound of their hooves dropped away until silence returned. Chasen landed on the pavement and looked up at the candlelit window. Something must have passed between the candle's flame and the window because the street flickered for an instant, and when Hutriel looked down again, Chasen was gone. For the slightest of moments, Hutriel's heart rose. Had his friend seen reason after all? Had he come to his senses and flown away?

All hope withered and died in Hutriel's bosom as quickly as it had flared and blossomed. Chasen had not seen his own folly and escaped to find reality, he had entered the room and his first action was to open the curtains wide. Hutriel could see the encounter taking place quite clearly now, and it made him feel sick because in his mind's eye he saw the inevitable outcome as clearly as he could see Chasen now. The one they called *the Ripper* removed a map from a black tube, unrolled it and laid it on the table. Then he placed candlesticks at each corner to stop it from rolling back up again. Hutriel saw Chasen leaning over it, analysing it, scrutinising it intently. Hutriel knew that look well, he'd seen Chasen develop a battle plan or plan a rescue in the same way. The minutes passed and Hutriel transferred his attention to the Ripper.

He was standing with his back to the fireplace. No flames leapt and danced there – it looked like a big square, black mouth. Hutriel wished that it would come alive and swallow the man, but that was never going to happen because this was his world, dark and evil, without any real light or hope. It was so plain to see. This creature had turned Chasen, whispered sweet words of escape and revenge into his ear. For that, he would be punished. Hutriel did not know how just yet, he would have to speak with Judas and maybe even a higher power first, but he would pay for the taint he had placed in Chasen's heart.

Hutriel was too far away to see the details of the map and he decided that the only way to truly know what was really happening, or about to happen, required that he be much closer to that infernal room than he was currently. Chasen and his conspirator were deep in conversation and Hutriel did not fear being discovered. He flew down on half wings, gliding over the rooftops in a wide arc, so that he could approach the street from the other side. There was a small terrace outside each of the second-floor windows. In the real world, high tea might be taken there during the summer, or pleasantries called out to passers-by on the street below. Hutriel landed on the terrace of the house next door. He could see and hear what both of them were saying now.

"So then, Jack, you know that there is a way out of these Fields, and all you require is for me to take you into the Key Room, and from there you can escape into the real world?"

"It is that simple, Chasen. Once there, I can pass through the Key Room, and use any number of souls nearby to make good my escape."

"What is your secret?"

"That I will not tell you, angel. My side of our bargain is simple – once I have escaped, all hell will break loose with me. There are minds out there that rejoice in my actions and desire to recreate them. Hospitals are full of feeble individuals that wish to be me. Escaping these Time Fields is the first hurdle. Judas will be disgraced and punished. His tenure at the Black Museum will be terminated and what will those who sit above him think when the streets are overrun with ancient evil? You will be released from your servitude at the very least and, would it be too much of a stretch of the imagination to suggest that you could apprehend him, cause him some pain before taking him before his master? It would look very good for you."

"Enough with your scheming! I know the plan and what we will both gain. All we need do now is to arrange a time. I will take you to the Key Room, and then you may do what you desire."

Hutriel winced at Chasen's final words, and his heart sank. Chasen was going to turn the streets of the world outside red with innocent blood just to spite Judas. Hutriel launched himself into the air and took up a position on the rooftops nearby. He had a clear field of vision in all directions so he would see Chasen take to the air. Then it would be over for one of them, and the pain would stop.

Jack the Ripper rolled his map up again carefully and slipped it inside his map tube. It had taken him hundreds of years to piece together the information on it. Doorways, openings, passageways to other Time Fields and most importantly, the key to each place of imprisonment.

He would call them all forth, and then destroy their key so that there would be no going back. It would take so much time to recreate the Time Fields, eyes would be elsewhere, and throats would be unguarded.

He watched as the angel stood up and walked to the door. It knew so little of this place. If it had only studied it, worked it out, and used it to its own advantage, this meeting would never have happened, and Jack would be locked away for all time. When the angel finally departed, Jack let out a sigh of relief. Then he sat down in one of the large red leather chairs and started to sharpen his knives.

Hutriel saw Chasen, his old friend, heading away from him, in more ways than one it seemed. This was something that only he could do. It would bring him great pain to see Chasen torn apart by Michael or one of the other Archangels. So, he leapt into the air and set himself on a course for conflict. When Chasen was close enough, Hutriel challenged him.

"Brother! You may not continue on this path. We must settle this now, here in the darkness that you have created between us."

Chasen pulled up quickly, his wing curling to catch every breath of the fetid air around him. As he hung there in the grey sky, Hutriel saw in his face that there would be no going back now. Chasen had passed the point of no return. His voice and his words might say otherwise, but his eyes could tell no lies.

"I cannot stay a moment longer! I will not stay, we have been trapped and lied to, there will be no return to the City of the Heavens for us, we might as well join the ranks of the Morningstar!"

Hutriel powered across the space between them and raised his sword. Battle was joined. Chasen's flaming sword appeared in his hand and they closed with each other. Both were wary, both knew the other's strengths and weaknesses. Chasen had lost all reason at that point – he did not see his old friend anymore, merely an enemy that stood between him and his freedom. The fight started in the air, but Hutriel knew that to continue here would mean death for him. Chasen was far too strong and his skill with the blade was well known. Hutriel, however, was an intelligent opponent. He visualised the end of the fight and plotted a safe and short passage toward it.

Chasen had chosen might and anger. Hutriel wanted only to save his friend. He hoped that it would tip the balance in his favour when the time came. Hutriel dropped out of the sky, snapping his great wings open just feet above the ground. Chasen would follow and press his advantage, attacking from above, and from the side. Hutriel pushed on. He flew down the street – he could see the sheen of the damp on the cobblestones reflecting the blur of his face, he was that close. Then, he lifted his shoulder, angled his wings and shot upwards. The dome of St Paul's was to be the battleground, and he circled it once, scanning the skies for the inevitable attack, and then landed at the top.

The night was still. Smoke and fog had joined to place a dark blanket over the streets and there was the faint sound of boat horns in the distance. In the real world, outside the Black Museum, there was something good about the city. It had life and energy, there was positivity there, and even in its darkest hours, it remained a beacon and stood firm against evil. Just as Hutriel was standing now.

Chasen dropped out of the sky and landed directly in front of him. He did not say a word, only raised his sword and attacked. Hutriel parried and steadied himself. The onslaught would be terrible, but he must not lose his footing, or it would be over. Chasen fought savagely. Backhand followed forehand as he sliced at Hutriel's body and then for his wings. Attack after attack came and Hutriel allowed his friend to manoeuvre him so that Chasen had the higher ground. From this position there could only be one winner. The high ground was the killing ground.

Chasen pushed him further and further down the slope of the dome. The moment was near and Hutriel knew it. One more parry, one more death blow to deflect. Chasen leapt across the divide and raised his sword for the final blow. Hutriel chose that moment to fall backwards. He put his life in God's hands then. If Chasen were too close he would die; if Chasen were not close enough he would suffer the same fate. The arc of the dome allowed Hutriel to spread his wings and the sudden pull of gravity sucked him away from his opponent's blade.

Hutriel sped downwards then just as he fell over the edge of the dome, he reached out and grabbed the ledge that ran the whole way around St Paul's. Once his fingers found their grip, he held on as tightly as he could. If Chasen had followed him, as he hoped that he would, he should appear within seconds. Hutriel took a deep breath. What followed would require perfect timing and a lot of luck. Then he sensed, rather than saw Chasen, and he gambled, thrusting his sword straight upwards into the empty air. Chasen flew straight onto its point and the force of the blow ripped Hutriel's sword from his hand.

Hutriel found Chasen on the ground that led up to the main entrance. He was horribly mangled; his limbs faced backwards, and his mighty wings had been destroyed in the fall. The deep slash in his stomach was black and crooked but there wasn't much blood. Hutriel imagined what must have happened to his friend's body after he administered the mortal blow. In his mind he saw Chasen bouncing and slamming from rooftop to rooftop, onto slates and spire, then down and down, clipping the walls and finally smashing onto the steps.

Hutriel's heart was broken, along with a few bones, and his wings had been dealt some healthy blows during the fight, but he was still alive, and he knew what he must do. He could not leave Chasen's body here. The Archangel Michael would need to be told, and the Master of the Black Museum, DCI Judas Iscariot. Hutriel lifted his friend's corpse from the ground and jumped into a sky full of static and dead lightning. The journey back to the Key Room would take longer than usual but it suited him. It gave him more time to hate himself.

29. THE SHIFTING SANDS

Black Shuk watched the birds skimming across the surface of the pond. There were two versions of each one – the real birds – and then the dead, black reflection that rushed up to join with its living partner for a fraction of a second, as they dipped their beaks into the water. He was resting amongst the reeds at the water's edge. They grew tall and straight in this part of the country and created the perfect place in which to hide. He had been running for most of the day and had decided to rest here and sleep. The freedom of birds had always interested him. Their world was fraught with danger, of course. They looked carefree and beautiful when on the wing but theirs was a perilous existence. They were constantly scavenging for food and scraps. Then there was the threat of predators. On the ground, foxes and cats preyed on them ruthlessly, always waiting at the base of trees to catch the falling young, and often, creeping along the branches to eat the sleepers and the nest bound. Above them, in their natural environment, they fared no better. Bigger birds preyed on the smaller, and cuckoos planted their young into the nests of others.

But they were free, or as free as a creature could be, he thought.

He dreamt each night of his own liberty, and of the moment when his curse was lifted. He longed for the day when he could set his snout to the wind once more, and travel between the worlds of man, and through the distant lands of the Fae. He had become a wretched thing of late, consorting with the scum of both worlds. He looked down at his paws and the great claws that had ripped so many throats, and he felt sick to his very stomach. How had he been brought so low? He had not seen a female in many years, and he realised that his line was all but dead now. And why? What had caused that fateful moment in the church? It was still a mystery to him.

Long, long years of self-reflection had done nothing to help him find an answer to that question. He'd replayed that fateful day's events over and over again in his mind, and even today, he could not understand why he had been driven to kill the congregation of that church. Where had the fire come from? He'd never been able to conjure it before. He knew that he could disappear at will and bring on a mist or fog if he needed to, and he knew so many of the other creatures' languages – but fire?

He remembered drinking cool, refreshing water from his favourite rock pool and feeling the wind on his fur. Often, he would sit on the shifting sands and watch the white smudges in the sky amble by for hours. Nothing disturbed him, the world grew older in front of him, and he was content. But one day, something had called out to him as he sat there, and he had been unable to resist it. The words were alien to him and sung by a voice that he did not recognise. And, in what felt like the shortest of times, he was there, amongst the pews and the people, raging like the beast he was, biting, tearing, and ripping. Blood sprayed all over the walls – they screamed and screamed and still he could not stop.

Then the Holy Man lifted his iron cross and Black Shuk could not move. He was held fast, and he panicked, as any creature that is caught in a trap will do. That was when the fire came, and the world he knew changed forever. The flames and hellfire scorched the flagstones and charred the walls, and through the heat haze he saw two great forms in the air above him, locked in combat. The stained glass windows groaned and cracked with the intensity and energy of the conflict. Two powerful forces were fighting each other, but for what, and why was he here? He was not part of this fight; he was merely witnessing it. He felt strange and detached.

The battle raged on and the walls began to vibrate. The plaster fractured, causing white dust to drift into the air, and then the tiles fell from the roof. Many of the congregation were killed by these sharp, slate missiles.

When he came round, he was at the base of a tall oak tree, far away from the church, wet with blood, and singed by fire. His head was heavy, his ears were still ringing, and he felt that deep sense of dread from being part of some act of great evil. When he stood and looked around, the surrounding countryside was empty. It was still daytime, but the daylight was darker somehow.

It looked as if night had fallen, but when he looked up into the sky, the sun was still hanging there; the Moon had not come to call yet. It was clear to him then that he had been used. He had been manipulated and a powerful spell had been cast over him. And then he discovered that his precious gift, his magic, had been taken away from him, and he howled at the sun. No matter how hard he tried he could not summon an opening. He could see none of the secret pathways or any of the hidden roads anymore. He was trapped.

A fox came to the water's edge nearby and its loud slurping pulled Black Shuk from his reverie. The birds had gone, and the sky was empty. He had waited long enough; he must return to the church once again and claim the reward for his horrible crimes. When he stood up and revealed himself, the fox flinched, lowered, and braced for attack, eyes locked. Black Shuk almost smiled at the look on its face when he said,

"Don't worry, I've already eaten."

The fox recovered from its near-death experience very swiftly and melted away into the countryside. A distant rustle and the slight movement of a bramble bush at the corner of the field told Black Shuk that it had moved very quickly and covered a great deal of ground. He was impressed. He stretched, then loped away into the night, keeping close to the stone walls, and using the deep shadows of the undulating ground to hide his passing. The church was not far and as he got closer, he tried to quieten the argument in his mind. He didn't want to kill the queen, but he needed the Golden Torque. He could not achieve the one without the other, and what of the curse? The torque would lift it, and the church and their priests would be furious, and then what of the Iceni and their infernal druids? They would waste no time in placing another spell on him once they saw the queen's body.

When he arrived at the lone tree on the brow of the hill above the church, he sensed that all was not as it should be. The spell that he had cast was still in place, but something had affected it. Black Shuk sniffed the air and growled. The church was empty when he entered; he expected as much. His prisoner had escaped. So, he sat down near the pulpit. Scattered on the floor at his feet were little lumps of moss. Boudica's blood was still on a few, but the freshest moss was clean. Her wound had healed completely – it might even be that his saliva had helped speed up the process.

He decided not to chase after her. She may have escaped directly after he had left and if she travelled fast, she would be well out of his range by now. The question was, how did she escape? He padded around the church, sniffing here and there for signs of her escaping but there was nothing. It was only when he returned to the pulpit that he got some vague sense of her. He stepped up onto the dais and explored the steps that led up to the pulpit – her scent was stronger here. When he got to the stone column next to the pulpit, he could read the scene quite easily.

Boudica had climbed up the column using the holes and the chips on the stonework. Then she had leapt up and caught hold of one of the wooden beams. From there she had only to run along the length of it to a hole where the birds flew in and out. When he had cast the spell in the first place, he had not wanted to imprison the birds, so he left a small hole in his spell, one that the Queen of the Iceni had found and – *exploited.*

So much for the liberty of birds, he thought.

He returned to the floor and lay down. There was no use in reacting blindly now. The Iceni would mobilise against him; they would hunt him down and kill him. There were many of their kin in the ground, mauled and murdered. Their revenge would be swift and certain.

Without the torque, he was stranded. Alone and vulnerable. His great plan was at an end.

Maybe it was right that I should perish in this way; have I lived too long?

He gnawed at a piece of human bone that had become stuck in his paw – it was in deep, and it would poison him unless it was removed. As he worked away at it, teasing it this way and that, he made the decision to wait until the man that had set them both on this perilous path came to see the body of the Queen of the Iceni. As payment for regicide, he would offer up the power of his people.

He had to wager everything on this last throw of the dice. Boudica may have already made it to safety, but there was a good chance that she had fallen on the way, succumbed to her wounds, or simply did not have the strength to complete her escape. There were so many variables, but he had to hope for something, or else, what was the point? In a way, he was glad that she had escaped. He had not wanted to kill her.

The time of the meeting was near. The man that had set the wheels of this entire bloody endeavour in motion was nearing. Black Shuk decided to wait for him outside, in the dell, just behind the church. Once the man entered, he would make himself known, and then take the Golden Torque by force and disappear into the wilds. He had plenty of time to work out how to unlock the power. There must be some other way to release it, and then, maybe, he could live again, away from the madness that he was in part responsible for.

Black Shuk rose and tested his paw against the cold stone. He'd gnawed at it for most of the night and finally, the splinter of bone had come free. When he put his weight fully down upon it, he felt no pain. Then, he slipped away, just as he had arrived, in the darkness and under the cold gaze of the White Woman in the blue-black sky above. As soon as he had crossed the threshold of the church, the timbers in the roof creaked, as though a great pressure on them had suddenly been released. He looked back at the building he had turned into a prison cell and felt a great sadness. His sorry story had started here. Hopefully, it would end here as well. The fire and the bloodshed he regretted with all his heart, and if he could make amends he would, but that was a concern for another day.

He turned away, crossed the grass on silent paws and took up his place of watching in the shadow of the dell. It was a cold night; the air was still and crystal clear, and the sounds of the countryside floated across the flat lands towards him. A sudden movement above the church roof caught his eye but Black Shuk did not react to it. He followed the flock of starlings up and into the night sky. The birds had discovered, finally, that the sky was open to them once again.

30. THE DEATH OF THE FUTURE KING

Lace could feel the angel's heart beating on her back. It was strong and reminded her of a scene in a film she'd watched where some Greek hero, or was it a Roman, had been wrongfully imprisoned and sentenced to a lifetime as an oarsman on a galley. The heartbeat sounded like the drummer that sets the pace for the oarsmen.

Boom, boom, boom, boom.

It made her feel safe, rather than reach for an oar, thankfully. They had been travelling for about an hour and a half and Angel Dave was flying in a relatively straight line now. They had followed the car through the East End of London and had been forced to turn sharply, again and again, as the car below took evasive action so as not to be followed. As soon as they had left London, the swerving became less and less erratic. The driver must have tried every trick in the book to shake someone following him in another car. Luckily, they weren't on four wheels – they were on two wings.

She was wondering how Judas was getting on with the Silent King and the Women of the Chapel. How far had he got with his investigations? Had any more of the Iceni been murdered, and if they had, would she be returning to Scotland Yard to find that the Black Museum was on a war footing? Then she started to think about the Gilded Goat and the Cunning Man. As a female in the Force, she'd seen and felt the effects of discrimination first-hand. What had become clear was that the Gilded Goat wanted to be a human, and he was prepared to make that happen, whatever the cost.

Inevitably, someone or something must have learnt of this and taken advantage of his desperate need. Lace imagined the Gilded Goat sitting in some dark room with a nasty piece of work whispering in his ear. Telling him, persuading him in honeyed tones, that for a price, he could be transformed and reborn. The Goat would have grabbed it with both hooves. And the price? That would have been huge of course because they knew that the Gilded Goat often held vast sums of money and on occasion, powerful magical objects. The Goat would pay, of course he would, even if the money wasn't his in the first place.

He wanted to be treated differently, to be accepted, and to be admitted to a world he felt excluded from. Once this case was wrapped up, she would seek him out, and try and clear it all up before the Cunning Man or the Gilded Goat's employers caught up with him first. She didn't have any more time for reflection though because Angel Dave banked sharply to the left and her stomach came up to meet her chin as they dropped out of the sky.

Morcant reached over to the digital display in the walnut dashboard of the Bentley and gently tapped the screen to turn the Sat-Nav off. There was a muted beep, programmed no doubt to be subtle and unobtrusive. He liked expensive cars because they would do anything you asked, and then disappear the moment you didn't need them anymore. If they could talk, the first thing they would say is, 'We are here to serve the master'.

Morcant slowed down, flicked the indicator, and turned right onto the country lane that would take him from the busy 'A' road to the church. The road curved first left, then right, and the trees on either side began to rise around him. Eventually, they grew so tall that their tops leaned over so that they could clasp each other and create a green tunnel that stretched away into the heart of the countryside. The hum of the steady traffic died away and all was quiet – at least for now.

The tall trees gave way finally to the fens and the flat lands, and it was while he was rearranging the package on the passenger seat that he saw the movement in the air directly behind him in the passenger side mirror. Morcant slowed down. The church was just around the corner, and he had a decision to make, and fast. He could go through with the plan, or brake and find somewhere to turn around.

The shape in the air behind him was an angel, one that he'd seen before.

Morcant looked for a place to turn the Bentley around but could not take his foot from the accelerator pedal. His foot felt heavy and as though it belonged to someone else. He was scared, as usual. He'd always been a coward, standing at the back, allowing the rest of his people to take the risks for him. He always froze at moments like these and now he realised that his fear had made the biggest decision of his life for him.

He pulled off the road and stopped. He could see the church clearly through the trees, and inside the church was the body of his dead mother and the great black beast that had done his bidding. Morcant reached across to the passenger seat and lifted the bag with the Golden Torque inside, then opened his door. Then it came to him, the answer to his problems. Why not order the Beast to kill the angel? It was genius and it was sharp. Don't kill two birds with one stone, kill an angel with a beast instead. He walked with purpose now across the grass to the small wooden gate, unlatched it and made his way inside.

Lace watched the man in the photograph step inside the church and her heart began to pound. Judas had been right! They'd all been looking the wrong way, or they had been made to look the wrong way. The attacks on the Silent King and then the reprisals on the Iceni had all been staged and arranged. She looked at Angel Dave and shook her head. Then they both set off to apprehend the one person responsible for the multiple murders, the carnage, and the conflict. As she approached the church her mind was racing, and she wondered if the death penalty existed in the worlds of the Fae – or was there something worse?

Morcant stepped inside the church and closed the door behind him. The stench inside the building was rank. The air was musty, and he recognised the waves of smoke, fire and burning flesh.

"Where are you, and where is the body of Boudica, Queen of the Iceni?"

His words echoed but were not answered and he started to feel the cold grip of fate on his neck.

"I have the torque! Bring forth the body and it shall be yours!"

Again, there was no reply.

"Where are you? I have it here! The key to your prison cell, here in my hand, it is yours – come forth!"

"I don't know who you are looking for *Prince Morcant of the Iceni,* but it appears that you've been stood up. Luckily, we're here. *We*, being the Black Museum of Scotland Yard that is, and you are well and truly nicked, you nasty little git."

Prince Morcant spun around. He was expecting them, but he had hoped to persuade Black Shuk to deal with them.

"The Black Museum? You have no power over me, I am a prince!"

"I think you've used that excuse one too many times, Morcant. Anyway, it's all over now, and you are going to have to face the music."

Lace took a step towards Morcant and removed her handcuffs from her inside jacket pocket, but before she could take another, there was a roar from the back of the church, and she froze. Angel Dave leapt in front of her, and his wings flexed out so quickly that the backdraft nearly knocked Lace off her feet. She stumbled and had to reach out for one of the pews to steady herself. Now, there were four of them in the church.

"My good friend here is called Black Shuk, and he is a fearsome foe, even for an angel."

"He might be fearsome to you, but he does not scare me. My line stretches back to the first of the Host and their blood runs true in me. Stay back, Beast and no harm will come to you!"

Lace had always seen Angel Dave as a bit of an odd-job-angel. Judas had always given him small tasks, errands really, but he was so much more than that.

"I advise you to stand back, angel! I have need of words with this one."

Black Shuk motioned towards Prince Morcant with his snout. His great fangs glistened in the gloom. He looked ferocious, but the tone of his voice told another story entirely. Lace looked on as the smile on Morcant's face started to drop like a stone dislodged from the edge of a well.

"If you kill them both, Beast, the torque will be yours. Only an Iceni can give it to you. Kill them and I will place it around your neck myself."

Morcant was trying to appear brave and in control of the situation, but his hands trembled. Lace moved forward to stand by Angel Dave's side.

"Black Shuk, this man is responsible for the death of many people, he's caused so much pain, and the Black Museum are here to bring him to justice. Whatever you agreed with Morcant, or were promised by him, we can talk about that, but we must take him, and if we have to use force, we will."

Black Shuk padded towards them with his head lowered and the sound of his claws on the flagstones was like the scraping of spears. Angel Dave lifted into the air and Lace produced her Asp and a can of Mace. They moved towards the great black beast together, and they drew strength from each other.

Black Shuk drew level with Morcant. The distance between them shortened. Its eyes were glowing red, and Lace could feel a great heat coming from it. She must have flinched because Angel Dave whispered to her.

"Fear not, Lace, we are its equal."

Black Shuk stopped suddenly, and then with a swift turn of its powerful head, bit Morcant on the shoulder. The prince howled in pain and dropped to his knees. The bag he was carrying fell to the floor and there was a muffled thud as it hit the ground.

"Stand back, angel, and you too, soldier of the Black Museum. I mean neither of you any harm, there has been far too much blood spilt on his account. I was promised the contents of that bag in return for my services as his assassin and murderer. It sickens me to say it out loud. He came here to collect the dead body of his own mother, but I could not kill her, and she has escaped – and best of fortune to her!"

Morcant groaned and whimpered as he heard his own story being told. His face was turning pale, and his eyes were creased with pain. Lace could see that blood was seeping through his jacket – his condition was worsening, and she wanted to keep him alive – very alive.

"Black Shuk, he's dying, but he must face justice. We can make sure that living will be far worse than dying for him."

Black Shuk opened his jaws and Morcant slumped to the floor.

"And why must I release him? I can take my payment now and leave his corpse on the floor for the rats."

"Yes, you can, but I have an idea that might serve us both better."

"I'm listening," said the Beast.

"If I heard correctly, the torque only works if it is given *by his hand?"*

"That is so, but I can take it now, and learn its power over time. My kind live long and there are many that will help me if asked."

"Why go to all that trouble? Let us have him, alive, and my friend here can persuade him to give it to you."

"The angel can do that?"

Angel Dave landed softly, and his wings folded behind him.

"There are angels in the North, Black Shuk. They have great and powerful magic. They could unlock the torque for you. It … well … it will mean *intense* and *excruciating* pain for the Iceni male, but that, I think, is a price you are willing to pay?"

Black Shuk placed one gigantic paw on Morcant's back and pressed down. Morcant whimpered and then started to cry.

"I will give it to you! Release me and let me live, and I will give you the torque."

Morcant pleaded with the Beast. He whined and mumbled, and he sobbed and cried. Lace could see small bubbles of blood forming on Morcant's lips, so she raced forward, retrieved the bag, and removed the torque.

"Get up!" she roared into Morcant's ear.

"Give this to Black Shuk, and we will save you from his jaws, and from the Angels of the North."

Morcant got to his knees and then, using the stone steps that led to the pulpit, pulled himself upright. He was pitiful then – gone was any semblance of the man who had entered. Here was the boy that wanted to be king but had not the strength to take the crown. His blood had turned the left-hand side of his blue suit-jacket black and he was unsteady on his feet. Lace thrust the torque into his hand, and then raised the Asp she was carrying, just in case Morcant had one last trick up his bloody sleeve.

Morcant took the torque, and then turned to look into the great red eyes.

"By my own hand, a prince of the Iceni, I pass on the power of my tribe to you. By the power of the

Great Oak and the Ley Line Cross of Icknield, I give it freely and of my own will."

Morcant lifted the torque up and touched Black Shuk. The Beast shuddered, and then the torque appeared around its neck. It had grown to fit the wearer and Black Shuk twitched as the torque settled.

"Do we have a bargain then, Black Shuk? You have the golden collar, let us have him."

Black Shuk looked down on Morcant.

"The pain you have caused the Iceni – I wonder how your mother created one such as you! But that is not for me to dwell on a moment longer."

Black Shuk suddenly moved and wrapped one great paw around Morcant's neck, and Lace and Angel Dave feared the worst. But the Beast was true to his word and instead of finishing the job and removing the coward's head, he licked at his wound until Morcant passed out.

"The wound will heal, it won't fester. You may have him now. But before you do, soldier of the Black

Museum, why did you not attack me? There are two of you, the fight would have been swift."

Lace snapped her Asp back into place, short enough that it would fit back inside her jacket pocket.

"We're going to take him back to face the music, but it may be that we have run out of time already. In that case, I would ask a favour of you."

"A favour of me? I shall be gone before you take to the sky. The secret ways are open to me once again, I can see them clearly now, and after what I have seen and done, I won't be missed."

Angel Dave reached down, plucked Morcant from the ground and slung him like a bag of sand over one of his broad shoulders. Lace stood next to him and looked into Shuk's red, fiery eyes.

"We could have attacked and killed you and Morcant, that is true, but we're police officers, not killers. Besides, you owe me one now, maybe even two – it could even be three."

"How so?"

"You've got the torque, the Iceni prince will be punished, war can be averted if we're quick, and you're free, *blameless*. I don't even have to mention you in *my report*."

Lace left the last words hang in the air for a second and Black Shuk narrowed his eyes at her.

"So, it's blackmail then?"

"You're bloody well right it is."

"What do you require then, soldier of the Black Museum?"

"My name is Sergeant Lace and what I request – no, what I would like to ask of you – is that if I summon you, will you come to my aid? I will only ask once."

Black Shuk scratched at the stone with his claws. Outside, across the flat lands, a fork of lightning reached down and touched the horizon. A few seconds later, a rumble of thunder passed overhead.

"I will come when you call, Sergeant Lace. For now, let us just say goodbye. And to you, angel. Fly well."

And then he was gone.

"It's time we made a move too, Angel Dave. There's a brand-new Bentley out there, I'll race you back to the Museum!"

31. CUNNING IS STUPID

Judas had decided to stretch his legs. Lace was following one of their suspects, Nora was tending to the invalid that was Wulfric, Warden of the Church Roads, and the Silent King had gone quiet. It was the calm before the hurricane, he could feel it in his old bones and he needed a coffee, and to be left alone long enough to drink it. The Hallowed Ground was his favourite coffee shop. It was owned and run by a group of ghosts. Their coffee was amazing, but their conversation was a little on the thin side. That's why Judas loved it so much.

When he arrived, he found that his favourite haunt had been taken over by a group of South American tourists. At least that was what it looked like at first. Then Judas noticed the smell – it was faint, but he knew it well. It was the scent of the dead. It was like the Day of the Dead, without the raucous shouting and the confetti. He ordered a flat white and retired to the table furthest from the door. The ghosts moved around the café at half-speed, drifting here and there, moving from table to table, talking in whispers and exchanging baubles and symbolic objects. Occasionally, one of them would look in his direction. They were unsure of him, and he was beginning to feel like a goldfish. Judas thought about going over to the nearest group and introducing himself, maybe that would put them at ease. But he didn't need to, word must have reached one of the owners of the café and they had appeared at his table like Mr Ben's shopkeeper.

"Inspector, I hope that our friends from the south aren't annoying you?" said Hector, the ghosts' leader and head barista.

"Not at all, Hector. If my presence here makes them uncomfortable, I would be happy to leave."

"That will not be necessary, inspector, you are a valued guest and patron. They will lose interest in you shortly. It is not every day that our cousins encounter

Judas of the Black Museum. I should put the price of their coffees up!"

Judas smiled and nodded at Hector. One second the ghost was there, and then he wasn't, unfortunately, as his place had been taken by none other than Cat Tabby, feline gossip magnet, and all-round schemer.

"Inspector! Fancy seeing you here! I have always been lucky, you know. Our chance meeting here at this very moment in time proves it without question."

"I doubt that this is a chance meeting, Cat Tabby. Take a seat. Can I get you a drink, saucer of almond milk?"

Cat Tabby leapt into the chair opposite Judas and performed the cat's ritual of turning around three times, before sitting down. When he was comfortable and had given the room the once-over, Cat Tabby placed a small, perfectly manicured paw on the table and began to shuffle around the tiny bits of sugar that had been spilled. Judas could hear the cat's brain working ten-to-the-dozen from where he was sitting, so he said nothing and waited for Cat Tabby to work out if he could con Judas or get away with telling him a lie – or two. Finally, it came.

"Inspector?"

"Yes, Cat Tabby."

"I have heard, from a certain fairy that drinks in one of your favourite hostelries, that the Black Museum is looking to speak to a nasty little cove that goes by the name of James Murrell, often called 'the Cunning Man' by them that know no better. Would that be the case, inspector?"

Judas reached across the table, picked up the bowl that they had served his coffee in and raised it to his lips. It was still very hot, but it would not stay that way for long if people and characters from the Underworld kept coming to pay a call. Judas wanted to relax for a bit, but that was becoming more and more impossible as the day wore on.

"That's Sergeant Lace's case, Cat Tabby. She's away, chasing up a lead. Can I help, in the meantime?"

Cat Tabby leaned forward and licked the table in front of him.

"I like the brown sugar, not massively keen on the white stuff. The brown sugar makes a satisfying crack when you give it a crunch, have you found that yourself, inspector?"

"Can't say I have, but, if you're finished talking about the benefits of molasses in sugar, I would like to spend a bit of time inspecting my fingernails or planning how best to organise my sock drawer."

Cat Tabby's tail gave an angry little swish and his eyes narrowed.

"I'm wasting your time, that's what you think isn't it, inspector? What's old Cat Tabby doing here, waffling on about brown sugar and James Murrell. Well. It turns out that a friend of a friend told me that the Gilded Goat had been turned over by a sharp chap who had promised to make some changes to the Goat's appearance, something lasting, permanent if you like."

Judas pretended to look at something interesting over Cat Tabby's shoulder, but Cat Tabby was no fool.

"And, that the Gilded Goat had offered to pay the Cunning Man a rather large amount of moolah."

Judas sighed. "Today was looking pretty straightforward for me until you showed up and started using words like *moolah*. What do you want?"

"The Gilded Goat has disappeared, inspector. Word has it that he has vanished and taken a lot of money that belongs to individuals other than himself away with him. I as it happens, am one of those individuals, and that Goat has trotted off with a small fortune of mine. Seeing as you and I are acquaintances, it was put to me that I should come and have a quiet word with you, and express our concerns."

Judas shifted in his chair. His scar had begun to itch, very faintly, but it was there, and it was a good indication that all was not well.

"How much, Cat Tabby?"

"Well, inspector…"

Cat Tabby started to prevaricate, but his tail gave him away.

"Dick and I had a good run at the summer fayre down near the Roman fort, some weeks back. Made a fortune actually, enough to buy a Wisdom Stone and have a few japes too."

Judas could tell that Cat Tabby was lying – there was something else, but he wouldn't get it from the fickle feline, not now at least.

"I can't help you with this. Sergeant Lace has been handling the case. When she gets back, I'll let her know to come and look you up, okay?"

Cat Tabby arched his back so high that the backs of his front legs nearly touched the front of his back legs.

"I don't suppose you can tell me when the good sergeant will be returning then?"

Judas shrugged. His coffee was producing less and less steam and he was getting a bit miffed because he was giving his free time away, again.

Cat Tabby dropped to the floor and started to pad away, but he had only taken a few steps when he stopped and turned to face Judas once again.

"I know where Murrell is right now, inspector, I know who he's with and I hear he's been making some unsavoury comments about our mutual, hoofed friend. Also, I hear that he's well acquainted with some people who know a thing or two about dead trolls in the sewers."

Judas took a deep breath and pointed back at the chair that Cat Tabby had just vacated. The cat didn't need to be asked twice, and in the blink of an eye he was back and searching for some more brown sugar granules on the table. What had been the perfect start to the day had gone downhill rapidly. Judas signalled to the ghost behind the counter and pointed at his drink. It was as warm as a jogger's armpit, and not fit for consumption.

In the time it took for another beverage to bite the dust, Cat Tabby told Judas everything he knew, and then the little purring troublemaker wandered away, leaving Judas with two cold cups of coffee on the table and an itching scar. Judas sat for a while and tried to make sense of what Cat Tabby had told him. He'd put the case of the dead troll to the back of his mind – he'd had to because the Silent King and the Iceni had bulldozed their way through his caseload. But crime, like life, went on, and he had a duty to all the Underfolk. So, the Gilded Goat had disappeared, and Murrell had surfaced. A coincidence? Not likely.

Judas flagged a cab down outside the Hallowed Ground, and after the usual banter about what a poor job the mayor was doing and road closures, the cab headed south of the river. After a relatively uneventful journey, the cab pulled up outside Tooting Bec tube station. Across the road is the Wheatsheaf. It is an enormous old boozer, arranged over four floors, has a small beer garden, and has even modernised a little, so as to provide small rooms for backpackers. It sits at the junction of two very busy roads. One heads down the hill and towards the South Downs, and the other goes to Streatham.

The main floor is achingly trendy now – the bar staff don't serve the hoi-polloi anymore, they have been forced to search for their refreshment elsewhere. Through the bar is a large dining room. White tablecloths are stretched over some of the smaller tables

– those that look directly onto the chef's workstations are at a premium. The staff are cool, bearded and covered in tattoos. If you need a job and you have ink on your neck or your hands, you are in. Beards are optional. Judas threaded his way through the crowd, mostly human, but here and there was a face he recognised. He took the stairs at the back two at a time – no doubt his presence had already been communicated to the regulars in the *'Pocket Room'* upstairs.

No matter.

The doorman, a short barrel-chested gnome, saw Judas coming and opened the door for him. The smoke from many pipes – clay, briar and hookah – filled the air. Some of the cloud was quite pleasant but Judas paid it no mind. He'd been tricked by the smoke once too many times in the past, and he had work to do. The Pocket Room was so called because you could get anything here, it was always in pocket. If you wanted to pay someone to do a job for you, the money always went into the pocket. Bribe someone, you put them in your pocket and so on.

The drinkers and the smokers were huddled in their own little groups, no doubt cursing the visitor from the Black Museum or trying to put a spell on him. It had been tried before but his gift from God made him impervious to witchcraft or spellbinding. Judas made sure that everyone knew he was there, and then he took a seat at a small table in the corner. He only had to wait a minute or two before his guest arrived.

James Murrell, the Cunning Man, stepped into the Pocket Room and made his way to the bar. He had not noticed or gauged the atmosphere of the room and was all smiles. When at last he realised that something was not quite right, the smile on his face went back into storage. He was served at the bar and then he turned and saw the Black Museum waiting for him.

"Inspector Judas Iscariot of the Black Museum, as I live and breathe. What brings you to the Pocket Room, may I enquire?"

The Cunning Man's accent was awful. He was a semi-educated man that had convinced himself that the better one spoke the more loot one could extort. Judas disliked him immediately.

"Sit down, Murrell."

"I would be delighted, sir, momentarily of course. I have a small piece of business that I cannot step away from. You will be here over the course of the evening will you not?"

Judas stood up quickly, grabbed Murrell by the throat and then casually stuffed him into the seat opposite. Murrell tried to look offended but no one else in the Pocket Room was going to help him and incur the wrath of the Museum.

"Sit there and shut up, Murrell. I haven't got all night. Where is the Gilded Goat, and where is the money you stole from his place?"

"Me, sir? No, I think you have drawn a blank the size of a tablecloth there if I might be so bold. I have no idea as to the Goat's whereabouts, and as for money, sir, I am no thief."

Judas grabbed Murrell's wrist and turned it so sharply that the bones cracked. Murrell let out a little sob and went as white as the tablecloth he had been referring to.

"Right then, Murrell, shall we do this the right way, or shall I take you down to the Black Museum and throw you into the Time Fields? You know what they are and what they contain. I'm sure there are a few in there that would like to say hello again, a few that you helped to shuffle off this mortal coil."

The Cunning Man grabbed his own wrist and muttered a few spells under his breath. The crack that his wrists made as the bones meshed back together was twice as loud as the initial break and it caused some at the next table to drink up and retire to the bar. Murrell looked down at his hand and flexed his fingers. All seemed back to normal apart from the little finger, which stuck out at an odd angle.

"You should get someone with some medical knowledge to have a look at that you know, Murrell."

The Cunning Man sat back in his chair and smiled, revealing two uneven rows of yellowing teeth. He had a broad forehead and intelligent eyes, blue in colour, with long feminine eyelashes. His lips were full and his nose small. He was good looking in that school bully sort of way. Judas had seen so many men like him, and he knew exactly how to play him.

"You offered the Gilded Goat something, didn't you?"

"I did. The Goat wanted to become human, walk on two legs properly, lose the horns, grow fingers and toes, the whole shebang. I told him that I knew one spell that could achieve the results he wanted but it would cost him."

"Then what?"

"He sought me out at my lodgings, we made a deal, and he returned the following day with payment. He wanted me to do it there and then! I told him that I needed time to prepare, assemble the necessary oddments and chemicals, the stages of the Moon needed to be observed. It couldn't be rushed, I told him."

"How much did you ask for your *services?*"

"A spell like that, inspector? I asked for something magical and something physical, that was all."

Judas took his silver coin from his pocket and began to rub his thumb across its face in small circular movements.

"Go on."

"Well, a couple of days later he shows up carrying a Wisdom Stone and a three-way mirror. I'd never seen anything like it. To have one would have been a miracle, but two in the same room! He wanted that spell to work so badly, inspector. He was giddy and kept doing that thing that he does with his hooves, that little shuffle thing."

"And then what happened?" Judas was starting to get that uneasy feeling and his scar was heating up.

"I tried the spell, made all the right shapes, uttered the words and drew the symbols. It worked! But then it didn't, the initial transformation was perfect, but then it started to wear off and the Goat went crazy. Saying that I was teasing him, trying to extort even more from him. I thought there was going to be an altercation, so I called my man in, to protect me."

"And just who is this man?"

"Seldon is my bodyguard, inspector, he is a Half-Golem from the East, Poland I think."

"And where is this Seldon now?"

"Oh, he is around, just taking care of a few errands. He should be here *any minute*, actually."

"Save the theatricals, Murrell. My bodyguard's bigger than yours. He carries a flaming sword and makes people disappear just by looking at them. Get on with it."

The Cunning Man looked a little perturbed but carried on, nonetheless.

"The Gilded Goat snatches up the Wisdom Stone and the mirror and then starts shouting that I was a fraud. I never knew the Goat had such a wicked tongue on him – he was bleating so badly that I feared he would do himself an injury."

"Or drop the mirror?"

"The thought never crossed my mind."

"I bet it didn't."

"He was out of control, inspector! I feared for my life, and his, wandering around these dangerous streets alone and in such a state, so I asked Seldon to escort him home. It was the least I could do."

"So, now you know where the Gilded Goat lives and you know what he had hidden in his house. Sounds a little suspicious don't you think, Murrell?"

"Only if you have a devious and uncharitable mind, inspector."

Murrell was hiding something, that was a plain as the bulbous nose on a goblin's face, but Judas had other questions that needed answers.

"Cat Tabby tells me that you know something about trolls and sewers."

"I move in strange circles, inspector, what can I say."

"Look, Murrell, charming as this is, I don't have all night, so unless you want me to arrest you and then reacquaint you with some old, dead friends back at the Museum you'd better start talking."

Murrell was a pale-skinned man, but Judas could have sworn he dropped a couple of shades right there and then.

"There is a warlock that lives out near Richmond, nasty piece of work. Well, this warlock hears that there is a piece of special land nearby, and on this land is a 'Tree of Ages'. The warlock knows how powerful a tree like this is and he wants it, badly. Only problem is that the land belongs to the trolls. He tries to hoodwink the trolls, offers them some paltry sum and the trolls tell him where to go. Then, the idiot tries to spell them off the land, but trolls don't respond to threats or showground magic, and they threaten the warlock. So, the warlock asks someone to mediate for him."

Judas leaned forward and placed his elbows on the table. His scar was beginning to burn, and he had a horrible feeling that he knew just who the warlock had instructed to get the land and the tree. Murrell leaned back in his chair. He didn't like the look that had just appeared on the inspector's face, but he pressed on with his story. All the while, glancing at the door in the hope of seeing his golem.

"The mediator arranges for the troll leader to meet the warlock and to talk their problem through. Only thing is, the warlock took a couple of his witch friends along and they did the poor troll in, dumped the body in the sewer, and now the trolls are after the warlock and the mediator."

"And this mediator … walks on all four legs and has whiskers that can sniff out a groat at 100 paces?"

"Why yes, inspector. It is none other than Cat Tabby."

"I'm going to wring that bloody cat's neck!"

Murrell pushed his chair back quickly and stood up. He certainly was cunning, and he was fast.

"Can I presume that our conversation is at an end, inspector? Do I have your leave to…*leave?"*

"Yes, but I will want to speak to you again. Don't disappear!"

Judas remained seated for a while. He continued to trace small circles with his thumb on the flat silver coin and wondered to himself just how things had turned so bad, so quickly.

32. THE TIPPING POINT

Morcant was furious with himself. Why had he trusted that hound? Why had he not planned for this eventuality? The Beast was always going to try to steal the torque! He should have foreseen it, made a contingency plan, or something!

The angel and the sergeant had shoved him into the boot of his own car. So now, here he was, laying on his side with his knees pulled up to his chest, whimpering and sobbing like a child – in the dark. The Bentley ran so smoothly and quietly that Morcant felt that he was somewhere else entirely. The darkness was tight and close, the soft leather of the car's interior was not unpleasant to lay upon, and the smell … he could have been in the saddle room back at his mother's stable. He thought of her then and hoped that she had succumbed to her injuries and was even now slipping into the mud at the base of a ditch somewhere.

Morcant tried to change his position in the boot of the car because his arm was starting to register the sensation of pins and needles, and as he shuffled around, he felt something hard and rectangular press into his ribs. In their haste to bundle him into the car they had forgotten to remove his phone. And, they had not bothered to tie his hands either. How pathetic he must have looked to them. Well, that was their mistake. He might be locked away inside this beautiful prison cell, but he could still start a war.

Morcant removed the phone and placed his index finger on the screen. A blue light appeared in front of his face and Morcant smiled because the inverted pyramid at the top of the screen showed him that he had a full signal. He sent his older sister a message to tell her that he had been kidnapped by the Silent King's men, and that their younger sister was also in grave danger. The enemy was making their final move. He signed off with a plea for her to avenge him if he should not return.

Morcant started giggling to himself. At one point he felt like sending an emoji, but that would have been far too flippant, and he stopped himself just in time. Then he sent a coded text to his baby sister's mobile phone, followed by an email to a courier service in East London.

Princess Oebfinn was sitting in the bay window of one of the Iceni safe houses that overlooked the Thames. She liked seeing the water. It calmed her and took her mind off things. There were so many guards in the house and so many weapons. The druids were everywhere too, casting spells on the doors to make them invisible and impregnable. Everyone was tense, all they talked about was the Silent King and his army of Resurrection Men. She missed her mother and the tranquillity of normality. Her mobile phone bleeped, and she picked it up, but there was nothing important on that sliver of silicon. Just one text, and that made no sense. Princess Oebfinn tapped the screen to open the text bubble and when she did it activated the spell that Morcant had placed inside her phone.

The blast ripped her head off and turned the room she was in inside out. The guards on the first floor all perished and so did three of the Druid Council. Limbs were strewn everywhere, and blood turned the white walls pink. Only a handful of the Iceni escaped with their lives, and it was with heavy hearts that they passed on what had just transpired. Their beautiful princess had been executed, and many Iceni had fallen.

As the few remaining Iceni retrieved the bodies of their dead from the rubble, a young man dressed in the uniform of a Shoreditch cycle courier – ripped cargo shorts, retro 2000AD t-shirt, dreadlocked hair and two nose piercings – was delivering a padded envelope to a security guard at a marina in the Docklands. He skidded to a halt and leapt off his trusty steed in one fluid movement. Then, he flipped the flap of his satchel and rummaged around inside it. He found what he was searching for and swapped the package for a signature. Then he mounted his bike, pressed his radio to his ear, heard the controller screeching the location of his next pick-up and disappeared. The guard read the address on the package, logged the delivery in his book, and then called the owner of the boat to let them know that a package had arrived for them.

There was no answer from the boat even though the log showed that they had not left the marina in two days. The guard decided to pop it round to them because *service above and beyond* always earned the guards a few extra quid by way of a bonus from the boat owners come Christmas time. Sweet Rosey was tied up at the far end of the dock. She was in amazing condition; her bows were smooth, and her timbers were well polished. Her brass work glinted in the sun, and even the seagulls seemed to respect her because there wasn't a fresh green splat or dry white calling card to be seen on her roof. When the guard reached the steps that led down to the cabin door, he started to smell something. At first, he thought it was the chemical toilet, they sometimes leaked, or it could be that there was something clogging up the bilges. Rats were incredible swimmers and if they smelled food, they would find a way to get inside a boat.

He tried to peer in through the windows, but the curtains had been drawn and the window shutters were locked in place, and the longer he stood there, the worse the smell became, and by the time he had reached the far end of the barge he was forced to use the thick end of his tie to cover his mouth. The lock on the hatch had been forced and the guard knew that he had a duty to investigate. He hoped that the owners had just left some food out and it had gone off in the heat, but he had a horrible feeling in the pit of his gurgling stomach that it would not be the case. The hatch door eased open on well-oiled hinges, and before he had taken a step down the smell charged up the steps from inside the cabin to burn his nostrils and sting his eyes.

There were bodies everywhere. Great brown pools of sun-dried blood punctuated the carnage like oversized full stops, and the air was thick with fat black flies. His presence at their banquet caused them to buzz angrily and he had to wave a hand in front of his face to deter them from dive-bombing him. The guard vomited all over the deck, and then himself. He gagged and belched, spittle and phlegm dribbled from his mouth and nostrils and his eyes were full of tears. It was too much for him and he fell backwards, smashing his head on the dockside. When the other guards found him, he was barely conscious, and when they looked inside Sweet Rosey, they understood why.

He still had the package in his hand; he was gripping it so tightly that his knuckles showed white. The shock of what he had just seen had paralysed him with fear. The other guards managed to free it without ripping it too much. When they opened it, they found a single sheet of headed writing paper. It was thick and expensive, not something you would find at a newsagent. At the top was the Iceni flag, embossed and touched here and there with blue paint. The colour was unmistakable. Written in a well-practised and educated hand were the words: *Resurrect This!*

The envelope was resealed straight away and then delivered to the Silent King on his barge nearby, and brief moments later, a message was despatched to the Iceni, summoning them to battle.

33. THE BATTLE BRIDGE

Princess Fedelmid marched up to the front desk at Scotland Yard and screamed at the desk sergeant. It took him completely by surprise and he dropped a mug of tea onto the keyboard of his computer.

"I must speak with the Master of the Black Museum, right now!"

Sergeant Bond didn't know whether to reach for the wet wipes or reach over the desk and lift the woman from the ground by her neck. He chose to count to ten instead.

"The Master of the Black Museum, now!"

The veins in the woman's neck were standing out and she was gripping the edge of the wooden counter so tightly that it began to splinter. Bond was one of the experienced old heads that knew of the DCI on the 7th floor and reached for the phone.

"Sir, we've got a young woman down here that looks like she might explode if she doesn't get to see you sharpish."

Bond listened to the voice on the other end.

"Your name, miss?"

"Fedelmid."

"Her name is Fedelmid, sir. Yes, of course, sir, right away. If you'd like to go to the lift, princess, it's floor seven."

As the young lady marched over to the lift doors, Bond shook his head and then his keyboard, causing the droplets of tea inside it to rain down on his paperwork, which in turn caused him to mutter something under his breath that stopped his colleagues dead in their tracks.

Judas was waiting for Princess Fedelmid. He knew from the tone of Bond's voice that all was not well, and that he should prepare for the worst. When the lift doors opened, he had to take a step back. He had underestimated her anger and she was quick to impress upon him the gravity of the situation. At first, Judas could not separate the cursing and swearing from the other words that were spewing from her mouth. Her eyes were wild, and he could tell she had been crying. She could not stand still and occasionally she gave an involuntary twitch; she was agitated and angry, and the time for reason had passed her by. Something terrible had happened since they last met.

Judas did not dare lay a hand on her – he wanted to reach out and comfort her, but he knew better. Instead, he walked away from her towards the office, hoping that she would follow him because he didn't want to have to drag her there. Judas made his way to his desk and sat down. She followed, still shouting, sobbing, twitching and gesticulating. Every step she took forward was accompanied by a look over her shoulder – she was afraid and expected some danger to be drawing closer. It took her the best part of ten minutes to calm down. When Judas learnt what had just happened to her family, he was surprised that it was only ten minutes. Finally, spent and overcome with grief and anger, Princess Fedelmid collapsed into the chair opposite him and skimmed her mobile phone across the table like a stone across water.

"Read what the Silent King has done to my family and my people! He has drenched the halls of my house in the blood of our children, my own sister has been killed, and now he calls us to battle, knowing that we are weakened and few."

Judas picked up her phone and read her messages. Each one was worse than the one before it. He kept reading and his heart sank. The Silent King had butchered the queen, apparently, killed the heir to the throne, kidnapped Morcant, and had murdered the youngest princess, along with half of the Druid Council. And now he wanted to finish the job, once and for all. Judas didn't have the Silent King down as the sort of ruler that would attempt something like this. He wanted to suggest to Fedelmid that there may be another explanation, ask her to wait, take a moment, but it was useless. He'd failed to avert the war that would tear the Under Folk apart. The Black Museum would lose its power, and the streets of the Underworld were about to become a battlefield. Many would lose their lives, as reprisals took place and opportunists filled the void left behind.

"Where is the battle to be?"

"Battle Bridge, Judas, where else could it be?

"King's Cross then."

"Will you come to see us die?"

"I'll come, and I'll do whatever it takes to stop anyone from dying."

34. KING'S ANGER

The area behind King's Cross station was once a no-go zone. Addicts scored their bags of smack and other nicely named narcotics on those dark and dirty streets. Half of the stuff they bought was cut so many times that the highs got lower and lower. These daytime ghosts would do anything for a fix, literally anything, and were abused because they were weak and easy prey for the dealers and the punters. After giving their bodies and their dignity away, they went in search of a vacant alleyway in which to lose their minds. Once there, behind the overflowing refuse bins and the sad, stained mattresses, they injected themselves and slipped away.

Across the road, the ladies of the night and the rent boys wandered up and down after dark, looking for love and settling for cash. It was a dark place where dark deeds were three-a-penny.

The only things that look a little seedy these days are buns and bagels. King's Cross is clean, it's chic and it's what every property magnate wants more than anything – it's trendy. The area is called the *Railway Lands* now. Central Saint Martin's Art School has relocated to King's Cross too, and has been followed by urban workwear emporiums, selling designer overalls and two-tone beanies. Fast-food chains are everywhere, and outlet stores for expensive trainers and gym gear appeared almost overnight. Trees have been planted and the canal has been given a wash; conservation has replaced crack cocaine and *Charlie*.

It's vibrant and nearly always busy, but not tonight. The revellers and students all seem to have heard the calling of some silent horn and slipped away, back to Shoreditch and Hackney. The trains are still running though and the rumble of their carriages on the steel tracks drifts across King's Cross like lazy thunder. The army of commuters are still charging across the station concourse with tickets in hand, ready to fight each other for seats that face forward, or one that is far away enough from the toilet.

Everything looks normal – but it isn't. Two armies have come to King's Cross, and only one will be leaving it.

The events of the last few days have sent shockwaves through the Underworld and unsettled the Under Folk. First, there was the abduction of the Queen of the Iceni. Then, murder followed murder, tit-for-tat it seemed, sightings of great beasts started to circulate, and long caravans carrying fairies and their folk travelled away from the city along the Church Roads. There was an assassination attempt on the Silent King, the cold-blooded murder of a princess and talk in the taverns that 'Old Scar Neck' was losing the streets. War was imminent. The Iceni and the Silent King had reached the point of no return; neither side could turn away any longer.

Judas was not in a good mood as he walked past St Pancras. The combination of the current black mood of the Underworld, and the rank atmosphere in the

Black Museum and the Time Fields made him feel uncomfortable, and off balance. This case had aggravated the status quo, turned everything upside down and reopened lots of old wounds. His scar was aching all the time and he felt tired. Dead tired. When he arrived at the ground chosen for the battle, the forces of the Silent King were already there, waiting and expectant, and from where Judas was standing, heavily armed and ready for blood. He couldn't see the Iceni yet, but they would come, they had no alternative.

Judas walked towards the Silent King's army. He could see Meg and the other Women of the Chapel standing to one side of their king. Meg made eye contact with him, and he tried to read her face, but the Meg he knew was not here today. He recognised several Lords from some of the other prominent Under Folk houses. It was funny – two weeks ago they would never have allied themselves with the Silent King. They had more to gain now though. Fight by his side, and it would weaken the Iceni so dramatically that they would then be able to walk in and take what was left of their operation, without so much as a scuffle, or a cross word.

When Judas was near, one of the Silent King's men walked out to meet him.

"My Lord wishes to know if the Black Museum is here to observe – or to fight? And, if it is the latter, on which side?"

Judas took a deep breath.

"Does the Silent King have the relevant documentation for a gathering of this size?"

The herald looked uneasy; he wasn't expecting this.

"We are here to wage war, not to attend a fayre."

"That's as maybe, but you still need a pass or a letter of permission to assemble in a public place. If you don't have one, I'm afraid you'll have to disperse."

"Disperse?"

"Yes, it means to move away from the area without annoying the residents, and not to leave any litter behind, axes or swords, that sort of thing."

"This is no time for jests!"

Judas stepped closer to the herald and looked him directly in the eye.

"I take my job very seriously indeed. If you don't get moving, in say, ten minutes, I'll have to start arresting."

The herald shook his head and then turned smartly around. Judas watched him return to his Lord's side and then pass on the message. The Silent King shook his head. It was only a small movement, but Judas knew what he was thinking. The king turned to one of his men and words were exchanged.

Not long now thought Judas.

He was in no man's land as usual, and he wished that he had Michael with him. The big Archangel was a pompous idiot at times, but he did put the fear of God into most creatures. The Silent King's men were deploying now, and Judas guessed the reason why. He turned around and watched the Iceni approach. It didn't take him long to count their numbers, the recent war of attrition had slimmed their ranks to the point of military emaciation.

Princess Fedelmid rode out onto the battlefield and Judas had to give her marks for style and courage. She was standing bolt upright in an Iceni war chariot, her red hair was free and dancing in the wind, and her arms and face were covered in symbols, drawn on by a scribe of the Druid Council, of course. Fedelmid was outnumbered, but the way in which she was conducting herself would make her people stand with her, and her mother – wherever she was – proud.

"So, Judas Iscariot, Master of the Black Museum, you have come to see the fight. Has the Silent King surrendered yet?"

Fedelmid was as scared as everyone else. Judas could see it in her eyes – they were wild, but the flames that usually danced within them had been extinguished.

"I have just informed the Silent King that he must remove his forces from the battlefield, or I will be forced to start arresting his men. Just so there is no confusion on this, that goes for you and your army, too.

You have the best part of 15 minutes to retire, my lady."

Princess Fedelmid started to laugh.

"And just where is *your* army, Master of the Black Museum?"

Judas removed his wallet from the inside pocket of his Frahm City coat and flipped the top flap open to reveal his warrant card.

"There it is, my lady, the most powerful force in the city."

Princess Fedelmid looked down on him and she studied the card.

"We cannot give way, Judas. You must see that. There are spies and informants all around us, passing on our news and movements to the other great houses of the Under Folk. Retreat and our bones will be picked clean before we cross the river. As for our wealth and power, all will be gone if we turn-tail and run."

"You're forgetting that you will lose even more than that. If you cross the field and fight, you'll lose your lives as well."

Princess Fedelmid shrugged and gripped her spear tightly.

"My mother would fight – so must I!"

"Fedelmid, please, your mother was a great warrior and tactician, but she lost the battle of her life and chose to run rather than watch her whole tribe be turned to red mud."

"That much is true, Judas, but she never betrayed her family. Can you say the same thing?"

Judas heard her words and sighed heavily. There would be a battle here because neither side had the guts or the sense to walk away. Princess Fedelmid nodded to her charioteer and he flicked his whip with expert skill, cracking it just above the lead horse's ear. Judas watched them coast over the paving stones toward the old Granary building and then stop in front of their soldiers. She would be making her last speech now, a call to arms. A call to death would be more fitting.

He put his warrant card back inside his coat pocket, and then looked at his watch. The minute hand had just touched the number 10 when his mobile phone started to scream.

"Sir! It's Lace! I have him, the one we were looking for."

"Where are you, Lace? All hell is about to break loose here, I need you to bring that little monster to me now, as soon as possible, put the blues and two's on, whatever it takes."

"Give me five, sir."

Judas put his phone away and ran over to the one person he knew that could buy him the time he needed.

"Meg! I need a word with you."

"The time for words is over, Judas. We have been mightily wronged by the Iceni – the carnage, and the bloodshed they have caused, the attempt on my Lord's life! They cannot go unpunished. The Black Museum must stand aside, or you will face their fate too."

Judas was about to start pleading when his last chance for peace was ripped away from him.

Queen Boudica of the Iceni, red-haired warrior and a champion of old Albion, charged onto the battlefield on a horse so white, it looked like it had been made from clouds. A cheer from the Iceni went up! Shields were smashed with the butts of spears and cold, hard steel blades were scraped across the ground. Boudica raised her sword and let out an enormous roar, and then she dug her heels into the horse's flank and trotted towards the Silent King. When she was within speaking range, she pulled the horse's head up and it stopped smartly.

"The Silent King of the Resurrection Men! You are a thief and a liar, you are one with the worms, you have murdered my children and brought about the destruction of my people. Breaker of promises and spreader of lies! Look at me now and see your great plan in tatters. The Under Folk shall hear of how you reneged on our agreement, and then stole the Golden Torque. How you hunted my people down with your great black pet, Black Shuk, that infernal Hell hound, and how you brought war to the city."

Judas decided that it was best to leave the two main protagonists to it. The longer they shouted at each other, the more time Lace had to deliver the real culprit. The Silent King raised a hand, and a hush fell over the assembled troops.

"You dare speak to me of deceit, woman! It was I that gave you the means to escape the Romans! It was I that created the Golden Torque and I that helped you to rise. And what payment did I ask for this? For everything? An hour of your time, once a year, to talk, nothing else! It was you that reneged on our agreement, you that set us all on this red path. How you can stand there and throw your gauntlet down at my feet after all you have done! Madness has come to live with you, Boudica, and you have made it welcome!"

The ranks of both armies started to fidget and shuffle as uncertainty rippled across them. Was the enemy really the enemy? Was the force opposite responsible for this, or was it them? Boudica looked uncertain and pressed on.

"And who then set the Black Beast of the Fens on me at the races? Who killed my eldest and then planted the bomb that obliterated my youngest child?"

"It is my purpose to bring back the dead, not to increase their number," the king replied, gravely.

"And what of your red-eyed assassin? I suppose he invited himself to your war?"

"I know nothing of the creature, only that it has ripped the throats from my people and fed their bodies to the offal pits."

Judas felt the mood of the moment swinging in the balance. Holes in each of the leader's arguments were growing; neither seemed so sure of their position now.

"Your creature abducted me to stop me from meeting you at the great tree, on your orders I suppose, so that you could say that I was the hostile force and had tried to get out of our agreement. You have become weak and low. Have you grown bored, Silent King? Does war excite you? Has the taste for peace and order gone stale in your mouth?"

Judas dragged his eyes away from the regal Punch and Judy show for a second and looked at his watch again. The dialogue between the king and the queen seemed to have been going on for much longer than the three minutes since he spoke to Lace. He needed more time and it looked like their speeches were nearing a natural break. The king did not believe the queen, and the queen did not believe the king. One of the Silent King's generals hurried to his side. Seeing this, Boudica turned her horse around and trotted away. Then, there was the sound of two horns and both sides started to walk towards each other – and annihilation.

The distance between the two armies was shortening. A lone arrow hissed into the air. Was it a signal, or had someone gone too early? Judas wished that Michael was here – he'd even take Angel Dave or Williams or Joachim – but the sky was clear and still. Judas was still in the middle and he was in danger of getting a crick in his neck through checking the progress of the Iceni and then the Silent King. He thought about getting his warrant card out again, but that bluff was a busted flush, so he started to walk, but he didn't get very far.

The Bentley came out of nowhere, headlights on full beam and the horn blaring, and when it skidded around, the boot caught Judas just above the knee and sent him flying. The armies halted, unsure about whose side the Bentley and its driver were on. Then Lace jumped out.

"The next person to take a step forward gets six months for assaulting a police officer!"

It confused the warriors and made Judas want to laugh out loud, but that would have ruined the moment.

"Have you got him?"

Angel Dave landed on top of the Bentley and the roof creaked inwards under his weight. Lace shot him a look that would have killed a horny bullock and cocked her head to one side.

"Really? You couldn't land on the ground?"

Angel Dave looked embarrassed and more than a little uncomfortable. Lace walked around the car and opened the boot. Judas got up and dusted himself down.

Then he ambled over to her and looked inside the boot. He reached into it and lifted Prince Morcant of the Iceni out, throwing him on the ground between the two forces.

"There is your enemy! This – this little bastard, brought you all here. It was his thirst for power and the throne that set him on his path. The blood of the Iceni, and your people, my Lord, is on his hands. Well, mostly his hands."

Morcant stood up quickly. He looked dishevelled and appeared distraught. His eyes were wild. He searched for a friendly face but saw none and began to tremble.

"My people! I have been kidnapped, held by the Silent King's men, made to listen to the tears and the laments of my dear brothers and sisters as they have been murdered. They made me watch as they killed my mother, the queen! Defend me my people, I am your king!"

Silence swept across the battlefield. Even the banners and the flags dared not rustle in the wind, then, a horse whinnied, and the Iceni forces started to part. Something or someone was advancing from the rear, and when Morcant saw who it was he dropped to his knees.

"So, my boy, it was *you!*"

Queen Boudica rode out, and the world held its breath.

"Mother! Thank God you are alive!"

"You can remain quiet now, Morcant. The gravity of this situation demands that words must now be had, that you may not hear."

Boudica's voice was as cold as the tip of a mammoth's tusk. The look she gave her son was not much warmer. She was so pale and looked very small. It was clear that she had suffered greatly; livid red scars were visible at her neck, and long dark scratches stretched away down both arms. Dark circles had replaced her blue face paint, making her handsome, proud face, appear gaunt and wasted. For all this, the wounds, and her pained, tortured expression, she was still an imposing figure – and many of her people chose to look away, rather than meet her eye.

Boudica turned to the Silent King, and then to Judas.

"My lord, may I ask you and the Master of the Black Museum to join me?"

Judas nodded.

"I would be honoured to accompany you if it means that war can be averted, my lady. I will bring my Second of course. Lace!"

Lace zipped up her bomber jacket and gave Angel Dave a nod, as if to say, 'I won't be long,' and then she walked away with Judas.

The Silent King did not move so swiftly. He was suspicious. Was this all some elaborate theatre, a *ruse de guerre*? He surveyed the ground, looking away to all four points of the compass, searching the darkness and the shadows for evidence of new deceptions. Finding none, he turned to his advisors, and after a hurried discussion, he rode out to join the queen. A parley was about to take place, leaving the forces of the

Iceni and the Silent King's armies staring into each other's eyes across a no man's land marginally wider than the carcass of a male whippet.

The German Gymnasium restaurant was nearby. It should have been open, bulging at the seams with guests, all of them sampling the German cheese and sausages, and the dark Austrian Holstein. There should have been revellers outside, families up from Kent or Essex to take in a show and complain about everything being dirty and way too expensive. Instead of life and light there was only darkness and silence. The same magic that had cleared the battlefield and turned the passers-by blind to what was happening was at work here too.

Boudica dismounted and walked over to one of the vacant tables outside the German Gymnasium and sat down. Minutes later, the Silent King appeared and joined her. Neither looked at each other or uttered a single word.

"My lady, my lord. Sergeant Lace apprehended Prince Morcant in a church, a church that has a particular tenant – a big, black beast of a tenant. Sergeant Lace, would you like to tell the king and the queen what happened?"

Lace edged forward, cleared her throat, and then started to tell them both about how a boy had talked with a great black wolf with red eyes about killing his own mother, and then giving the animal a great treasure in payment for the deed. The Golden Torque was the treasure, and Morcant had persuaded Black Shuk, that it, *the torque*, could set the Beast free.

"The Golden Torque was not his to give." The Silent King spoke softly but his words carried.

"How cruel it is to be cast away by one's own child. How devastating it is to know that my own flesh and blood wanted to see me dead, ripped to pieces by some foul hound. How sickening it is to hear his words, and see his face, and know that every word is a lie. I am not the queen I thought I was."

"And what of the Golden Torque, my lady? It rightly belongs to me."

Judas and Lace looked at each other, and then into the queen's face. She sat upright and looked the Silent King in the eye. Then she smiled, a broad, happy smile that had no place being there, but no one minded.

"Yes, it does, my lord king. And, by the look on the Master of the Black Museum's face, you may need to explain to him how that happens to be the case."

The Silent King looked up at Judas and then waved a white hand across the table to point at a chair opposite his own.

"When the queen was defeated in battle, it was not enough for the Romans. They scoured the battlefield for her body, tortured anyone they found alive, but none of her people gave her up. Romans can't just win a battle, they must find the leader of the forces that stood against them, and then take them back to Rome, so they can be shamed and humiliated. It isn't enough to win, they must destroy – utterly. It's pathetic really, but there you go. I found her, and what was left of her forces and family and chose to offer her a way out. An escape from the Romans."

"Which I took, gratefully."

The Silent King nodded to Boudica and resumed his tale.

"The Golden Torque was mine. It could do nothing for me, so I offered it to the queen."

"Why? Why save her and her family and give them a weapon of such power?"

The Silent King laughed. It was a dry and hollow sound that reminded Judas of the wind through rushes.

"Love, of course, Master of the Black Museum. *Love*."

Judas looked across at the queen and knew that the king's words were true.

"We arranged to meet at the Great Oak on the Icknield Way. Once a year, and at the same place, and at the same time. The terms I set, purely selfish of course, were that Boudica was to come alone, and that we would talk of what we had achieved, and what we had done with our long lives, and on occasion, what the future held for each of us. When you live as long as me, knowing that someone is there, travelling along the same long path, someone that will not fade away and disappear as so many of my friends have done, it gives you purpose and meaning, and stops you from drifting in life, and dreaming of death."

The queen nodded in agreement and breathed a great sigh.

"I know how you feel," said Judas. "All my close friends got together, formed a secret criminal enterprise, and then tracked me all the way from the Holy Land to blessed Albion, in the hope of killing me."

The Silent King laughed his little hollow laugh once again.

"The crime you committed, Master of the Black Museum, warranted your destruction, at the very least. You will find no sympathy here. Respect for your more recent actions, yes. Sympathy? Not a chance in Hell."

Judas pretended to be insulted, but only a little.

"It was only a peck on the cheek, but no one ever forgets, do they? And it was a long time ago. But enough of the Mills and Boon and the trip down memory lane, what are we to do with Prince Morcant?"

The queen cleared her throat. Even this small action seemed to bring her pain, and Judas noticed the concern on the Silent King's face.

"It is true that the pact I made with the king has been broken. It is also true, that much blood has been shed. The creator of the carnage and the person responsible for nearly bringing both our houses down is, unfortunately, a member of the Iceni royal family. He is also my child, and I must take the blame for his actions. I offer you my head, Silent King of the Resurrection Men. Take it now, and we can end this war, and afterwards, hopefully, you may look kindly on the Iceni that still survive, give them safe passage to one of the other realms perhaps?"

A stray dog appeared and sniffed at the table, hoping for some left-overs, or a scratch behind the ears from some friendly hand. It received neither and thought about cocking its leg to relieve itself but decided, wisely, to move on. After the cur had disappeared, the Silent King spoke. His voice was strangely quiet. Judas had met the man a few times now, and where there had been strength and discipline before, there was now a deep sadness.

"The binding spell that I cast over you, Boudica, and your family, is not something that can easily be broken or undone. I made a bargain with you, but I did not ask for *your head* specifically, if you broke your promise. The terms were simple: the Golden Torque must be returned to me and the neck that wears it shall go under my axe. In short, if you have the torque, place it around Morcant's neck. I will complete the ritual and you and your people may go free. My Gods will be satisfied, life will go on, and then, possibly, a new bargain can be made."

Judas stood up quickly, he didn't need to hear anything more. Boudica would plead for her son's life, but the king would never accept it. Then she would realise that his death would mean that her tribe would live. It was a harsh thing to contemplate, but Boudica was a warrior, and she would make the right choice.

Lace was standing nearby. She was keeping an eye on everybody at the table and their seconds. Seeing, without appearing to look. It was good to have someone watching your back at times like these.

"Where is the torque, Lace? We need it back."

Lace looked uncomfortable.

"What is it, Lace?"

"Well, sir, I let the Beast take it."

"What do you mean, you let the Beast take it?"

"Well, sir, it's odd, I know, but it made sense at the time. Black Shuk could have killed me, and Angel Dave if it wanted too, but it didn't. We were this close to walking into that church and not walking out again. We came to an agreement, sir. Morcant was dying right in front of us, I had to give the Beast something in return for his body. I made Morcant give Black Shuk the torque. He wears it now and apparently it enables him to travel through magic doors, or something. Before Angel Dave and I made our way back here, I made it promise me something. That it would come to my aid if I needed it."

Judas smiled and went back to the table.

"We can get the torque back for you but there is something that we need, *from you both*. The reputation of the Black Museum has suffered of late, due to that little git Morcant up there, I want it restored, and I want you two to speak up on our behalf, when and if the situation requires. Secondly, and this is more like a bit of housekeeping really, can you get your armies to disappear and hang up their spears and whatnot?"

The Silent King nodded, and Queen Boudica of the Iceni, smiled for the first time since she held the reins of her chariot.

"So, now that we're all agreed, where exactly will this handing over of the torque and the swinging of the axe take place?"

The Silent King stood up and faced Judas.

"Where it all began of course, inspector. I will take you and your sergeant, and if the lady allows, I will take her son too."

35. A ROPE OF SERPENTS

The Great Oak stood at the top of the hill. Only a stone wall, no higher than the head of an adult ram, dared approach it. The tree was called sinister and frightening by some. To others, it was heroic and spectacular. The truth was very simple: the tree was all those things, depending on how the tree felt. Many people, ramblers, hikers, and Ordnance Survey junkies had all remarked on the strange sensations they experienced when standing close to its vast trunk, and the light that streamed through its branches was the bane of many an amateur photographer. Beautiful images were spoiled by strong lights that emanated from inside the tree's dense canopy during the hours leading up to the penumbra. Pictures were taken and then developed, only to reveal that half of the image was blurred, or a light flare had suddenly pulsed through the camera's lens, creating white holes that looked like tunnels in the air. Why did this happen? It happened because the Great Oak was a 1000 doors – a jumping-off point, a meeting place, and a bridge to fantastic realms and strange worlds.

Lace was standing nearby taking in the wonderful view and trying to make sense of the moment, trying to put all the pieces together so that they resembled something like a coherent story with a beginning, middle, and an end. Of course, she was failing miserably. What passed for normality inside the Black Museum and in the world of the Under Folk, was anything but normal. Endings had a habit of coming first, monsters did go bump in the night, but it was usually because they were incredibly clumsy and had tripped over something, and there were happy endings, but they came at a price.

The rain had been intermittent since they had all arrived. Normally the wet stuff fell from the sky; she hadn't experienced the horizontal or diagonal variety before and was having trouble finding a place to stay dry in.

Lace was still feeling a little bit sick. One second, they had been standing in King's Cross, and the next, they were here, in East Anglia somewhere – *apparently*. The Silent King had cast his spell so quickly that it had caught her unawares. She was used to travelling along the Church Roads but that was a walk in the proverbial compared to what had just happened, and she was a bit embarrassed that she was the only one that needed to find a quiet place to retch on arrival.

Judas and the Silent King were deep in conversation when she rejoined them. Much of what they were saying made no sense to her and she realised very quickly that she would have more luck trying to start a conversation with a deckchair. Prince Morcant was tied to the trunk of the Great Oak; his clothes had miraculously disappeared, and blue symbols had appeared all over his torso and legs. The rope he was secured to the tree with seemed to shiver and twitch and it was only when she took a closer look that she realised it was made of grass snakes. She found them both disgusting and beautiful to watch in equal measure.

"This is old magic, Sergeant Lace. Binding someone or rather something like him with chains or steel would be of no use. The old ways are still the best way."

The Silent King was very light on his feet and Lace nearly jumped out of her skin when he appeared at her side.

"My apologies for disturbing you."

She was about to answer, but suddenly became tongue-tied. What exactly should she call him? She went for a catch-all and hoped that she wouldn't offend.

"That's quite all right, your *highness.*"

"You are the Black Museum, Sergeant Lace; you need not address me in that fashion. 'Sir' will be fine. Now, we must call on the Beast, and hope that it answers you. How will you do it?"

"I haven't got the foggiest sir, I forgot to ask."

"Worry not, Sergeant Lace. He swore an oath on the Golden Torque, simply call his name and demand that he fulfils his obligation."

Lace was expecting something more intricate, involving runes and flashing balls of light perhaps, so she was a bit disappointed that all she needed to do was to shout his name into the wind a couple of times. Judas watched her perform the act of summoning from his seat on the stone wall behind the tree. It was peaceful there; the wind made the Great Oak's branches creak, and its leaves rustle. The air was still and warm, and Judas realised that the fabric of time was being manipulated around him. The sky was darkening, and the stars were coming to bear witness, like some million-strong celestial jury. Morcant felt it too and began to whimper; his bonds reacted to his sobs by tightening even further. The blue shapes on his body started to move now, turning around, fading in and out, and then locking together. The moment was at hand.

Lace joined Judas by the wall. They had done everything that they could to help solve the case and avert a civil war in the Underworld of the Under Folk. It was out of their hands now; whatever happened next was the responsibility of the Silent King and a great black beast with red eyes. Lace was hot and tired, and she wanted to sleep, but couldn't take her eyes from the scene unfolding in front of her. The king nodded to them both and walked away to take up a position on the path, in the open ground away from the tree. He was pale and steady, like a standing stone in the night. An axe, a great double-headed monster of an axe, had suddenly appeared in his hand, and each time he hefted it, Morcant cried out, and was silenced immediately by the rope of serpents.

Judas was thinking about the witch again. He had met her on the Ley Line Express, and formed an attachment, and it was at moments like this when the air was still, and the world was quiet that he missed her the most. He wanted to get back on that train and ride it away, but God had not finished with him yet. Maybe he never would. Was Lucifer the Morningstar right about everything? Was his crime truly unforgivable, and should he just give up and down tools, see what happens? Judas didn't get the chance to get any more maudlin because at that very moment, his scar started to burn so badly that he jumped up and placed a hand on his chest.

"I think our guest is about to arrive."

The Silent King raised his axe high above his head and then brought it down smartly onto a tree stump. Half of the blade disappeared. Then there was a sound like a wooden door being smashed to pieces, and Black Shuk materialised.

"I thought that I would have a bit more time to stretch my legs and reacquaint myself with the hidden pathways. No sooner am I on the wing and I receive a summons! Why am I here?"

The Silent King stepped forwards and inclined his head. It was not a bow, it was more of an acknowledgement, and Black Shuk returned the compliment. The Silent King was the first to speak.

"The Golden Torque sits well on you, does it do as you command?"

“It works well enough, although it is reluctant to allow me to cross certain borders. I should like to know more about why that is.”

“It is simple: the torque is mine, and I alone can unlock all of its power.”

Black Shuk’s hackles rose swiftly.

“Yours? I think not, it was given to me by that wretch under the tree.”

“And who gave it to the one that the wretch stole it from?”

Black Shuk started to circle the Silent King, and he in turn reached out for his weapon. Judas had seen situations spiral out of control when great forces like the two in front of him came to blows, so he took a deep breath and charged in.

“Hang on!” shouted Judas.

“Look, big black beasty, or whatever it is that you call yourself. Now is not the time for a measuring of your manhood competition. We are not here for conflict, and we are not thieves, we have a proposition for you. If you agree to its terms, you get to keep the

Golden Torque, for eternity and a day, and maybe, just maybe, *if you're nice*, the Silent King, that's him with the big magical axe, will unlock the rest of the torque's power for you."

Black Shuk growled and continued to pace back and forth. His red eyes were wary and calculating.

"Go on," said the Beast.

"Brilliant. Look, we need the torque to complete a spell. Once that's done, the Queen of the Iceni, a close friend of yours I believe, or something like that, gets to live on, the prince gets his comeuppance, and you, Black Beauty, can lope off into the Far Realms to your heart's content."

"And just what is it that you want?"

"Allow the Silent King to remove the torque, just for a second or two. The king will perform the ritual and that's it, everyone's a winner."

Black Shuk stopped pacing and looked directly at Judas.

"I know you. You are called the Betrayer, and the Master of the Black Museum, and warden of the Time Fields. That is correct is it not?"

Judas was starting to get an uneasy feeling in the pit of his stomach. The Beast's snout was twitching, and his eyes were locked on to him. Something was going on behind those red pools of heat. Judas feared the worst and started to regret wearing his navy Kilgour suit. Black Shuk edged closer.

"Is it true that you can pass through these *Time Fields* at will?"

"It is."

Black Shuk seemed to relax – his hackles dropped, and he closed his great mouth, hiding those sharp, yellow teeth. Judas would regret acting so swiftly afterwards. Black Shuk sat down and laid his great head down on his front paws.

"I will allow you to take the torque from my neck if you promise, on Sergeant Lace's life, that you will return it after the ritual is complete, and, that you will take me to a certain place in the Time Fields so that I might speak with one of those who resides there."

Judas was a bluffer, a fibber, and when the need arose, a champion liar, and he knew that something was not right, but he didn't have any room for manoeuvre, or Archangels up his sleeve.

"I think that can be arranged."

The Beast growled once again and looked straight at Lace.

"Will he keep his word, sergeant?"

"I believe he will, I take him at his word, and he's never let me down."

Black Shuk turned back to the Silent King and bowed his head. The king then reached out and laid one hand on the Beast's neck and with the other, he took hold of the Golden Torque and began to sing. His voice was deep, and it flowed away from them all like a great river. Twisting through time it went, speeding up and then dropping away, and towards the end it became little more than a whisper. When it was over, he stepped away from Black Shuk and in his hand was the Golden

Torque. His spell had taken a lot out of him. He looked gaunt and emaciated, but there was something different about the Silent King now. His body was covered in green leaves that the moonlight had turned silver. His clean-shaven face now wore a beard and his long dark straight hair had curled and shortened. Once the transformation was complete, the Silent King looked across at Morcant. His voice was still clear and deep but now there was a slight burr to it.

"Release him!"

The rope of serpents that bound Morcant to the tree dropped away and disappeared into the long grass. Their job was done, and they raced away to the streams and the hedgerows they called home. Morcant was still frozen, however. His body was paralysed but his eyes were very much alive. They rolled and darted this way and that, still searching for an escape, but all doors had been closed to him long ago. The Silent King motioned towards the tree stump and the axe. Morcant's body obeyed the king's summons, and he shuffled over to the stump, knelt, and laid his head upon it. The Silent King reached down, placed the torque around Morcant's neck and then lifted the axe.

Black Shuk twitched, sensing some betrayal or subterfuge. It wanted the torque back, and it wanted it back intact. The Silent King read his thoughts and sought to reassure him.

"It is only the neck that will be damaged, *I promise*."

Black Shuk nodded and then the king brought the axe down on Morcant's neck. His aim was true and his technique perfect; there would be no hacking around and multiple swings at this execution. Morcant's head rolled off the stump and dropped into the grass. He would not be buried with his brother; a ditch, possibly even a bog would be his grave and no headstone would ever be placed over it. Prince Morcant of the Iceni was gone, and his name and his deeds would never be spoken of again. The Silent King lifted the Golden Torque from the stump and placed it back around Black Shuk's shaggy neck. Judas walked out into the path; they were very nearly there – or so he hoped.

"That's that then! The prince paid the price, Black Beauty gets the shiny necklace, and a tour of the Time Fields, the Black Museum gets a few extra Brownie points, and the king gets the queen, or am I being too familiar, my Lord?"

"Goodbye, Master of the Black Museum, and Sergeant Lace. I wish you both well and thank you for uncovering the real enemy. War would have been … unwelcome. And to you, Black Shuk, travel well and travel far, you'll find that the torque will obey you in all things now. I must take my leave of you all, there is much healing and rebuilding to begin."

Black Shuk didn't bother to bid anyone farewell, he disappeared as he had appeared, suddenly and accompanied by the sounds of doors smashing and splintering. Only Judas and Lace remained. When they looked for Morcant's head, that had disappeared too.

"Now what? We're in the middle of the countryside, my GPS is down for some reason, and I can't see a signpost. I'd say we were lost, *sir.*"

“Don’t worry, Lace, I hear from his nibs that there’s a lovely pub just over that hill, and we’ll be able to get something to eat and drink, and they’ll sort us out with a taxi to the local station. Then it’s back to London as quickly as we can. We need to find the Gilded Goat. I’m not happy about his disappearance, it doesn’t feel right to me somehow. The Cunning Man has more to do with this than he’s letting on.

“Then, there is the Museum, something is wrong in there. It’s been acting out of sorts, I keep getting a feeling that it might be sickening for something. I can’t quite put my finger on what or who is causing it. Between you and me though, it better not be Mr. Aleister Crowley and his mob, or I’m going to get very mauve with them.”

36. DEATH OF THE MUSEUM

Judas and Sergeant Lace had taken rooms at the pub after their exploits at the Great Oak, both agreeing that getting back to Scotland Yard could wait until the morning, and after a good night's sleep and a hearty breakfast, including more coffee than was good for them, they caught the mid-morning train back to London. The journey was swift and *sans* delays – for a change. The carriages on the train were half empty and there were lots of spare seats. The driver or conductor, whoever was in charge of the environmental controls, was obviously feeling very generous and had pumped the heating up so that most of the travellers had fallen asleep, at least once, and were arriving at Liverpool Street station feeling very relaxed, slightly off the pace and like a bear at the end of winter.

After alighting from the train and clearing the ticket barriers, Judas ordered Lace to take the day off.

She refused at first, citing the case of the Gilded Goat as a very important reason to get back to work, but Judas pulled rank and Lace reluctantly agreed. His former sergeant, a large, barrel-chested Welshman with a heart of gold and a tremendous upper cut was the same; he would fall asleep standing up if it meant staying at his post. When Judas had time to reflect, sometime in 2030 with the way things were going right now, he would look back on the men and women that had served alongside him and try to work out just what it was about policemen and women that made them fight so hard to protect the people who hated them. Was it a calling? Nurses and doctors healed because they felt that they needed to. The police stood in front of people that spat in their face, and then they wiped the spittle off and the following morning, helped the spitter to jump-start his or her car in order to get to work, or an interview.

He watched Lace disappear into the bowels of the city to catch whichever tube she needed and then walked out of the station. He'd had more than enough fresh air of late but just wanted to stretch his legs and get a feel for the city again. The noise of the city helped him to think: the cars and the buses vying for control, the grey traffic channels, the whirr, and the buzz of a billion conversations, random shouting, the pigeons, the crackle of the police radio, buskers and the roar of planes slowing down as they approached one of the capital's many airports. It centred him.

He was pleased to be back, but something felt wrong, and it was only when he stopped to look at a rather fetching grey two-piece suit in a shop window that he realised what it was. The sky was nearly empty; the angels were missing. Normally, it would be like the angel Northern Line up there, busy and overcrowded, but not today. There were still some angels spoiling the perfect sky but not nearly as many as there should have been.

Judas hailed a black cab and jumped in. He needed to get back to the Yard quickly. There aren't many ways to frighten an angel, in fact, there is only one way to put the fear of the Almighty into an angel of the Second Fall, and his name is Michael – the Archangel Michael. Judas promised the driver of the cab an extra £20.00 if he would break a few laws to get him to Scotland Yard as fast as possible. When the cabbie refused, Judas showed him his warrant card and promised to fix any speeding fines that he racked up, or had racked up in the past, and offered him £30.00 instead.

When Judas stepped out of the lift at the 7th floor, he almost stepped back inside. He knew that Michael was here, not twenty feet away. God's vengeance, God Almighty's all mighty killer of devils, demons, and dapper detectives, if he got the chance. There was also a smell in the air that he thought he recognised. Judas decided to leap rather than look and sauntered down the corridor with as much bravura as he could muster and entered his own office.

He was standing at the window, looking out at the city. His great wings were folded back, and his heavily muscled arms hung down at his sides. There was a great stillness about Michael. He was capable of incredible acts of ferocious violence that only those who had witnessed them first-hand could truly contemplate, and Judas, who had seen them, recognised the calm before the storm and he started to get nervous.

"So then, little snake, you are still full of the serpent's sap. Even far away and beyond the limits of your own comprehension, in places that you could not imagine, I have heard rumour and gossip from some of my kin. They tell me that you have been cavorting with 'Little Horn' again. Have you opened your ears to his sugar-coated words, or could it be that you are losing your balance on the tightrope you tread? One look at your face tells me that you are on the edge again, little man. There is theatre and movement in the darkness of your eyes, you question everything but know nothing, it is now as it was when first we met. You look confused and drawn, Judas, stretched too thin and hollow."

Judas tried to appear positive and brave but when faced by a superior force, in more ways than one, the intelligent option is always to take a breath and a step backwards, that way you can see the blow coming and have the energy to avoid it. The Archangel knew something that he didn't, he had the upper wing and Judas had heard that tone in his voice before. Now was the time for quiet and humility. The time for running and hiding wouldn't be far behind. Judas took his deep breath and pressed his lips together. Holding his tongue was a very hard thing for him to do, but he was getting better at it. Practice makes perfect, apparently. Michael looked at him and Judas bit his lip even harder.

"Enough of these trivial words, I am here because something grave has occurred. You feel it also, don't you, little man?"

Judas walked across the room on wobbly legs. Fortunately, his one good chair was near at hand, and he brushed away the dust that had settled upon it and sat down.

"Michael, I've been away on a case, trying to save this city from tearing itself apart. I've been doing my best to make sure that the world of the Fae and the Under Folk doesn't spill over into the world of the mortals. I've been busy, and when I return, I find that the sky is empty, and someone has forgotten to pull the chain on the 7th floor!"

Many years ago, not long after Judas had been plucked from the floor of the olive grove and mended, Michael had flown into Judas's life, and passed on a special message from God. The message wasn't written on a scroll, or delivered in the rackety, wheezing voice of some otherworldly oracle. Michael's message was a physical one and Judas heard it loud and clear. God didn't want Judas to get confused about the gift of his newfound immortality and his indestructability. It was important that Judas knew why he had been spared and what was expected of him. Michael decided to break Judas in two, and then trampled what was left of him into a bloody pulp. Then, Michael sat down by the pool of hammered human and produced a harp. He then proceeded to pluck and pick and twang away on it until the sun rose, waiting patiently for Judas to recover.

Judas remembered this and much more. They had fought side-by-side in the sky above London to defeat the Black Sun Magicians and in the tunnels under the Colliers Wood slave market. They had even journeyed into the stars on more than one occasion and into the depths of time, and through Hell, to fight dark shadowy creatures and spirits that the world would rather not know about. For all this, Michael was a winged robot. A 24-carat, dyed in the wool, 100% do it all by the books, cut no corners, angel with an attitude.

"When you looked into the sky just now, and you saw that the angels were gone, did you think that it was because I had come? Did you think that the refugees from the Second Fall had flown away, lest I do them damage and smite them from the air? I have no time or inclination to do any of those things. They are beneath me, these fallen angels, they are petty, they are but mere echoes of the truth and beauty that they once were. I was called here by one of your servants, Master of the Black Museum. An angel, one of my own, has been murdered – here, in these Time Fields. Why, and how, Judas? This is your kingdom and what happens here is your responsibility."

Judas sat up quickly. He'd had a good night's kip and a full English, with fried eggs and a side portion of scrambled. He was feeling sprightly and ready to roll but he was still feeling raw, and very aggrieved that Prince Morcant had managed to turn his world upside down, and he didn't like the big, feathered fellow's meaning. It was never a good thing to interrupt Michael. Not many had done so before and lived to tell the tale but the jibe about the Museum and the Time Fields had rubbed him up the wrong way and he let fly before thinking.

"*My Time Fields?* I didn't magic them into being, I did not create them from the jawbone of a mythical ass or a sacred mermaid's tear, and nor did I stock this malicious menagerie with all of London's evil. Look to yourself and your master for that! And what is this talk of the death of an angel? The only angels here are the ones that you sent to keep an eye on the Morningstar, the ones that interfered in my work, and nearly had my new sergeant killed. The angelic duo on a romantic city break, to my knowledge, are both still inside."

The Archangel was unaccustomed to be spoken to in anything louder than a whisper and his face registered his displeasure. Judas took one step back and prepared for the worst.

"Do not confuse my inaction for confusion. My heart is heavy and my anger is cold. If you were any other being, or creature, I would destroy you utterly. I could crumble your very atoms, mortal man, and cast them into the void, not even the stars would mark your passing. But I am not here to rage against you, although I should like the exercise. I am here because an angel of the Host lies dead inside your *Room of Keys.*"

Judas interrupted.

"Key Room."

"I do not care what it is called! Idiot!"

Judas had never been able to control his own tongue; if he survived this encounter, he made a mental note to have a word with the witch from the Ley Line

Express. Maybe she had a charm that would keep his lips in check?

"Take me inside the *Key Room* now! There is work to do."

Judas felt like asking Michael to say *please* but thought it might be a sarcastic bridge too far. Instead, he walked out of the office and down the corridor to the door to the Black Museum. Michael filled the corridor behind him; Judas heard some of the wall panels creak and the neon tubes on the ceiling crack as he passed. He'd have to square the damage with the superintendent first thing. The Black Museum did need modernising, but Judas didn't think that putting *Destroyed by Archangel* would get the sign-off he required for new furnishings.

Judas reached the door to the Black Museum and took his black swipe card from his jacket pocket. He swiped it through the jaws of the lock, the door shivered and opened, and Judas and the Archangel entered. The outer room of the Black Museum was cold and dark. It contained hundreds of photographs showing the scenes of notorious crimes, crude drawings made by prison inmates, wicked looking knives, coshes, hammers, pliers, screwdrivers and all manner of despicable weapons. The exhibits, for that is what they were, whispered in low voices, muttering and murmuring to each other. Judas often spoke with them; they had knowledge of how crimes were committed and where the bodies were buried. They were useful, so he let them stay.

The smell that Judas had detected when he got out of the lift was stronger in here, and he noticed that Michael flinched when he smelt it too. The Key Room was in the room behind the door on the far side of the Museum. Judas unlocked it with his card and stepped inside. The main feature of the Key Room is the vast table that stretches away into darkness. On it are thousands of items. Some are easy to identify – daggers, hat pins, wooden stakes, revolvers, and bottles of liquid marked poison or hazardous – others are much more difficult. A brick sits next to a scrap of paper, next to the paper is a rusty nail, further down the table is a peacock's feather, the handle from a suitcase, and so on and so on. These objects are murder weapons or the murderer's calling card, or maybe what was in the killer's pockets when he or she was executed.

On any other day they would be interesting, but not today. On the other side of the room is an angel and he is carrying the body of another of his kind in his arms. Tears have stained the living angel's face; his eyes are red and there are dark shadows beneath them. The dead angel appears to have died badly if a death can be described as such. A black stain covers its chest, and its wings are mangled, the once handsome face is battered and bruised, an eye socket has been smashed and the black hole stares out. Michael is the first to speak.

"Hutriel, how has this happened?"

Hutriel stirs when he hears the Archangel's voice. He was somewhere else, far away, beyond the worlds of the living. He has been flying through darkness, searching for reason and forgiveness. His friend died at his hand; the sword thrust took Chasen by surprise and carved a hole in his chest, but it is the fall that broke him. Hutriel opens his mouth to speak. There is a pause, and then he starts to tell the tale of the fall of Chasen, a warrior angel of the Host.

"My Lord Michael, blessings upon you. Here is the body of Chasen. It was my blade that killed him. He had gone mad. A darkness was on him, this place and the Time Fields killed him long before I did. He had taken to torturing the souls beyond this room. Again and again, I watched him from the shadows, a once bright and brilliant mind turned to poison by the whisperings of the evil inside. He had formed an alliance with the one they call the Ripper. Their aim was to release the others and destroy the Time Fields. I stood by and watched them hatching their evil plan, hoping that Chasen would see the error of his ways – but he didn't. I will never recover, my Lord; I have taken a life of one of the Host and I offer myself up to your judgement."

Hutriel had been carrying the body of his friend across the Time Fields and had not put him down since he died. Michael stepped across the room and took Chasen's body from Hutriel, who then slumped to the ground and began to sob. Michael looked down on him. He held Chasen with one arm and with the other he reached down and placed a comforting hand on Hutriel's head. Judas heard Michael say something, and then Hutriel closed his eyes and went to sleep.

"Did he speak the truth, Michael?"

The Archangel turned to face Judas.

"Which part, Judas? The torturing of the inmates, the plans to destroy the Museum, his collaboration with Jack the Ripper?"

Judas could not keep eye contact with Michael and knew from the tone of his voice that he was angry and more importantly, he felt responsible for the dead angel in his arms.

"Michael, I'm truly sorry that Chasen is dead. I won't lie and say that he was amazing, and a true son of the Host, the truth is that we didn't like each other much, but I didn't wish him harm and I feel that I am somehow to blame for his death. As you said before, the Black Museum is my kingdom, and an angel has died on my watch. I will do whatever you ask to make amends."

Michael surprised Judas then with a smile that burned the gloom away, then he placed one of his huge hands on Chasen's head and closed his own eyes. When he reopened them seconds later, the smile had gone.

"I have looked into Chasen's mind and then into his heart, and what Hutriel said was true – unfortunately. I must take his body to the City in the Heavens and lay him to rest there. I think that it would be unkind to leave Hutriel here now. Will you release him from his engagement, Judas? I would see it as a favour."

Judas waved the suggestion away.

"Of course, Michael, Hutriel is free to leave at any time, and you owe me nothing."

Michael nodded and lifted the sleeping form of Hutriel from the ground, and then, carrying both angels, he left the room and seconds later Judas felt the building shake as he flew into the sky. The stench that had hung around the 7th floor disappeared straight away, and then the Black Museum shuddered because it had lost its warders and it knew that Judas was angry.

"If you can hear me, Jack, I hope you can, know this. Your time is nearly up and I'm coming in there as soon as I finish this case, and I'm going to chain you to the floor and make you sorry that you whispered your evil words into that angel's ears. Hide if you can, but anyone or anything that helps you gets the same treatment."

Judas slammed the door on the way out and returned to his office. He made himself a cup of coffee that he didn't really want and then sat down. His hand found his silver coin and his thumb began to make the first of a thousand rotations across its face. He closed his eyes and tried to imagine the death of the Black Museum. If God would not let him go, one way or the other, would the destruction of the Museum at Michael's hand mean that he would have to move on?

"I'm not that lucky," he said to himself.

Judas reopened his eyes and stood up, grabbed his Frahm City coat from the coat stand, and went home.

37. THE SEARCH

Judas woke the following day in his flat. The cleaner had been during the week and the place was spotless. He showered and dressed and turned LBC on so that he could hear Nick Ferrari tell him about what was happening in the capital, and beyond, over a bowl of power-packed wheat something or other. Today's talking point was the NHS and people gluing their hands to the roads. He wondered how they would react to some of the things that had happened over the last week if they ever came to light. That was what he was here to do, keep everything going nice and easy, make sure that God's children weren't scared or eaten by the children of the Underworld. A thankless task so far.

Later, the bus arrived and Judas boarded. He decided to sit downstairs today. The skyline could amuse itself. It was a mercilessly short commute for some reason. Traffic flow had dribbled away to almost nothing and the usual stopping and starting every five seconds to wait for drivers who had strayed into the bus lane to remove themselves was non-existent. Judas arrived at the Yard feeling better for it and decided to smile at the Duty Sergeant this morning instead of his usual scowl. Sergeant Lace was already in the office, studying the newspaper, feet up on the desk and cradling a real, proper coffee from one of the Fair Trade right on and down with the kids coffee shops nearby. Lace looked up at him.

"There's one on the side for you in the kitchen, sir, and a Danish, if you fancy it."

Judas didn't need to be asked twice and mere seconds later he was drinking the coffee and trying without success to keep the currants from falling on to his new jacket. The sticky little bleeders hung on for dear life and were a devil to get out, he had to be on his guard against them. They sat in silence for a short time then, enjoying the peace and the relative quiet. What they'd seen and done over the past week had been strange and incredible, even by Black Museum standards. But they didn't have time to contemplate it for long because the old phone on the desk started to scream at them.

Judas reached out for it and placed the receiver to his ear. The voice at the other end told him that an important message was waiting for him in the mortuary. Bloody Nora, the Black Museum's specialist mortician and pathologist was not given to theatre, so Judas knew it was as important as the message suggested. Ten minutes later they entered Nora's kingdom and made an astonishing discovery. A packet of orange-flavoured Hob Nobs had been placed on her desk and underneath the box was a letter. Judas marvelled at the fact that the box had not been opened or stolen. The letter must be very important.

Judas cracked the wax seal on the back of the letter. Nora was inclined to write everything down on paper, she didn't like computers for personal notifications and had developed a bit of a flair for calligraphy and such. The letter ran to two sides and the basic gist of it was that while Bloody Nora had been tending to the injured Wulfric, Warden of the Church Roads, she had become intrigued by his stories of what happened there. How they worked, where they went, the Ley Lines and different realms that they connected. She was as giddy as a schoolgirl to see them and had decided that there was no time like the present. Nora had nursed Wulfric back to health and he had agreed to take her on a tour of his fiefdom.

Bloody Nora went on to say that she would return at some point because she had her pension to consider. She believed that in terms of line managers, he was hers and she was sure that he would sign off her leave request, which was in the top drawer of her desk. There was one last thing she needed to let him know about, but it would be best explained by opening compartment six on the wall.

Judas left the office, munching on his second biscuit; Lace had already consumed three. Judas opened number six and pulled the stretcher out. On it was the Gilded Goat, dead and crumpled. Lace looked down at the Gilded Goat's face. His strange eyes with their sideways pupils were still open, and she was unable to close them. One of his horns had been ripped off – whoever had done it was strong as well as being a nasty bastard. His clothes, the joy of his life, were dirty and ripped, and there was a stab wound in his neck. The blade would have been short and wide to make that sort of wound.

"Poor Goat, I thought we could keep him safe; it must have happened when we were in the countryside."

Judas nodded in agreement. The Gilded Goat was one of the good guys – he wasn't evil, he traded in stolen goods, was the best and most well-known fence in the Underworld, and he was also a friend to the Black Museum and a good, reliable source of information. He would be missed.

"It looks like the Gilded Goat was unable to evade the people he stole from. This is no accident though, when I spoke to the Cunning Man, I made sure to tell him that he needed to return the goods he'd chanced upon, and quickly. If I was a betting man, I'd say that Charles Murrell was responsible for this."

Lace pushed the trolley back inside compartment six and locked it.

"If you told this Cunning Man to give the Gilded Goat his money back, why kill him as well?"

"I think that Murrell is a nasty piece of work, Lace. He pretended to fudge that spell, the one that would turn the Goat into a human. He could have done it I reckon, but he didn't, he wanted more money, and he knew that the Gilded Goat had it. He took him home and cased his house, stole the goods when the Goat was away hiding from the people he was fencing the stolen items for, and then killed him to make it look like they'd caught up with him. The goods have disappeared, everyone will think that the Goat either stashed it all away or spent it on Oswald Boateng suits. Either way it's gone. Murrell has it, every blasted piece of it, but he won't have it for long, not if I have anything to do with it. Unfortunately, you and I need to get on a plane and go and see someone else first."

38. LES BEAUX VOYOUS

Marseille was hot and sticky. The roads were packed, and Gallic tempers were fraying. A car had broken down on the bridge above Vallon des Auffes and the normally quiet and tranquil little fishing port was hearing the outside world crashing in on their lives with a vengeance. French fishermen gathered around one of the cabanons to talk and to complain to each other about the noise. The cabanons were small, rustic sheds, useful for storing fishing tackle or black-market booze and cigarettes. They were also the perfect place in which to hide. That was what Simon the Zealot had been told, anyway. His recent foray into smuggling had started well, he'd been able to move quite a bit of stock and made a bit of cash that he was planning on using to help him get a foothold in the lucrative drugs market in the South of France. He'd worked it all out, paid the right sized bribes to the right guards on the docks, he'd even purchased the services of an ex Foreign Legion enforcer to watch his back. The only problem had been that the legionnaire wasn't watching his back, he was drawing a target on it.

Henri was a big chap with hands like shovels. He boasted that he dug graves with them for anyone that crossed him. He was also one of the Beaux Voyous – the French mafia – and he stitched Simon up like a kipper. They were in one of the storerooms down on the dock loading their ill-gotten gains into an old Renault flatbed truck, just Simon and Henri. The legionnaire went for a smoke and returned mob handed. Simon had jumped through a window to make his escape and ended up in the sea instead. The gang emptied their firearms into the water; thousands of rounds hit the surface, but Simon's luck held and none of the bullets hit him.

When the Renault pulled away from the storeroom with all his property on board, Simon considered following. In his mind's eye he saw himself bursting through a door and laying waste to the gang, but Simon was not a fool, and he knew that he had already outstayed his welcome. He was presumed dead; it was probably best that it stayed that way. He swam to a buoy and clung to it for at least an hour. The water was so cold that it turned his legs off, but he knew that one of the gang, maybe more, would be hanging around the storeroom just in case he'd grown some gills. When a small fishing boat passed by on its way to its moorings, Simon cast off from the buoy, caught hold of one of the fishing baskets hanging over the side and was pulled to safety.

The first place Simon tried was his apartment, but Henri was camped outside it drinking beer with some of the locals. There was no way past him, so Simon went to the only place that he hadn't told Henri, or anyone else about. Old habits die hard, and Simon was always expecting the tables to turn on him, so he had hired one of the fishermen's cabanons and hidden his escape kit there. He was dry now and had finally stopped shivering. His teeth hurt where they had chattered so much and there was still some water in his ear that bubbled and popped. All things considered, he was in good shape. He was dry, had a full stomach, and had drunk half a bottle of vodka. The sleeping bag he'd purchased was warm and he'd slept surprisingly well. All he needed to do now was to wait for nightfall, make his way to the train station and head for Spain.

That was the plan, but shortly after midday, Simon had to make another. Henri was a whistler, he whistled as he worked and whistled as he walked. His favourite tune was the *Legion is Marching to the Front.* He couldn't go a whole day without performing it, and this is what saved Simon's life. He heard the strange tune coming from down on the jetty, not more than 100 metres away, and through a hole in the tin wall he saw Henri and another couple of goons talking with one of the old fishermen. After a quick chat, the fisherman turned and pointed straight at the hut he was hiding in.

Simon did not panic; he'd lived too long for that. He lifted his small rucksack up, put it on and slipped away through a metal panel that he had already loosened, just for situations like this one. They would be able to tell that he had been there – the food wrappers and the vodka would not lie for him. He ran up the lane nearest to the shed, heading upwards and away from the water. Once he was on the bridge he had a chance but if they intercepted him in these close, winding streets? Well, that was a different story entirely.

Simon's luck eventually ran out precisely eight minutes and forty-five seconds later. He'd heard someone approaching and presumed that it was one of his pursuers. It turned out to be a middle-aged man running to the local bar to make the kick-off between PSG and Lorient in the French Cup. Simon had picked up an old paint tin from the gutter. It was half full of water and heavy. As soon as the man rounded the corner Simon swung it at his head. The tin missed its target but caught the man on the shoulder instead. Unsurprisingly, he started to shout and within seconds, his friends, all wearing PSG replica football tops stormed out of their bar and came to see what all the fuss was about. The noise was better than a giant neon arrow for Henri and the others. They followed it to its source and found Simon pinned up against the wall and trying as hard as he could to make them understand that he didn't like or follow Lorient.

Henri waded through the supporters and when he reached Simon, he whispered a few words into the ear of the man who had just escaped wearing a tin of paint as a hat. The shouting and shoving stopped instantly, and all the PSG fans disappeared back inside the bar, closing and locking the door behind them. The match was much more important than getting mixed up in Le Milieu business. Henri ordered the others to find a suitable alleyway while he softened Simon up a bit. Fortunately for Simon they were back quickly, and he only got hit six or seven times. Unfortunately, they'd found the perfect place to do the really hard work in and it was just around the corner.

The alley was narrow and smelt of urine and cheap alfresco sex. At the far end, a stack of empty metal beer barrels created a wall, turning the alley into a dead end, in more ways than one. Henri tied Simon to a lamppost and then, to the applause of his co-workers, pissed all over his prisoner. They were having so much fun at that point that they didn't notice the tall dark-haired man and young woman approach. Henri was taking his shirt off in preparation for the beating he was about to administer when he suddenly realised that they had an audience. He fired off a few choice phrases, and when the mysterious couple did not disappear, he decided to try something else instead.

When a trained killer like a French Foreign Legionnaire attacks, you need to be better trained than he is or things get messy, and it's usually the one person not used to wearing a white Kepi that suffers. He sized the stranger up and couldn't see anything that caused him concern. Henri was feeling so sure of himself that he shouted over his shoulder to his audience.

"When I have finished kicking this guy's balls all the way up to his mouth, I'm going to make him eat them, and then maybe we could have some fun with the woman."

The visitor spoke quickly and in perfect French.

"The man you have tied to the lamppost is coming with us. I'd prefer it if you didn't make things difficult."

Henri stopped smiling. Something was wrong, but he couldn't put his finger on what it was. They were in a dark alleyway in a very dangerous neighbourhood, outnumbered, and yet these two strangers weren't afraid.

"If you want this pathetic little fool in the piss-stained slacks, he's all yours. Right after I kill him."

"That's not going to happen. Look into my eyes. You know what's going to happen to you if you don't go now. It won't be pleasant, and it will hurt – a lot."

Henri was too cock-sure of himself to back down and instead, made his move. He had planned to chop at the man's head with his hand and then kick him in the stomach, but it didn't happen that way. The other man was far too quick for him and caught Henri's foot in one hand and smashed his kneecap to pieces with the other. One of the other valiant souls decided to get involved and raced over to defend Henri; he got to within a yard of him but no closer. Sergeant Lace whipped her Met Police standard issue muscle breaker (the ASP extendable baton, in layman's terms) out of her pocket, snapped it to its full length and then swung it with such force that not only did it break the man's shin bone in twelve different places, it also lifted him off his feet and he remained on the floor until long after DCI Judas Iscariot and Sergeant Lace of the Black Museum at Scotland Yard had left the crime scene.

The other men had seen enough and ran away.

"Hello, Simon the Zealot. You look well, the South of France agrees with you. How have you been since the last time you tried to kill me?"

Simon was in no mood for festivities. He had been roughed up and used as a toilet, all his money had been stolen and now, here he was, tied to a lamppost in some fishing port and being rescued by the last person on Earth that he wanted to be rescued by.

"It's all so very amusing, isn't it, inspector? All so hilarious and gay. I have to say thank you for saving me from a savage beating. I don't want to, Lord knows it hurts, I think that I would rather take the kicking. In fact, can you call them back and give them another go? I won't be offended."

"It's *chief* inspector these days, Simon. I got a promotion for solving a case. Some idiots, following an even bigger idiot, were chopping angels' wings off. Turns out that they were all being used by a small, dapper German magician to help him go about destroying London and then the rest of the world. I got a pay rise too."

"Very drole, *chief inspector.* Can we get on with whatever this is? My trousers are really starting to pong, and my left arm has gone to sleep."

"Sergeant Lace, would you be so kind and cut the poor chap down?"

"Certainly, sir, it would be my pleasure."

Two days later, Judas and Sergeant Lace escorted Simon the Zealot to the Key Room inside the

Black Museum of Scotland Yard. After his rescue he had been incredibly loquacious. Lace had offered to gag him, but Judas knew what lay ahead for Simon and let him chirp away. But now that they were here it was time for silence and for Simon to find out why he had been saved.

"The angels Hutriel and Chasen were the warders of the Time Fields. They kept an eye on things, made sure that there was nothing for me to worry about, but they are gone now, and I need a replacement."

Simon looked puzzled and confused.

"You want me to work for you? In here?"

"That's what I love about you, Simon. You're sharp, sharper than a diamond tin-opener, in fact. Want me to show you around?"

"This is another joke, isn't it? I say yes, and then you sink me to the bottom of the North Sea with a mountain on my chest, just like John."

"Simon, the Time Fields need someone to watch over them. It won't be easy. There are even worse creatures in there than you. It will be dangerous. I chose you for this task because every time I ask someone or something good at heart, pure and honourable to take up the keys to the Black Museum, they end up getting hurt. So, this time, I choose a two-faced, nasty little piece of work like you instead. You owe me your life now. I can take it if I want, whenever I want, so this is the deal: you will work your way into the confidence of Jack the Ripper and anyone else I ask you to get close to, and you will inform on them for me. Understand?"

Simon was already making plans to escape; he knew it and he knew that Judas knew it too. For now, though, he'd do as he was bid and put the time to good use. He may even learn how to free John the Baptist from his watery grave; all things were possible if you wanted them enough.

Judas watched him closely, he knew Simon so well that he could have written down exactly what Simon was thinking without lifting the pen from the paper. He could keep an eye on Simon, keep him close and make him work. Simon was a brilliant confidence trickster. People believed him and trusted him, and as one of Judas's oldest enemies, he had the perfect cover.

"I will do as you ask then, chief inspector."

"That's good to hear, Simon. Why don't you have a look around. Sergeant Lace and I need to organise something. I'll be back shortly to give you the grand tour. And, before you think of running off, this floor is contained, there's no getting off it unless I say so, okay?"

Simon scowled, turned away, and pretended to look at some of the artefacts on the long table. Judas and Sergeant Lace returned to the office where they made the obligatory mug of coffee and sat down to discuss the case of the Gilded Goat.

"I want you to lead on this one, Lace. Find out where the Cunning Man is and what he's doing. Then we're going to watch him and if we find that he had anything to do with the Gilded Goat's death, we're going to be handing him over to our new friend in there. That okay with you?"

"It certainly is, sir. Can Simon be trusted though?"

"Simon believes that he's the smartest person in the room. Always has done and he always will. He's predictable and that works for us. I don't trust him a bit, Lace, but he'll be useful for a time, and he owes us his life. It's going to take a while before he works out a plan to either get us killed or break out. I'll have worked out what to do with him by then.

"Now, let's find out who really killed the Gilded Goat!"

THE END

ALSO, BY THIS AUTHOR:

JUDAS THE HERO

THE CHILDREN OF THE LIGHTNING

THE CURIOUS CASE OF CAT TABBY

OLIVER TWISTED

THE BLIND BEAK OF BOW STREET

If you've enjoyed this book, please do consider leaving a brief review of it on the Amazon website. Even a few positive words make a huge difference to independent authors like me, so I'd be both delighted and grateful if you were to share your appreciation,

Many thanks, Martin

Printed in Great Britain
by Amazon

75692797R00261